CRY WOLF

Previous Titles by Michael Gregorio

Fiction

The Hanno Stiffeniis series

CRITIQUE OF CRIMINAL REASON
DAYS OF ATONEMENT
A VISIBLE DARKNESS
UNHOLY AWAKENING

The Sebastiano Cangio series

CRY WOLF *

Other Titles

YOUR MONEY OR YOUR LIFE

Non-fiction

INSIDE ITALY
FIFTY SHADES DEEPER INSIDE ITALY

* *available from Severn House*

CRY WOLF

Michael Gregorio

This first world edition published 2014
in Great Britain and 2015 in the USA by
SEVERN HOUSE PUBLISHERS LTD of
19 Cedar Road, Sutton, Surrey, England, SM2 5DA
Trade paperback edition first published 2015 in Great
Britain and the USA by SEVERN HOUSE PUBLISHERS LTD.

Gregorio, Michael author.
  Cry wolf.
  1. Park rangers–Fiction. 2. Earthquakes–Italy–
  Umbria–Fiction. 3. Mafia–Fiction. 4. Wolves–Fiction.
  5. Suspense fiction.
  I. Title
  823.9'2-dc23

ISBN-13: 978-0-7278-8467-1 (cased)
ISBN-13: 978-1-84751-570-4 (trade paper)
ISBN-13: 978-1-78010-617-5 (e-book)

Except where actual historical events and characters are being
described for the storyline of this novel, all situations in this
publication are fictitious and any resemblance to living persons
is purely coincidental.

All Severn House titles are printed on acid-free paper.

Severn House Publishers support the Forest Stewardship Council™ [FSC™],
the leading international forest certification organisation. All our titles that
are printed on FSC certified paper carry the FSC logo.

MIX
Paper from
responsible sources
FSC   FSC® C013056
www.fsc.org

Typeset by Palimpsest Book Production Ltd.,
Falkirk, Stirlingshire, Scotland.
Printed and bound in Great Britain by
TJ International, Padstow, Cornwall.

This book is dedicated to the memory
of
Fabrizio Reali Roscini & Damiano Corrias

ACKNOWLEDGEMENTS

Cry Wolf was inspired by a series of shocking events which changed our lives. We wish to thank inmates of the maximum-security prison of Maiano, Spoleto, who helped us to understand how the Mafia works, while we taught them creative writing. If not for them, we might still have been writing historical crime fiction.

MAIN CHARACTERS

POLICE OFFICERS (in order of rank)

General Arturo Corsini, Special Ops Commander, *carabiniere*, a.k.a. the
    Legend
Alfredo Dandini, Captain, *carabiniere*
The Supervisior, Special Ops Co-ordinator, *carabiniere*
The Watcher, Special Ops undercover agent, *carabiniere*
Antonio Sustrico, Brigadier, commander of the *carabinieri* in Spoleto
Eugenio Falsetti, Special Constable, *carabiniere*

NATIONAL PARK POLICE

Marzio Diamante, Senior Ranger with powers of arrest
Sebastiano Cangio, Park Ranger with powers of arrest
Loredana Salvini, Cangio's girlfriend

CRIMINALS

Don Michele Cucciarilli, 'Ndrangheta clan boss
Zio/Zì Luigi Corbucci, 'Ndrangheta lieutenant
Raniero Baretta, 'Ndrangheta soldier
Ettore, 'Ndrangheta *picciotto*, a new member of the clan
Corrado Formisano, 'Ndrangheta former hitman
Andrea Bonanni, 'Ndrangheta drug dealer

POLITICIANS

Donatella Pignatta, the Queen, elected President of Umbria
Paolo Gualducci, the Queen's secretary
Maurizio Truini, Mayor
Cesira Truini, Mayor's wife

MAGISTRATE

Calisto Catapanni

BANKERS

Cosimo Landini, director of the bank
Ruggero Franzetti, manager of the bank

CIVILIANS

Lorenzo Micheli, student, anarchist
Federico Donati, student, friend of Lorenzo
Riccardo Bucci, student, friend of Lorenzo
Davide Castrianni, student, friend of Lorenzo

Wolves howl for three reasons:

- *As a rallying cry for the rest of the pack*
- *As a signal to let the pack know of a wolf's location*
- *As a warning to other wolves to stay out of the pack's territory*

They also howl when they are in pain.

EARTHQUAKE

*T*he Apennine Mountains in central Italy are often plagued by a 'swarm'.

That's how experts described the series of earthquakes that hit Umbria that summer. The first one weighed in at 4.5 on the Richter scale. Almost seventy per cent of the buildings in the region were damaged, but not too seriously. There was another quake three days later, but that one was only 4.1. On 22 September, there was yet another one, even smaller this time. Only 2.4, a man from the Ministry of Civil Defence announced. The danger zone begins at 5.0 on the Richter scale.

People had been sleeping in their cars for weeks, and they were exhausted. The 'swarm' appeared to be diminishing. The danger was over. That seemed to be the message.

Most people slept in their own beds that night. At 03.02, another earthquake struck. It measured at 6.1. The real problem wasn't just how big it was, but how long it lasted.

It went on rumbling only four miles beneath the earth's crust for almost a minute.

Everything that wasn't new fell down.

The man from the Ministry appeared on the TV news next morning, saying that Umbria had been declared a 'disaster zone'.

A telephone conversation was recorded by police at 04.27 that night.

A: 'Did you hear the news?'

B: 'I just popped a bottle of Moët. We'll be partying till doomsday.'

A: 'Churches, houses, bridges. We'll have to rebuild the whole fucking lot . . .'

B: 'Billions and billions! And that's just the Italian government. There'll be more once the Europeans get their fingers out . . .'

A: 'We'll be swimming in champagne!'

No criminal intent could be inferred from the telephone call between two businessmen, who happened to be laughing shortly

after a massive earthquake in which thirty-six people lost their lives.
No legal action was ever taken against them.

ip/00/395 – Brussels, 11 April, 2011.

European Commission approves emergency aid for earthquake-hit region in Italy.

Today the Commission approved an increase of €75 million in the budget for the parts of Italy most affected by the earthquake in autumn 2009.

In February 2010 the Commission, acting on the basis of Article 87(2)(b) of the EC Treaty, approved outright grants for firms in the worst-hit areas in Marche and Umbria which had made investments in the immediate aftermath of the disaster. It is now apparent that the total assistance of €46 million falls far short of what is required to meet compensation requests. The Commission has therefore decided to match the €75 million provided for in the Italian Budget Act for 2010/2011. The aid has been deemed eligible for the exemption provided for in Article 87(2)(b) of the EC Treaty.

'NDRANGHETA

Think of Italy as a long riding boot, and Sicily as a ball. The toe seems to be kicking the ball into the Mediterranean Sea. It is a visual symbol of what has happened in recent years. Cosa Nostra, the original Mafia, gained power and influence after aiding the Allied invasion of Sicily in July, 1943. But there were other mafias in Italy, and some of them have expanded rapidly in recent years, smuggling tax-free cigarettes at first, then running drugs and guns, controlling rackets and extortion, prostitution and illicit gambling.

The Camorra controls the bay of Naples. The Sacra Corona Unita rules in Puglia, while smaller organizations, such as the Mafia del Brenta, reign over the rich Venice hinterland. But the most powerful mafia is the 'Ndrangheta from Calabria in the southern 'toe' of Italy.

It was the 'Ndrangheta that kicked Cosa Nostra into touch.

The 'Ndrangheta clans were violent, ruthless and greedy. They infiltrated the rich, industrial north of Italy, controlling the drug trade in Lombardy and Piedmont. Today, they supply the whole of Italy and the rest of Europe. The drugs in your home town come from South America, Asia, Africa. They are imported and distributed by the Calabrian 'Ndrangheta.

The 'Ndrangheta earns thirty-three billion euros every year tax-free, one-fifth of the total tax revenue that Italy generates. The word 'Ndrangheta is a corruption of the Greek *andranghatia* – *andros* (man) and *agathos* (brave) – and it prescribes a criminal code of fierceness coupled with absolute obedience. The 'Ndrangheta is formed of 'Ndrine – criminal clans or 'families'. At least 160 'Ndrine are known to the Italian police, generally by the surname of the *capo*, or boss of the clan. They are spread all over Italy. Each new recruit starts out as a *picciotto*, a 'kid', and works his way up the ladder by showing his courage, following the orders of his section boss who is known within the clan as *zio* or *zì* (uncle). The head of a clan is the *don*. He may be the oldest and wisest man in the family, or he may be the youngest, the wildest, the most ambitious, the one who has wiped out all of his rivals.

All the 'Ndrangheta needs is the opportunity to move in.

On 23 September, 2009, the earthquake in Umbria provided an opportunity.

Before that date, rural Umbria had been of no interest to the 'Ndrangheta. But as EC money began to flow into the area and the reconstruction started, everything changed.

Some people came to help the victims.

The 'Ndrangheta came to help themselves.

ONE

December, 2011 – London

Sebastiano Cangio was heading east on the Central Line.

Most of the passengers jumped off at Tottenham Court Road, which was where the lovebirds got on. The guy had an Afro hairdo which added six inches to the five-foot-two-inch frame cruel Mother Nature had dealt him. The woman was thinner, taller in flat-heeled pumps, her black hair braided with multi-coloured strings. They weren't as young as they wanted to look, but the kiss they exchanged the instant they sat down was the biggest tongue-in-throat job that Sebastiano Cangio had ever seen.

He hated travelling on the Tube. Anything could happen down here, and no one took a bit of notice.

The woman's hand was inside her lover's jeans, and a couple of kids sat fiddling with their mobile phones. A woman on the opposite bench was working on her laptop, totally absorbed. An Asian in a blue uniform and matching turban was flicking through the pages of a free newspaper. There was something about Italy on the front page, but it was too far away for Cangio to read it. Almost everyone had ear pods shutting out the world.

All Cangio had was a plastic folder. He slipped a sheet of paper out of the folder and pretended to read it. He was heading out to the Docklands for an appointment with an American couple who had walked into the property agency the day before. They were interested in buying a top-floor flat with what the agency described as 'stunning views' of the slate-grey waters of the stinking River Thames, and a 'breathtaking' panorama of the low-rise south London skyline on the far bank.

He glanced up without thinking.

The man's purple tongue came sliding out of the woman's mouth.

'You fancy doin' it there, then?' the woman said.

The man was gazing at something above Cangio's head.

'Why not?' he said. 'I'd do it anyplace with you.'

The train began to slow down. Then it pulled in at Bank and the pair got off.

Cangio crossed the aisle and sat down where the lovebirds had been sitting. The seat was still warm. There was an advert next to the Central Line route map. He'd seen a lot of these ads on Tube trains in the last few weeks – pictures of Venice, Florence, Rome. The Italian tourist board was trying to woo the British holidaymaker away from Spain. This picture showed a fabulous view of a long, curving sandy beach and a pretty hill-top town that Sebastiano Cangio recognized.

Soverato.

Just seven months before he'd been stretched out on the sand at Soverato beach, drying off after a swim, watching the girls stroll by at the water's edge, when a family of four had arrived. They'd hired two deckchairs and a beach umbrella. The kids had dug a sandcastle while the mother prepared lunch, and the father had thrown a handkerchief over his face and taken a nap. They hadn't been there long when a Ducati motorbike pulled up on the promenade. The man riding pillion had jumped off, strode down the beach still wearing his crash helmet, pulled a pistol from his belt and shot the sleeping man in the face. Not once, but five or six times.

And still, the man wasn't dead.

He had dragged the blood-soaked handkerchief from his face, staggered to his feet and tried to run away, barrelling down to the sea and into the water, blood pouring from the wounds in his face and throat. The killer had splashed after him into the shallow water. People had screamed, running away in panic, but the killer had ignored them. He'd hooked the pistol in his belt, grabbed the man by the hair then smashed his face repeatedly against a rock until the water turned red and the man lay floating in his own blood.

Everyone had looked the other way as the killer sprinted back up the beach.

Everyone, except Sebastiano Cangio.

He'd been paralysed, shocked.

The crash helmet had turned his way for an instant, and he'd seen a lizard tattoo on the killer's neck. The gun had come up and aimed. *Click* . . . If there'd been a bullet left in the pistol, Cangio would have caught it. The killer had shaken his head then run up the beach to the waiting motorcycle.

You couldn't stay in Soverato after something like that.

The TV news that night had announced that the victim had

been a local 'Ndrangheta boss. There was a *faida* going on, they'd said – a new generation was taking over, stepping into the driving seat.

His mother had bought him a plane ticket for London that night: one-way from Lamezia Terme. He had tried to say no. He was supposed to be defending his PhD thesis at the University of Catanzaro three weeks later. He'd been working hard all spring and summer to put together the photographic portfolio, heading up into the Sila mountains two or three times a week, checking out the various dens. The wolves were roaming wild for the summer and the cubs were growing, starting to hunt, so it was easy to document the habitats that they had abandoned.

'There are no wolves in heaven,' his mother had said. 'Go to London and stay there, Seb. The mafiosi will slaughter each other before too long. I'll let you know when it's safe to come home.'

The feud was still going on, one or two dead each week, his mother reported, sometimes more.

Goodbye, PhD.

Goodbye, *Canis lupus italicus*.

He had found a job with an estate agency easily enough. He had a master's degree in ethology, the branch of biology that deals with animal behaviour, but they didn't give a damn about the life cycle of the Apennine wolf. His English was good enough to sell flats, and that was all they cared about. Could he sell two or three flats a month? He thought he could, so the interviewer came to the punchline. There was no salary, the woman said, just luncheon vouchers, an Oyster card if he had to use the Underground, and he'd be paid one per cent of every sale.

'How much do flats in London cost?'

The woman smiled at him. 'Anywhere from one-fifty for a bedsit to six or seven hundred for a two-room flat with a view.'

'Seven hundred thousand pounds?'

She nodded while he did the maths in his head. Three flats at an average of three hundred thousand, and he'd be making nine thousand pounds a month. He didn't think twice. 'I'll take it,' he said.

'You can rent a bedsit from us for one-fifty a week,' the interviewer added.

'One hundred and fifty thou . . .'

'Pounds,' she said, not getting the joke, and they shook hands on it.

The bedsit was a dump. A basement room in a Victorian terrace near King's Cross. After a fair start, he hadn't sold a flat for three months. His bank roll was running low. He was going to have to smooth-talk the Americans today. The asking price for the 'stunning views and spectacular panorama' was five hundred thousand, five hundred and fifty pounds. 'You can give them a fifty quid discount,' Claire Maunders, the office manager, had said as he'd picked up the sales folder from her desk the night before.

Talk about making life easier!

He'd been checking his email ten times a day. He was waiting for a reply to the application he had sent off five weeks before. He hadn't said a word to his parents about it. His father would have said he was crazy, his mother would have cried her eyes out trying to dissuade him. One night, while trawling the Internet, looking for news about wolves, he had checked out the Italian Parks Administration site and an announcement had caught his eye. They were recruiting rangers. All you needed was a degree in animal biology to gain admittance to the two-month training course. He would never have considered joining the police or the *carabinieri*, but a park policeman was a different proposition. You looked after animals, protected forests and mountains and warned off poachers. There was no chasing after criminals.

And where there were forests and mountains, there were wolves . . .

He was sick of London. Anywhere in Italy would do. Any place that didn't stink of chips and beer and worn-out fitted carpet.

Anywhere except Calabria.

TWO

January, 2012 – Rome

Alfredo Dandini had never been there after dark.

He had never seen the place so empty, hadn't realized just how huge it really was.

He stood beneath the massive colonnade, looking out across St Peter's Square, trying to figure out which of the two fountains was the one that the Legend had called the *fontana antica*. There was no way of telling the two fountains apart. They looked identical, except for the papal coats of arms.

As church bells chimed four a.m., he stepped out from behind the column and walked towards the nearest fountain.

He had never felt so exposed in his life. There were lifesize statues of a hundred angels, saints and patriarchs along the parapets on all sides of the square. Anyone could be hiding up there, watching.

Why had the Legend chosen such a place for a meeting? Did he already know what was going on?

It had rained for most of the night. The paving stones gleamed in the first flush of dawn, mirroring the crushing mass of Michelangelo's huge basilica and dome directly ahead of him.

He reached the safety of the fountain with a sense of relief.

He glanced behind him, then looked all around. A weak light was shining in the Vatican guardbox at the end of Via della Conciliazione, but there wasn't another soul or light in sight. He lit a cigarette and dragged the smoke deep down into his lungs.

It wasn't like the Legend to be late.

'*Alfredo!*'

It might have been the voice of God calling out to him.

Alfredo Dandini dropped his cigarette and went to meet the man who stepped out of the shadows, the man he had served so faithfully for the last five years.

'*Signor* Generale . . .'

'*Signore* will do,' the older man cut him off.

'*Sì, signore.*'

'Why aren't we both at home in our beds, Alfredo?'

It was hard to know where to start – even harder to act the part. 'They're out to get you, sir. The magistrates in Milan have opened a file, and your name is written on the cover.'

The Legend took a deep breath. 'What do they have on me?'

'They're questioning the way you operate, sir. Too many men, too much theatre, they say. The press is always on the scene when you arrive. They're talking about the costs, the long-term gains.' He paused for a moment. 'Your reputation's growing, *signore* – you should have expected it. There are people who are jealous; others who would want to step into your shoes.'

'Why are you telling me this?'

'If you go down, sir, many of us will go down, too. I was part of those operations.'

The Legend looked away. 'I won't forget your loyalty,' he said.

'I'm proud to have been of service,' Dandini murmured, hoping that he hadn't gone too far.

The general was quiet for some moments. 'As if criminals and the Mafia weren't enough,' he said, 'I have to defend myself against Italian magistrates as well. I won't give up without a fight.'

Dandini lit another cigarette as General Corsini walked away cross the square, his footsteps echoing around the vast empty space until he vanished between the enormous columns like a wraith returning to the grave. He stood by the fountain for a few more minutes, shivering with cold, and with something else, too – an emotion he couldn't easily put a name to. He flicked his cigarette into the fountain.

Was it a sacrilege to use the holy fountain as an ashtray? he wondered.

Was it any more sacrilegious than what he had just done?

THREE

March, 2012 – Turin

They looked like Palestinian terrorists going into action.

They were all wearing the same uniform – a black hoody, a *keffiyeh*, jeans.

'Be careful, Giovanni!' one of the girls cried, wetting her knickers for the fucker.

Giovanni, my arse! Lorenzo thought. He could be anyone, a police spy, even.

'I'm ready,' Giovanni shouted to the boy below him.

It was a trick they had used before, it seemed. As the boy below stood up straight, Giovanni used the cracks in the wall to pull himself higher. The others cheered as he stood like an acrobat in the circus, a paint canister in his hand, stretching in the direction of the CCTV camera. He pressed the aerosol button and hit the lens square in its electronic eye.

Red paint dripped to the pavement like blood.

'The camera's dead!' someone shouted, and the whole gang

started screeching and prancing about as if their team had scored a goal.

Lorenzo didn't join the throng. He watched Giovanni jump to the ground like Braveheart, hoping the bastard would fall flat on his tits.

At every demonstration there was a 'Giovanni' in the thick of it, organizing the ranks, giving out orders, telling everyone what to do, as if he'd seen it all a thousand times before. They were French or German as a rule, members of the Black Block who came creeping out of the woodwork whenever there was something to protest about. Jean, Juan, Johann, or just plain Johnny-boy, the Italians found it easier to call them all Giovanni. It puzzled the cops, though. Giovanni was here and there and everywhere, just like the Scarlet Pimpernel.

'While the fuzz are seeing red,' Giovanni joked, uncovering his face, 'we get on with the revolution!'

All the others pulled their Palestinian *keffiyeh* scarves down, too.

All except Lorenzo.

He wasn't taking his green scarf off for anyone. Green for the woods and the hills of Umbria that he was ready to fight for.

Giovanni hit the metal roll-door of the garage with the flat of his hand and they all bent down to help him pull it up. A light blue Fiat Fiorino van reversed quickly out of the garage and pulled up on the pavement. The protestors crowded around the back of the van, stepping aside to let Giovanni through. Like Moses crossing the Red Sea, Lorenzo thought. They behaved like soldiers. They were disciplined, obedient to every word the foreign wanker said. Giovanni stood out in the crowd. He was tall and blue-eyed, with long blond dreadlocks tied back in a mangy ponytail. He spoke Italian well, but there was something not quite right about his accent. Maybe that was why the others obeyed him. He was exotic, charismatic, the undisputed leader of their group, even though they had only met him the night before.

'Sheep,' Lorenzo muttered.

He wanted to be in on the revolution, but not as a follower of all the Giovannis who were knocking around. He wanted to be the leader. He wanted people to follow *him*.

'All this for bottled water and Maalox?' Lorenzo sneered. 'They can't arrest you . . .'

Giovanni pulled his *keffiyeh* up over his face again, and everyone did the same thing.

Lorenzo did the opposite. He wasn't a mindless goon like this lot. No foreigner wanker was going to tell him what to do. An anarchist didn't take orders from anyone.

Giovanni turned on him, and Lorenzo saw a hint of a smile in his eyes. Was the bastard laughing behind his mask?

'This is the serious stuff,' Giovanni snapped.

Lorenzo grinned at him. 'You serving up snacks, now?'

The asshole had been giving orders since the night before in the pizzeria.

Well, Che Guevara had just fucked up! All this malarkey for pills and water.

Giovanni threw open the rear doors of the Fiorino. There was enough wood and iron in there to build a railway. The van was loaded down to the axles with clubs, iron bars, yellow construction workers' helmets, plastic binlid shields, Molotov cocktails, stones and gas masks.

'Unload it fast!' Giovanni shouted. 'Hide it round the corner. The paint won't block out the camera for long. If they realize what we're doing, they'll be on us like a ton of bricks.'

All the kids made a grab for something, and the van was empty within minutes.

Lorenzo stood by the door but he didn't help. He caught Giovanni by the arm, swung him around.

'Hey!' he shouted. 'Last night we were talking about a peaceful demonstration. We all lie flat on the ground and wait for the cops to carry us off—'

'That was last night,' Giovanni said, his blue eyes glaring hard into Lorenzo's. 'You're the guy from the country – Umbria, right? You should go back to shagging sheep there. This is urban war.'

Giovanni slapped his palm against the side of the Fiorino and the van drove back into the garage. 'Now, slow down, everyone. Nice and slow. Bring out the bottles of water and the boxes of Maalox stacked against the wall,' he shouted. 'That's what we want the coppers to see.'

Lorenzo knew what the Maalox and water were for. If you soaked your scarf with the solution it protected your eyes from the effects of tear gas and stopped you from throwing up.

Giovanni pointed his thumb at the camera. 'This is all they'll see. But when the moment comes for action, we'll be ready. They won't know where the ammunition came from.'

He pushed past Lorenzo, giving him a playful slap on his shaven scalp. 'They'll see *you*, that's for sure. Cover your face, you bumpkin!'

Lorenzo stood there for a couple of minutes, watching the kids walk slowly into the garage, coming out with plastic packs of mineral water and big brown boxes marked Maalox. Then, he turned away. The sight of the water made him thirsty, but you couldn't use the band's reserves to slake your thirst.

There was a fountain on the other side of the square so he went over there, ducked his head beneath the cold water gushing from a lion's mouth and drank from the tap. By the time he turned back, the protestors had disappeared.

Fuck them all! he thought.

When he got back home to Umbria, he'd do things his own way.

There was another CCTV camera above the fountain.

He didn't see it, blinded by the sun on his glasses.

FOUR

April, 2012 – Umbria

'I told you, didn't I?'

Still, Andrea Bonanni didn't get in.

One hand on the car door, a puzzled expression on his face. 'You know how it is, Corrà,' he said. 'We all say things to pass the time inside the slammer.'

Corrado Formisano gave him a smile. 'Climb in, Andrea.'

As Bonanni got into the car and made himself comfortable, Corrado gunned the motor then turned out of the car park heading for the mountains. 'You know me,' Corrado said. 'A promise is worth more than the Ten Commandments.'

They had shared a cell for almost a year.

There was one narrow window in the far wall, and the only thing you could see was the peak of a mountain far beyond the perimeter wall of the maximum-security prison. A regular torture. You saw the mountain every minute of the day, but you couldn't go up there. It reminded Corrado of a book he'd borrowed from the prison library, the one with pictures of the Greek gods. They had this thing about punishment. The gods had chained this punk next to a pool of water. He could see it, but couldn't reach it. In the end, he'd died of thirst.

'I'll take you up there one day,' Corrado had said as they sat by the window, blowing smoke out through the bars.

Today was the the day, though things were different now.

Bonanni rolled down the window and lit a cigarette. 'You didn't go back home when you got out, then?'

'I decided that I like it here,' Corrado said.

'How do you get by?' Bonanni rubbed his thumb against his finger. 'Money-wise, I mean?'

'My sister runs a bar, remember? She sends me all I need.'

'And you've never been back?'

'Not yet.'

'Got something going up here, then?'

Corrado shrugged his shoulders. 'I grow some veg, keep sheep and pigs.'

Bonanni flicked his fag out of the window as they turned on to a stony track. Before they'd gone a hundred yards, he'd lit another one.

'Can I ask you something?' he said, staring out of the window as if the trees and shrub were the only thing he cared about.

Corrado shrugged his shoulders. 'Shoot,' he said.

Bonanni turned to look at him. 'You were *someone* in there, Corrado. Someone *big*, I mean. A man who . . . who . . .' He struggled to find the right word, clenched his hand into a fist then shook it in the air, as if to say that *that* was the sort of man that Corrado had been. A clenched fist, invulnerable. 'And now you're growing fucking lettuce?'

Corrado waved his hand across the windscreen. An olive grove was giving way to a field that had just been ploughed. 'It's sheep or salad up here in Umbria. Just look at it. You can see what sort of place it is.'

That brought a snigger from Bonanni. 'There's other ways of living, Corrà. You don't have to grow no fruit and veg. Who's to know what the fuck you're growing? There's a serious market for weed up here. Perugia's a pot-head's paradise . . .'

Corrado smiled and nodded. They'd passed some good times together in cell forty-three. Andrea Bonanni was a talker; he had an opinion about everything. It was what you needed on the inside, but, well, now that they were out, it didn't seem right.

'I take it you're OK, then?' he said.

Andrea Bonanni didn't answer at once. 'I'm keeping busy,' he said.

Corrado kept quiet, waiting for the rest. All you had to do was wait. Inside a cell, or out of it, Bonanni would tell you everything you wanted to know if you had the patience. As the silence lengthened, Andrea said: 'I get along the way I've always done, Corrado. But now . . . well, it's . . . it's different. Better. I got guarantees, ain't I? I won't be going back in there again.'

'Guarantees? Is someone looking out for you?'

The car hit a bump and lurched to the side. The unpaved track was badly rutted after heavy winter rains that the sun had baked hard.

'There are people . . . you know, magistrates. They either break your balls or they leave you in peace. I play them along, use the fuckers. I give them a bit of news, they look the other way and hope I'll give them more. I run with all the line that they give me. I can snap it any time I feel like.'

Corrado turned his head and stared at his passenger.

Andrea Bonanni held his stare, a thin smile on his lips.

'How does it work?' Corrado said, as if he might be interested.

'I'm like a . . . sort of a . . . a consultant, like,' Andrea said.

Corrado let out a low whistle. 'One of the big boys.'

'One who intends to survive. I've spoken to this magistrate a couple of times. He's the one that sprung me. He's waiting for me to give him something juicy, the ambitious twat. His career got lost along the way in Umbria. I've got him eating out of my hand.'

'He hasn't given up on his ambitions, then?'

'It looks that way. Which is a bit of luck for me.'

Bonanni lit another fag, took a big puff and blew smoke out of the window. Then he leaned in a bit closer. 'If you felt like having some *guarantees* yourself, Corrado, they'd roll out the red carpet for a man like you.'

Corrado kept his eyes on the track, avoiding a pot hole.

'I'd give you a hand, of course,' Bonanni rattled on. 'Get in touch, know what I mean? Smooth the way, and all that. You know, have a quiet chat, say hello, see exactly what they might be offering . . .'

This was another version of the man that he had known inside.

A load of lip as always, but never one to shoot his mouth off. Now he was like a wheel rolling downhill fast. Making suggestions like that? To him?

Maybe Andrea was sniffing more than he was selling . . .

'You know,' Bonanni was saying, 'you made the right move staying here, Corrado. Peace and quiet, no pressure from the law, no one muscling in. I'm thinking of settling here myself. Life looks good in Umbria. It's just like home, but there's more money knocking about, rich folk building a decent habit, know what I mean? That's long-term earnings, regular business. They start on weed then move up. You can't beat an escalating demand, Corrado. Ask me, you're always better going with the flow. We could set up together, if you fancy it, make a fortune . . .'

On and on – he never stopped.

They passed the road sign, and he read it out loud. 'San Bartolomeo sul Monte, 783 metres above sea level. That'd look good on a visiting card.'

Another hundred yards or so, Corrado pulled into the car park. There was no one up else there. There never was when it was that cold up on the mountain.

Bonanni left the car door open as he walked towards the viewing platform. 'You can see for miles,' he called back, excited by the view.

Corrado doubled round behind the car and shut the door. You had to do things right. An open door could compromise a situation if you had to make a quick getaway. It was a question of order, discipline. That was the first thing he'd learnt when he started working with Zì Luigi thirty years ago.

No loose ends.

Bonanni was standing on what they called the Belvedere, a flat table of grey limestone, vertical on three sides, twenty or thirty feet high, projecting out over the valley and offering a fantastic view.

Corrado pointed down into the valley. 'You can see the prison better from here,' he said, taking a couple of paces to the left. 'That was our cell, there.'

Bonanni stared and nodded, but he didn't move. 'It looks like a grand hotel from up here. Except the windows are so small. You can't see the bars, either. Which one are we talking about, Corrà, the second from the end on the east wing?'

'The third,' Corrado said.

'You sure? I'd have sworn on my mother's grave . . .'

Bonanni's brow furrowed, an expression of puzzlement on his face.

It was the Force 99 that did it, because Corrado was pointing the pistol in his face.

Bonanni glanced back at the prison, as if he thought Corrado was going to kill him because they didn't agree which cell they'd shared.

Corrado felt the jolt and saw the bullet take a piece out of Bonanni's left ear.

The sight was off a fraction, or he was out of practice. Yes, that was it. He hadn't put anyone away for twelve years. He shifted the weapon a fraction to the left and squeezed the trigger again.

Dead centre.

A spray of red caught in the wind like a glorious sunset. Bonanni dropped on to his knees, then fell flat on his front.

Corrado lowered the gun and moved in close, making sure the fucker was dead. His own heart was ticking like a clock. He felt a surge of something tight in his chest and caught his breath. It had been a long time. Too long since he had shot someone. But now he felt the rush he had always felt.

The stench the body was giving off, piss pooling on the rock, the smell of shit. It always happened, an instant before or an instant after. The body emptying out, nothing else to give.

There was nothing like it.

He shifted the corpse with his foot, rolling it over, then went through Bonanni's jacket, taking his wallet, keys, some bits of paper, and stuffing them into his pockets. The less the coppers found, the better.

A minute later, he was driving carefully back down the mountainside.

It felt good to be working again.

When he got back home, the first thing he did was phone Zì Luigi.

'All sorted, boss,' he said. 'If he's talking now, it's to the angels.'

That was when Zì Luigi went berserk.

FIVE

I t was a cold, wet Sunday morning.
Another one . . .
Cangio thought of going for a walk, but then the rain turned
to sleet and the wind started gusting. There wouldn't be much to
see in any case, apart from the fox holes he had already mapped in
his notebook.

Another down side to London – there were no wolves.

He was watching the foxes with a growing sense of frustration.
For an Italian, they had been a novelty at first. You heard them at
night overturning dustbins, scavenging for food. Sometimes you
even saw them slinking through the back streets after dark. Foxes
in London? He had been amazed. It was a rare thing to see one in
Italy. Foxes were virtually extinct at home, while England was
overrun with them. There were half a million running wild, according
to the *Sun*, and a tenth of the fox population was living in the capital.
The problem was that 'urban' foxes were dismissed as a pest. If
you said you liked them, people thought that you were crazy.

He had stopped telling everyone that he studied wolves after his
first day at work. The other salesmen had started talking about Lon
Chaney Jr. He had never heard of the actor or seen the film until he
checked it out on Wikipedia. They'd called him 'The Italian Wolfman'
for a week or two, then finally decided that Seb was easier.

The Americans hadn't bought the flat in Docklands.

Canary Wharf was 'cute', they'd said, then disappeared as surely
as the wolves that had terrorized the British Isles back in the Middle
Ages. The other guys in the office had said that things were bound
to get worse before they got better.

'The crisis is walloping the property market,' Barry had declared.
He was the most seasoned salesman working out of the agency.
'Even London's a disaster. Who could have foreseen a thing like
that? The Arabs are buying like crazy in Singapore, Abu Dhabi and
Dubai, but they reckon Europe's on the slippery slope. They're

rubbing their hands, I bet, just waiting for our property prices to start free falling.'

'They'll be waiting till bloody doomsday,' Roger had said, his voice low, his eyes flicking in the direction of Claire Maunders, who was speaking on the telephone. 'You see how busy she is? All the customers want to do is *sell*. And the index price is going *up*, not down. I've only managed one bloody sale this month. A lousy bed-shit . . .'

Barry had secured a sale, as well: a penthouse with a view of Parliament.

Cangio was praying the Americans would come back, but he knew that the God of Property was no longer paying any attention to his prayers.

He looked out of the window. The rain was still lashing down.

He opened his laptop, checked the latest news from Italy. In Umbria there had been more earthquakes, not big ones like the one that had killed twenty-six people a couple of years before, but big enough to frighten the life out of anyone who felt them. His mother had told him they had even felt some of them down in Calabria, almost four hundred miles south of Umbria. It was like a train rushing past, she'd said. You heard a rumble, then the house began to creak and shake, and the light fittings started moving. The Apennines ran all the way from the Alps in the north to Calabria in the south. There'd been a 'swarm' in Soverato some years before. He still recalled the helplessness you felt, the fear that the house would come crashing down on your head at any moment. The only thing you could do was sleep in the car and wait for things to settle down again. If it was cold and wet in Umbria, he could imagine the hardship the people were going through.

He opened his UK email, but there was nothing of interest.

He checked his old Italian email, and half-a-dozen emails popped up.

The one marked Ministero dell'Ambiente was at the bottom of the list. He opened it first and something like an earthquake rumbled in his chest. He read it again, three or four times, then let out a howl like an alpha wolf, the leader of the pack.

'Bingo!' he cried, the Wolfman now, back inside his own skin.

He caught the Tube a bit earlier than usual.

It was Monday morning, everyone subdued after the weekend,

depressed at the thought of another working week, though Cangio didn't feel the weight of it. He gave a bright 'Good morning' to the girl sitting opposite who was giving him the once-over as he dropped into his seat and made himself comfortable.

She grunted something, pushed earphones deeper into her ears and closed her eyes.

'You're probably right,' he said, though she couldn't hear him. 'You've got a lousy day ahead, I bet.'

Claire Maunders was already at her desk when he got to the office. She didn't look up from the computer screen but she knew that he was there.

'Get me a coffee, Seb. Black, no sugar.'

Good morning to you, my dear Sebastiano. How are we today? Is all well with you, my dear Italian friend? Claire didn't waste her breath on small talk any more. Her time was too valuable for that sort of crap. Claire Maunders – Claire of the ravishing long legs, Claire of the swishing blonde ponytail – was his equal no longer. She had been promoted to sales manager on account of her amazing record.

A record *he* had helped to boost.

She had smiled at him one evening, asked him whether he was 'up for a drink, a Chinese meal, some fun and games in Soho'. They had ended up in bed, of course. London was like that. Fast and furious. You flirted, you fucked, you forgot. The morning after – yes, there'd even been a morning after! – Claire had brought him coffee in bed and told him to take it easy. She would cover the sales appointment he had fixed for nine a.m.

The flat had sold for four hundred thousand, and Claire had beaten Barry's annual sales record by a hair's breadth. From that moment on, there'd been no more drinks, no meals, no fun, no games. Claire had a career going for her. She was the boss, and he was demoted to making coffee whenever Claire was thirsty, running out for sandwiches if Claire felt a hollow spot deep down in her belly. Her favourite drink was a Bloody Mary. It wouldn't have surprised him to learn that she drank male blood by the pint. Then again, she was no better or worse than any of the other girls he had met in London.

Sick of London? Tired of life? Sick of London women?

These thoughts were rattling through his brain as he pulled her a *doppio espresso* on the genuine Italian Ariete coffee machine. He made a cup for himself as well, and wondered how to tell her what had happened the day before.

'Where's my coffee?' a sharp voice called.

He drank his own coffee slowly, savouring the expression that his announcement was bound to provoke on her face.

'Seb!' Claire's voice cut through the air again. 'Where – is – my – *coffee*!'

He picked up Claire's drink, carried it to her desk and placed it beside her computer, waiting for her to look up, thank him, maybe. But she didn't say a word, just kept on staring at the screen.

'I've got news for you,' he said.

She didn't react. Maybe she hadn't even heard him.

He leant forward, caught her ponytail in his fist, put his teeth to her neck and began to suck hard. She tried to pull away, but he held on tight. He hadn't been thinking of lovebites as a way of handing in his notice.

'What the fuck do you think you're doing?' she cried.

'A souvenir,' he said, letting go of her, seeing the burst blood vessels flowering on her lily-white neck. 'Something to remember me by.'

'A hickey?' She raised her hand and tried to slap his face. As the slap came winging in, he caught her by the wrist and held her firm. Her eyes were open wide, alarmed, as if she thought that he was going to hurt her.

'My resignation, let's call it. Signed, sealed, delivered.'

She glared at him as if she hadn't understood a word he had said.

'Tomorrow you can make your own coffee. I'm leaving.'

'Where do you think you're going?' she snapped.

'Italy,' he said, letting go of her, taking a step back. 'Umbria, to be exact.'

'Selling property?' she demanded, as if it was the only job worth doing.

'Working as a ranger in a national park,' he said.

'What about the Americans? They're ready to sign.'

'You look after them,' he said. 'I've got better things to do.'

'Like what?'

He didn't bother to tell her about the wolves.

A minute later, he was heading for the nearest travel agent's.

SIX

21 April, 2012 – Calabria, Italy

'It'll be like *Eldorado* once the funding starts to flow . . .'

Raniero listened carefully, wondering where the boss was going.

He'd heard about the earthquakes up in Umbria. He didn't know how big the last one had been, or if anyone had died. He only knew that Don Michele was interested in getting in first, before the other clans caught on.

'Luigi's up there, but things aren't working out the way they should. You'll go up with him next time. You've got a nose, Raniero – I want you to use it. Stick close. If he so much as farts I want to know. Are you listening?'

Listening?

Raniero had been waiting a lifetime to hear that voice saying those things.

He drained the coffee from his cup, the phone glued to his ear, and turned his face towards the turquoise sea beyond the picture-window of the hotel room. The slag he'd brought down for the weekend wouldn't notice a thing, but why take chances? Even so, it was hard to hide his excitement. He felt like a choir boy who'd been made up to bishop. He took in the news from Don Michele, fixed a smile on his face, then turned to look at the girl. Great face, great body.

She smiled back at him.

She respected men like him, she said. Real men who could handle themselves and show a girl a good time. She'd spent half the night telling him, working hard to keep him happy, hoping for a bonus.

'Is Luigi sick, or something?'

Don Michè was quiet for a bit. 'Luigi's still breathing,' he said at last. 'His brain's the problem. That's his trouble. He's stuck with old friends, old ideas . . . We're fresh blood, me and you, Raniè. We know we've got to change if we want to do business up there. *Adapt*, that's the key word. Luigi Corbucci don't think that way.

Truth is, Raniero, he don't think much at all. That man of his, Corrado Formisano . . . They shut him up too long in a small dark cage. Luigi gave him a job to do, the minute he got out, and didn't he go and fuck it up.'

Raniero heard a click of disappointment on Don Michele's tongue.

'They could have ruined everything up there.' Don Michele blew hard on his lips. 'We need to send the right men in, men who do what they're told and do it right. You keep tags on Luigi. Don't let him out of your sight. Push him in the right direction, but . . . Now, this is important, Raniè. Tell me if he doesn't take the hint, OK? Take Ettore up to keep you company. He's no genius . . . useful though, a solid worker. We need to get this ship on track, Raniè. You answer to me, and no one else. Right?'

What else was there to say? Zì Luigi would still be giving the orders, but it was just a front. Raniero would be standing right behind him, reporting back to Don Michele. Zì Luigi Corbucci was one step away from being 'retired'.

'This is really a . . . a great honour,' Raniero said, managing to smother the emotion welling up in his chest. He looked out to sea again as the girl turned towards him. Maybe she had caught the lilt of gratitude in his voice.

The boss was quiet for a minute. 'If everything goes the way I want it to go, Raniè, you may be running the shop up there in Umbria soon.'

Raniero held the phone in a trance, then realized the line had gone dead.

Don Michele's orders were simple – keep Zì Luigi on the straight and narrow; make sure Corrado doesn't blow the place apart. If he could handle the job, Don Michè would give him what he wanted: his own *commandamento* in Umbria, maybe, a cow that hadn't been milked yet.

Raniero glanced at the radio clock by the bed.

Ten thirty-three.

It would look good inscribed on a medal. Solid gold. The Madonna of Polsi, Queen of All the Clans on the front, the time and date on the back. He would wear it around his neck for the rest of his life. The miracle had been a long time coming, but here it was at last.

He turned his attention to the girl.

Tired of watching him, she was making the most of the breakfast tray the waiter had brought to the bedroom just before Don Michele phoned. She caught his eye, her teeth biting into a cream-filled croissant.

Raniero eased back in the armchair, opened his bathrobe and showed her what was growing under it. 'Get over here and chew on this,' he said.

The girl's eyes opened wide. She squeezed the cream from the cake across her lips, then fell down on her knees in front of him. He closed his eyes as he felt her hot breath on his flesh, but it wasn't her that he was seeing in his thoughts. He saw the face of Don Michele, heard Don Michele's voice, remembered the way heads turned when the don drove down the promenade in his red Ferrari, the throbbing roar of the mighty engine.

Raniero didn't want a red Ferrari.

He wanted a black one.

SEVEN

24 April, 2012 – Bari, Italy.

General Corsini checked his watch.

02.58 . . .

The breeze coming off the sea was freezing cold, but he didn't feel a thing.

Adrenaline was racing through his blood as the moment approached. He'd been watching the *Furore* for almost an hour. The rusty tramp steamer had docked late that afternoon from Lagos. Now, she was moored against the dock wall, outlined against the warehouses. Only her night lights were showing, red and green, the portholes dull black dots down near the waterline. No one seemed to be keeping watch on deck, but you learned not to trust appearances. A great deal of planning went into these operations. You could never entirely guarantee the outcome, but nothing had ever gone wrong before.

The pod in his ears had been silent for almost half an hour, which was a good sign. His men had spotted nothing suspicious through their night-scope binoculars.

02.59.

He started to count down the seconds.

Twenty-five, four, three . . .

He raised his hand to his mouth and blew hard on the whistle.

It was a trick he used, a game he sometimes played. It kept his men on their toes as they waited for the signal to attack, the tension building.

It might have been the start of a race as the assault teams came darting out from cover like an army of lethal black cats, each group of men with a specific job to do. They were all heavily armed with modified ArmaLite AR-18 rifles, Beretta pistols, serrated close-combat knives and stunguns, but the weapons were matt black, invisible in the dark.

There were only forty of them tonight, all picked by hand, specialists who excelled at climbing. A group of six dropped down on one knee at the foot of the gangplank, securing the position if anyone attempted to abandon the ship. Others swarmed like monkeys up the mooring ropes, while two more teams surged up extendable assault ladders that they threw against the hull. Corsini didn't look at his watch again, but he hadn't stopped counting.

Before he reached zero, they were all on board.

Shouts were heard as the ship's crew realized what was happening. Firing sounded and lightning flashed as the assault teams followed orders, discharging their weapons against anyone who pointed a gun or fired at them. Wisps of white smoke began to drift across the still, dark water.

Corsini felt a stab of nostalgia as he watched them in action. An officer in his position – head of the national Special Operations Command of the *carabinieri* – had to stand back and let the lower ranks do the work, but he would have sacrificed the privilege for half an hour just to be there in the thick of it.

There was another prolonged burst of gunfire, then silence.

It was broken seconds later by the sound of four sharp whistles – three short notes, one long one – as the different assault groups signalled that resistance had been overcome and that they were holding their positions.

General Corsini acknowledged the signal with his own higher-pitched whistle, then moved out from behind the tallyman's shed where he had been sheltering. He walked without hurrying towards the *Furore*, knowing that his men had the situation in hand.

'Well done,' he said into the microphone. 'I expected no less.'

By the time he reached the gangplank, his men were unloading the hidden cargo, the stuff that wasn't listed in the bill of lading, piling it high on the quayside. Crates of Chinese Kalashnikov copies, a mountain of ammunition, three grenade-launchers, boxes of pistols confiscated long ago by the police in Singapore, plus two large plastic wraps of cocaine from Turkey that must have weighed all of fifty pounds.

The assault leader stepped up, came to attention and saluted.

'No casualties on our side, sir. Three dead sailors . . .'

'Jack-tars shouldn't play with guns,' Corsini said with a tight smile.

'Seven more are locked up in their cabins, *sir*!'

The officer clicked his heels, and turned to his men: 'Hip, hip . . .'

'*Hooray* for General Corsini!'

It was hardly more than a quiet whisper, but better than a shout. In the midst of his men, he was the only one who wasn't wearing a flak jacket and black balaclava. When the reporters and cameramen arrived on schedule at four a.m., he didn't bother to change into his uniform. It was part of the performance. As lights came on and microphones pressed in on him, a pretty young journalist he had never seen before asked a question that broke the ice and got him off to a good start.

'Why are you dressed like a navvy, General Corsini?'

'Someone has to oil the machinery,' he replied.

When the laughter died down, standing in front of the arms cache, the prow of the *Furore* gleaming in the bright lights, he described the logistics of the raid, the timing and the number of men involved. Then he gave them a detailed rundown of the illegal treasure he had harvested, moving from a case of arms to a sack of cocaine, saying where it had come from and how much it was worth on the black market. He began to feel the cold now, but he was glowing inside.

As the show came to an end, the pretty young journalist leant close.

'I hope you didn't think I was being impertinent.' She smiled.

'The thought never crossed my mind,' he said.

'A blue boiler suit! It adds to your charisma, General. They call you the Legend, don't they? Your men, I mean to say.'

Corsini knew that the microphone she was holding hadn't been switched off.

'Is that what they call me?' he said.

He saluted, then walked away.

Corsini poured a shot of *baijiu* into the ceremonial cup.

He was tired but not yet in the mood for sleep, his mind still racing after the success of the raid on the *Furore*. Everything had gone exactly according to plan. It was time to celebrate.

He had bought the porcelain cup from an antique shop in Peking three years before while attending an international conference about Triads, tongs and street gangs such as the Black Bugs and the Flying Dragons. The *baijiu* came at no great expense from a small shop in Piazza Vittorio, Rome's own Chinatown.

How many other warriors had drunk from that cup after a victory?

He took a sip, savouring the rice liquor as it burnt its way towards his stomach.

How many warriors had drunk *baijiu* before a battle to give them courage?

There would be a battle, of course. If the magistrates in Milan had their way, the *Furore* would be the last in his long line of victories. They would try to get rid of him – want to pension him off, he supposed. Well, they were making a mistake if they thought they could outmanoeuvre him. He would defend himself. At any cost.

In any way . . .

He took another sip of *baijiu*, then opened his copy of *The Art of War*. He kept it on his desk the way a preacher keeps his Bible. It always amazed him to think that the book had been written three hundred years before the birth of Jesus Christ. The words of the Chinese general, Sun Tzu, had survived.

And *he* would survive, too.

He found the passage that he was looking for: *'Your attack must strike home like a stone hitting an egg. The principle is inescapable: the egg is fragile, the stone is not.'*

All he had to do was to find the right egg.

EIGHT

1 August, 2012

It would soon be dawn.

Venus cast silvery shadows over the grass in front of the house.

Sebastiano Cangio sat on the doorstep, a blanket wrapped around his shoulders, a cigarette in his hand. He hadn't been able to sleep, but he didn't regret the loss. Why sleep when you had Venus all to yourself? The planet had never looked so big. It seemed to be so close, you felt that you could touch it with your hand. It wouldn't last much longer now. The sun would soon edge over the horizon and Venus would fade from sight. Then birds would take the place of the bleating sheep in the darkness on the far side of the valley.

He loved the way that nature shifted modes.

One light came on, another disappeared. The echoes of the night gave way to the sounds of day. The sheep would drift into the wings, song birds would strut out on to the stage.

Umbria wasn't like London, that was for sure.

The city sounds were all mechanical: the rumble of the Underground, the sudden shudder beneath your feet as the first trains started running, police sirens fading as the daytime traffic began to swell, cars and buses churning out fumes as they crawled towards the city centre. Doors would slam inside the house, high heels clatter outside on the pavement, tourists rattling past with suitcases on their way to nearby King's Cross station. You soon forgot about the drunken shouts, the shattered beer bottles, the overturned dustbins, as the working day got into gear.

Cangio stared at Venus and he knew that he was in love.

He was in love with the night, in love with his job, in love with Umbria.

Even Marzio Diamante had won him over. The senior ranger had been in the park service for twenty-odd years, though he hated the forest and envied anyone who lived in a big city. When Cangio had told him he had run away from London because he couldn't stand it, Marzio had glared at him. 'What did the English do to you?' he asked.

Most of all he loved the wolves.

Most of all?

He wasn't certain whether he loved Loredana yet. It was best to keep his head on his shoulders. For the moment, he was prepared to admit that he *liked* her a lot.

They had met six weeks before in the bar where he always went for his breakfast. Italians don't make breakfast at home – they go to a bar, buy coffee and a snack, then leave the barman to wash up the cups. Enrico's was a regular stopping place for anyone who lived inside the national park. Cangio had been busy into the early hours the night before, working on maps, marking the territories of the three wolf packs that lived in the park, so he'd arrived at the bar a bit later than usual. He'd been standing at the counter, waiting for his second cappuccino of the day, when a girl had come rushing in, blonde hair tied back with an elastic band, jeans, yellow T-shirt and cowboy boots. She'd been out of breath, breathing hard.

'The usual, Enrico,' she'd called to the barman. 'Quick as you can,' she'd urged him, watching as the old man placed Cangio's cappuccino on the counter, then turned away and started loading ground coffee into the Gaggia, lining up the coffee cup and switching on the machine. She'd raised her eyebrows and sang on a rising note: 'I'm going to be la-ate!'

'What's the usual?' Cangio had asked.

She'd glanced at his cappuccino and said, 'Enrico's working on it.'

Cangio had pushed the cup and saucer towards her. 'I'm not in a rush. You have mine, I'll have yours.'

She had looked at him with surprise and interest.

'That's kind,' she'd said as Enrico had handed over her 'usual' croissant.

Then she'd smiled. Not at Enrico the barman. At *him*.

That smile seemed to light her up like an electric bulb. It had started on her lips, brought a flush to her cheeks, made her brown eyes glisten. As she'd sunk white teeth into the croissant, her breasts had moved energetically beneath her T-shirt. Even they seemed to be smiling at him, he'd thought, thinking of the estate agency for the first time in a month or more, remembering the way Claire

Maunders demanded her coffee and snacks, never saying please, never saying thanks.

'Fresh blood, Loredana,' Enrico had said. 'It took an earthquake to bring some new young lads to work out here in the wilderness. Seb's the new park ranger. Tall, dark and handsome. From Calabria, he says. Says he studies wolves, too. I'd shoot the lot of them if I had my way.'

Three minutes later, Loredana had roared off to town in her ancient Fiat 500. But before she left, she'd offered to give him a tour of the local churches. 'The ones that haven't fallen down,' she said brightly.

'Her uncle was the parish priest in Preci,' the barman told Cangio as they watched her go. 'She started ringing church bells when she was five. Up and down, up and down, holding on to the bell rope like a chimpanzee. She's a nice kid.'

Enrico had given him the details, too. Loredana Salvini, twenty-six years old, assistant manager in the supermarket on the edge of Spoleto.

'She had a boyfriend once,' Enrico had told him with a smile, 'but I believe she chucked him. You'd better watch yourself there, my friend!'

Cangio had met someone else for the first time in the bar that day as well.

If meeting Loredana had been exciting, the second meeting had been disturbing.

As he fished out his wallet, meaning to pay for his breakfast, Enrico had shook his head. 'It's already settled,' he'd said. Luckily, Cangio hadn't opened his mouth, but the thought flashed through his brain like lightning: Loredana! But then the barman had nodded in the direction of a man at the far end of the room. 'He paid,' Enrico said.

A middle-aged man that Cangio didn't recognize had been sitting alone at one of the tables. He'd worn a dirty workshirt and had an unlit cigar in his mouth, staring up at the television on the wall, his curly black hair unkempt and frosted with grey ends. He might have been good looking once, but now he had the time-worn look of a statue that had been corroded by wind and rain.

Cangio had walked towards him, intending to thank him for his generosity, wondering whether the man had mistaken him for someone else.

'Excuse me,' he'd said as the man looked up at him. 'You paid for my coffee.'

The man had crossed his arms and ignored the hand that Cangio offered him. 'That's right,' he'd said, not standing, looking up at him. 'Which corner of Calabria do you hail from?'

It was the accent that had taken Cangio by surprise, the rising cadence with a trace of a dialect he'd recognized but couldn't place. And it hadn't been just the man's way of speech that caught him off guard – it was his manner, too, which was stern, interrogative.

'Soverato,' Cangio had said, as serious as the man in an instant. 'You?'

The man had stared at him for some moments. 'I live *here* now,' he'd said with emphasis, as if he'd put the past behind him. He'd rolled the cigar from one corner of his mouth to the other. 'Why d'you leave Calabria? There are wolves down there, too.'

He'd definitely come from the south, from the Sila or Aspromonte mountains, maybe, where dialects changed so quickly that people living ten miles apart had trouble making sense of one another. Then again, when a man from the south doesn't want to talk, as they say down there, it's 'like pulling out boot-nails with your teeth'.

Cangio had decided to humour him. Why not, after all? They were two Calabrians who had chosen to live in Umbria. 'I left Soverato on account of an animal,' he'd replied with a smile, 'but it wasn't a wolf.'

'Call yourself a ranger?' the man had said, staring into his eyes. 'You should like all animals. Even the ones back home. That's what I'd have thought.'

He'd never looked away, never blinked, weighing every word that he'd said.

Cangio had tried to laugh it off. 'I wasn't a ranger then,' he said. 'I nearly got bitten by a lizard on the beach at Soverato.'

The man had raised his eyebrows, glanced at the TV, then looked back at him. 'Lizards on Soverato beach? That's a new one . . .'

'It wasn't on the sand,' he'd said, 'it was tattooed on someone's neck. Excuse me, but I've got to go to work. I just wanted to thank you for the coffee. Next time, breakfast's on me.'

Finally, the man had smiled. 'If there *is* a next time. A man could lose himself in the woods around here. They're almost as thick as the woods back home.'

When Marzio had picked him up outside the bar, Cangio had asked if he knew the Calabrian.

Marzio had shrugged his shoulders. 'Bit of a mystery, he is. Says his name's Corrado. He's been up here a while. Got a farm up on the mountain, keeps a few sheep, I've been told. We haven't swapped more than half-a-dozen words. A loner, if you ask me.'

Cangio had soon forgotten the incident as they'd driven around the park, checking the wire netting on the eastern border that protected the roads. There were always earthquakes, loose rocks that came tumbling down, a hazard to drivers.

Watching Venus, he'd decided that he was happy be a loner, too.

The house he was living in was perched on the side of the mountain with a view across the valley. It was a *casa cantoniera*, one of those big old houses you found dotted along the roads from one end of Italy to the other, all painted rustic red, each one marked with a metal plaque and serial number. ANAS, the metal sign said. The Azienda Nazionale Autonoma delle Strade had built the roads and houses back in the Fascist era. The woods all around it were teeming with deer, wild boar, wolves, eagles and an occasional bear.

'If you don't mind living on your own, you'll be all right,' Marzio had said.

Marzio knew Loredana, of course. He seemed to know everyone in the area. 'Don't try playing the big city boy with her,' Marzio had warned him. 'Loredana's bright. She could have gone to Rome, or anywhere, but she likes it here.'

In fact, that had been the first test.

'You moved here from London?' Loredana had said the first time they went out together for a pizza. 'What brings you to the backwoods?'

She had listened to him talk about his job for five minutes, then she'd smiled and said, 'I've never met a guy who studies wolves. Hey, don't they prey on innocent young maidens?'

'It all depends,' he'd said with a grin.

Then he had taken her up the mountain, and shown her the den.

'They're *tiny*,' she'd whispered, peering into the night glasses. 'The cubs are four days old . . .'

The first kiss had seemed inevitable.

She'd even asked questions. Why do wolves dig holes? Don't they run free on the mountains? He'd told her about the breeding cycle, raising the cubs, the pack taking to the hills, the young ones finding mates of their own. He couldn't remember the last time he had told a girl about his favourite animal, and he wondered whether it meant something.

In the end, he had come up with an answer: he'd been lucky.

And wasn't luck a funny thing? Such a strange kind of *luck*, too. The earthquake had brought him to Umbria. The wreckage, the ruins. If it hadn't been for the earthquake, he might still be in London and would never have met Loredana.

You couldn't tell anyone that, though.

I was saved by the earthquake . . .

They'd have punched his lights out.

He looked up.

Now, Venus was a ghost of a shadow. A new day was about to begin. Another day in Umbria. He felt like shouting out for joy, he felt so good. Then something his grandfather had told him popped into his head.

'Never tell anyone you're happy, Sebastiano. Don't even tell God. He'll try to take it away from you. We're supposed to suffer on Earth, remember that.' Then his grandad had raised his hands to the heavens and started to whine out loud. 'O, what a tragedy! What a terrible disgrace! Something bad's going to happen, I can feel it in me bones.'

His grandad had winked.

A golden crown of sunlight lit up the lip of the ridge. Cangio stood up, folded the blanket and raised his hands to the heavens.

'Oh, what a tragedy!' he moaned out loud. 'What a disgrace! Something bad is going to happen. I can feel it in me bones.'

In the woods on the other side of the valley, a wolf began to howl.

By then, Venus had almost disappeared.

NINE

4 August, 2012

'So, what are we looking at?'

The technician hadn't heard General Corsini enter the Special Ops video room, hadn't seen him move along the banks of monitors, glancing over the shoulders of the other video operators, then pass on to the next one.

'Sir . . .'

He pressed the pause button, meaning to stand up and salute, but the general's hand fell heavily on his shoulder and held him in his seat.

'Continue,' General Corsini ordered him.

The man in the white lab coat pressed 'play' and the action rolled on. 'This footage is from the NO TAV demonstration in Turin, sir. That high speed rail tunnel through the Alps is attracting all the media attention. A CCTV camera caught the Black Block up to their old tricks. There are a lot of new recruits, by the look of it.'

'*Italy's Got Talent*,' Corsini said, edging closer to the screen.

'I thought you'd want to see it, sir.' He pressed a button with a double-arrow and the video began fast-forwarding. 'This is the bit. Just look at what's happening around the van, and you'll see what I mean.'

He pointed to a light blue Fiat Fiorino that was backing out of a garage.

'They must have hidden it inside the off-limits zone a couple of days before the march.' He froze the frame, then zoomed in closer. 'They sprayed the camera, but the paint was cheap and runny.' He prodded the button and the film moved forward again in slow motion, advancing frame by frame.

The rears doors of the van were open, and someone was handing out gas masks, crash helmets and long wooden pick-handles. 'The registration plate has been identified. It belongs to an agitator from Monza that we've been following for some time. We can't identify any of the faces, unfortunately.' He froze the frame again and pointed with his finger. 'Except for this one. This lad here, General Corsini.'

A gang of masked and hooded youths in black clothes were crowding around the back of the van. There was only one exception: a boy in a green sweatshirt, hair shaved close to his scalp, an owlish pair of black-framed glasses on his nose and a green scarf dangling around his neck, who was standing beside one of the open doors of the vehicle.

'Watch what he does, sir,' the technician said.

The figures on the screen began to move again, hands going backwards and forwards, passing out clubs, masks, Molotov cocktails. There was no sound, no way of knowing what had been said. The boy in green grabbed the arm of one of the others, pulled him round and the two faced up to one another. They seemed to be arguing.

'What's going on?' Corsini asked.

'He seems to be trying to stop them,' the technician suggested.

'My guess is that he wants a mask and a billy-club.'

'Maybe, sir. But . . .'

The technician rushed the frames forward quickly, then slowed the film down to normal speed again. 'Here, the real action's over. The van's disappeared inside the garage, and they've hidden the gear. As you can see, sir, the one with the green scarf hasn't got a gas mask or a pick-handle. He's either careless, or stupid . . .'

'Directing operations, it seems.'

The technician cleared his throat. 'We stitched on a clip taken three minutes later from a camera on the other side of the square.' The video speeded up. 'This one's only black-and-white, sir, but you can't mistake him.'

'Stop there!' General Corsini whipped off his glasses and leant so close to the screen that his nose almost touched it. 'Now, go back slowly.'

Seen in reverse, the boy in the glasses wiped his mouth on his sleeve, drank from a fountain, stood up, then walked backwards away from the fountain.

'They seem to have left him on his own, sir.'

'Maybe he ditched them. Job done, he's off to organize the troops somewhere else. A lone wolf with a mission.'

'It's possible, sir.'

'Do we know who he is?'

'We've got him charted, sir. He turns up in quite a few protest videos. And he isn't always on his own. We've spotted three other agitators from the same town. A nascent cell, if I may say so, sir, though we've never seen them caught up in anything as big as this before.'

Corsini patted the technician on the shoulder. 'You've done an excellent job. The "Lone Wolves", let's call them. I want to know everything that you can find about them. Who they are, where they live, what they do.'

11.20

His morning capuccino lay on the desktop gathering dust.

General Corsini was studying the photographs and factsheets in the case file. One picture in particular had caught his attention. Those clear eyes peering out inquisitively from behind a pair of metal-rimmed glasses eyes were intelligent, alert, ironic. They stared with a bright twinkle directly into the general's eyes. The boy's lips were parted slightly, his head to one side, as if he were saying to the person who was taking the picture: *Hey, what's all the fuss about?*

Corsini read the factsheet that came with the mugshot.

Lorenzo Micheli, twenty-two years old. He still lived in the small town where he had been born – Spoleto in Umbria. A third-year student of philosophy at the university in Perugia, he was near the top of his class. The father was a left-wing trade unionist, the mother worked in an old folks' home. Lorenzo was a blood donor and a volunteer in a soup kitchen.

An angel, by all accounts.

The boy was a regular protestor in the region where he lived. If anybody was planning to build something up or knock something down, Lorenzo Micheli was in the front line carrying a placard saying NO! He had even organized a protest march in his home town against a proposal to construct a wind turbine plant in the nearby mountains.

Tilting at windmills?

General Corsi smiled as he read that Lorenzo attended classical music concerts when they were free, and philosophy conferences even when he had to pay. The close-up photo had been taken in Turin the day before the NO TAV march; he had been attending a two-day conference at the University of Turin regarding Socrates.

'A spot of philosophy, then a good old punch-up,' the general murmured.

There was another photograph in the file. Obviously shot at another protest march, the boy was wearing the standard Palestinian scarf over his nose and mouth – he seemed to favour the red one. The glasses looked out of place with the mask. Even so, dressed up for battle, Lorenzo Micheli looked menacing enough.

The scant material remaining in the file dealt with the three close friends who had gone on protest marches in Rome and Perugia with the Philosopher.

'D'Artagnan and The Three Musketeers,' he murmured.

Then, he opened the OS map and spread it out on his desk: UMBRIA.

A lot of things had been happening in Umbria in the months following the latest swarm of earthquakes. The national database kept coughing up odd statistics. Illegal arms had been seized in Foligno and Gubbio. Vast sums of money were pouring into the area as reconstruction work began. The banks in the province were having a high old time of it now that European money was involved. And not just the banks, General Corsini thought. Where there was cash, there were people who knew how to siphon it off: builders and planners, politicians and administrators, fixers and go-betweens. Plenty of controversy for Lorenzo Micheli and his crusading acolytes to get their teeth into.

He put the files aside and drained his cold coffee in a single draught.

Maybe he had found the 'egg' that he was looking for.

TEN

17 August, 2012

The abandoned badger's sett would serve as a den.

Cangio stopped by the roadside, studied the area through his binoculars. The area was isolated, easy to defend, perfect for hunting.

The first thing he had spotted in his new job was the pack of wolves that had taken winter shelter in the woods down on the lower slopes. There were droppings and piles of abandoned bones – birds, voles and even the ribs of a wild boar – spread over an area of a square mile. With the mating season about to start, and if everything turned out the way he hoped, he would be able to document and photograph the regeneration cycle – courtship, mating, digging out the den, the weaning of the cubs, the raising of the family. An article about the wolves in Umbria would have a better chance of getting into the *RRN*, *Rivista delle Riserve Naturali*, than the foxes he had left behind in London.

He didn't miss London one little bit.

The Sibillini Mountains were all he had been hoping for. For the first few months he'd been involved in civil defence work, helping to clear the rubble after the earthquake, but there hadn't been that much to do. The park was empty, more or less, and he had soon been allowed to get on with his job as a ranger.

Obviously, he had started out by taking a census of the wolf population.

He changed down to second gear, pulled into the turning space, and parked the ancient Land Rover, wanting to check the den's location from a different angle. It had been an uneventful patrol – no fallen rocks blocking the single-track road, no dead sheep, roaming bears or wild boars, just a huge crested porcupine sleeping slap bang in the middle of the road halfway up the mountain. Nothing to report, as usual.

It was a beautiful day. A cerulean blue sky above his head, a chill wind raking through the mountains. Wrapped up in his hooded, camouflage ski jacket, he peered through the binoculars, convinced that wolves would soon move into the area.

He intended to be there when they arrived.

It was a perfect place for wolves to breed. Scattered over the landscape were abandoned farms, forgotten churches and stone huts where shepherds used to sleep in the old days when they brought their flocks to graze up on the mountain top for the summer. Now the ruins were home to owls and a host of other birds, a perfect environment for a family of wolf cubs to thrive. Most of the people had gone, leaving earthquake-damaged homes and living in container boxes or wooden huts down in the valley. Nature was slowly taking possession of the land again, and no animal was better adapted to do so than the wolf.

He woke up every morning looking forward to the day ahead. And yet, for an instant, before he was wide awake, he had the strange sensation that if he opened his eyes he'd find himself back in his flat in London again.

He focused the binoculars, thought he saw a flash of movement near the hole.

Had the colonization started?

Cangio glanced at his watch. He should have been patrolling the woods further down the mountainside. A large herd of wild boar had been reported in the last week, marauding on the edge of town after dark. Complaints had been coming in about damaged fences, uprooted shrubs, ruined fruit trees and ravaged lawns. If a plant had a root, the boar would dig until they found it. The day before, Marzio had been talking about issuing hunting licenses to cull back the herd. Cangio didn't like the idea of shooting the boar, even if they were a damned nuisance, but something would have to be done about them, that was for sure.

The local hunters would be over the moon.

He packed up his binoculars and turned around. The Calabrian he had seen in the bar the week before was standing twenty feet away. While he had been watching the den, the man had been watching him. There was no way of knowing how long he might have been there, except by asking him, of course.

'Everything all right?' he asked, walking towards the man.

The man grunted something in reply.

'You're a farmer, aren't you?' Cangio asked him.

The man didn't answer him directly. 'I've seen you up here often. Looking for something, are you?'

There was something about him that Cangio couldn't quite put his finger on. He didn't seem curious but he was certainly inquisitive. He asked you questions as if he knew the answers already.

'There's an abandoned badger's sett over there,' Cangio said. 'I saw a wolf sniffing around it the other night. He'll be back soon with his mate, I reckon.'

The man's eyes never shifted. 'You going to shoot them?' he said.

Cangio couldn't hold back a laugh. 'They're a protected species,' he said. 'It's my job to protect the wolves. If they do decide to use the den, I'll probably have to cordon off the area for a mile around here to keep people away. How close is your farm?'

The man pointed to the west. 'More than a mile. Over that way,' he said.

'Don't leave any animals out at night,' Cangio warned him. 'Not even dogs. If wolves have got to feed a family, they'll kill anything in sight. Whatever you do, don't throw waste food on compost heaps. And for God's sake, don't try to feed them. They'll bite your hand off.'

A smile appeared on the Calabrian's face. 'Would I do something like that?' he said, then mumbled something about his sheep and turned away, leaving the ranger standing there on his own.

Cangio watched him disappear over the brow of the hill.

ELEVEN

18 August, 2012

There were just the four of them up there.

Which wasn't surprising, Zì Luigi Corbucci thought. Who the fuck would drive to the top of a mountain on a day like that? There was still no sign of the sun and it was freezing in the shadows.

Raniero and Ettore were sitting on the church steps wrapped up in their jackets, a life-sized lion reclining on either side of them. The stones lions had been guarding the entrance to the church since the days when Francis of Assisi used to come up there to pray, Cosimo Landini had chosen to inform them. But so fucking what? He hadn't come all that way to see a locked-up church.

Corbucci watched the two *picciotti* over Landini's shoulder.

Raniero and Ettore were fresh from home – Don Michele's boys – but they showed respect and did what he told them to do. Not like this old buzzard, Luigi Corbucci thought, staring into the face of the man with the silver-hair combover.

The banker was dressed for business: grey pinstripe suit, a trench coat worn loose, designer scarf with the label on show. They'd picked him up outside the station of the next town down the railway line – his idea. Cosimo Landini didn't want to be seen with them on his own patch. His face was the colour of battered beefsteak, blue and pink in the cold air. His hair kept lifting up like a silvery curtain in the wind.

'What's the problem, Landini?'

'I've been hearing rumours,' the banker said, looking him dead in the eye.

'What sort of rumours?'

'Other banks,' Landini said. 'We had an agreement, *Signor* Corbucci. I thought of you as a *privileged* client.'

'I should hope so, too.' Luigi nodded. 'The money we're putting up. But we need to get things moving . . .'

Landini cut him off sharply. 'Nothing happens overnight, *Signor*

Corbucci. It could take years. These projects have to go through so many planning committees. I understand how frustrating it must be, but that's the way it is. There are so many different levels, the local council, the regional authorities, the provincial government, the parliament in Rome. They all have to have their say. I'd be happier if we could speed things up, I assure you.'

Luigi Corbucci made one last try. 'You see that space down there?' he said, pointing to a field beyond the crossroads, white spots moving on a green board. 'We get rid of those sheep, put up a motel, catch the passing trade – travelling salesmen, lorry drivers, tourists. And that field next to it,' he pointed again. 'There's room for a four-storey car park with outside space for coaches. You make them pay for parking, obviously. A nice little town like this, you've got too many cars clogging up the centre. That's no way to greet your average day-tripper. We'll clean the place up then market it properly. You won't recognize this town in five years.'

Corbucci remembered reading somewhere that Hitler had said the same about Berlin before the Americans blasted it to smithereens.

'I believed that we were partners,' Landini was saying.

Partners in crime, Corbucci thought. Instead, he said: 'You need to speak with the movers and shakers, find out what they want, how much they're asking.'

'Me?' Landini objected. 'I'm a banker. I have a reputation in town. All this has got nothing to do with me.'

Zì Luigi took a deep breath, struggling to control his breathing. Landini had always known what he was getting into. That was what they were paying him for.

'Listen, Landini. Either you're in on the deal or you're out.' Corbucci turned and waved to Raniero and Ettore, telling them to start moving. Then he turned back to Landini. 'Make up you mind. I haven't got all week.'

The banker looked at him, a tight smile playing on his lips. '*Signor* Corbucci, don't tell me how I ought to run my business. I've helped you as far as I can.'

The soldiers were moving towards the car.

Raniero pointed the key, pressed a button and the clunk of opening doors sounded thunderously loud in the crisp, cold air.

Landini's face was set hard when he reached the car. 'Conditions here may not be what you're used to,' he said. 'But when in

Rome . . . You know the expression? There's nothing more that you can do to persuade me. You'll just have to wait.'

Luigi's face changed colour, his mouth changed shape, his eyes were two dark slits. Raniero wondered what would happen next. You could never tell with Zì Luì. It might be one of those tricks he used. If what Raniero had seen was anything to go by, Zì Luì would smile a big smile and win Landini over.

As Zì Luigi's hand went into his pocket, Raniero relaxed.

Here come the cigars, he thought.

The next second, Zì Luìgi was pushing an automatic in the banker's face.

'Nothing can persuade you?' he swore, and pulled the trigger.

There was a loud *click*, and that was it.

The banker stared at Zì Lugi, amazed that he was still alive, perhaps. Zì Luigi stood there like a block of ice, the gun still pointed at Landini's face. Then he started fiddling with the pistol, trying to release the clip, getting nowhere.

He's lost it, Raniero thought as he stepped behind the car.

No guns, Zì Luigi had told them, and the fucker had come up loaded himself?

Raniero pressed the catch and the boot yawned open. Don Michele would go bananas. He leaned inside the boot and came up with the jack. He hefted it for an instant, then smashed it into the back of Cosimo Landini's skull with a single blow.

The banker let out a sound like a punctured football. He sagged down on his knees and coughed up bile, a river of blood flowing down the back of his rain coat. Raniero watched and waited, expecting him to fall. When he didn't, he slammed his foot into Landini's shoulders and pushed him on to his face. Blood spots rained on the ground as he fell.

'Watch my fucking shoes,' Zì Luigi growled, stepping back.

He didn't seem to comprehend what he'd done, Raniero thought. Stick a gun in a man's face, you have to kill him. He'd never trust you again; stitch you up the first chance he got. Zì Luigi had fucked up, just like his mate, Corrado Formisano.

'I had to do it. You see how the fucker treated me?' Zì Luigi muttered, pushing the pistol deep into the pocket of his coat.

Raniero nodded, wiped the jack on Landini's coat then threw it into the boot of the car, where it landed with a clang. 'What now, Zì Luì?' he said without drawing a breath.

'Let him bleed,' Zì Luigi murmured, pulling out his smokes, offering one to Raniero, then to Ettore. 'We don't want to leave a trail of red drips as we drive through the town, do we?'

Zì Luì still didn't seem to get it. They'd killed the banker who was handling the deal, steering it through the planning committees. Who would Don Michele blame when he heard the news?

They stood there smoking, no one saying anything, then Zì Luigi crushed his fag beneath his shoe. 'He's bled enough,' he said. He stood there watching as Raniero and Ettore tipped the body into the boot of the Mercedes.

'Get rid of this heap of shit, Raniè. Take him up to Corrado. He'll know what to do with him.'

'Corrado?' Raniero stopped dead. 'You reckon that's a good idea, Zì?'

Zì Luigi bristled. 'You got a better one? He may as well make himself useful. He owes me after that mess he made with Bonanni.'

Exactly the same mess you've just made with Landini, Raniero thought.

'Whatever you think's best, Zì.'

'You can drop me off in town.'

'Aren't you coming, Zì? Corrado's bound to ask,' Raniero said.

Zì Luigi waved his hand dismissively. 'I've got nothing to say to him. Let him think I'm still pissed off. That'll sort him out. If it wasn't for me, he knows he'd be wearing a concrete waistcoat. Just tell him what to do, and make sure he does it.'

They drove back slowly down the hill, coasting through the hairpin bends, the dark woods pressing in on either side, broken now and then by an olive grove or a field where cows and sheep were grazing.

'This place is a paradise,' Zì Luigi said as they pulled up at the main road intersection, Raniero in the driver's seat, looking left and right for a gap in the traffic. 'Been growing olives here for a million years, they have. They make the finest oil in Italy. It's almost a pity to cover it with concrete.'

They dropped him in the centre of town then drove away.

'Where does this Corrado hang out?' Ettore asked.

'Next stop's on the far side of the valley,' Raniero said. 'Fasten your seat belt, Ettò. We don't want some traffic cop pulling us over, do we? Not with the cargo we've got in the boot.'

TWELVE

The same morning

The mayor smiled at his face in the bathroom mirror.

That final blast of ice-cold water after a hot shower was better than a whipping. It cleared your head of all the stuff you'd gobbled down the night before, helped you forget that you hadn't slept more than a couple of hours.

What a night it had been! The official celebration dinner after his recent re-election. The councillors and members of the election committee – no wives, of course – all waiting for him to order his meal when he stood up and headed for the loo. He could imagine the looks that had flashed round the table when Sandra Panetti had come traipsing after him a minute later. Women couldn't keep their hands off him. She had followed him into the men's room and smiled coyly as he stood there pissing in the bowl.

'Thanks, Maurizio,' she'd said.

'For what?'

'You know what.'

'There'll be a letter in the post tomorrow,' he'd said, giving himself as shake, 'making the appointment official.'

'Did anyone protest?'

'Who, for instance?'

Sandra'd shrugged. 'The Opposition, for instance.'

Truini had put his hand to his ear as if he was hard of hearing. 'With sixty-three per cent of the vote, who'd throw something like that in my face?'

He had just started to fasten his zip when Sandra stopped him.

Truini clenched his teeth and flashed another glance in the bathroom mirror.

'Opposition?' he asked his reflection.

Sandra hadn't put up any opposition, that was for sure.

Fingernails scraped on the bathroom door.

'Maurì, it's the phone,' Cesira whined. 'The blue one.'

His wife never knocked. She scraped like a rat, timid but furtive, knowing she was going to get on his nerves. Just like the people who worked for him at the town hall. They all scratched on the door of his office, leaving him to decide whether it was a knock or an earthquake rattling the fittings.

'Who's calling?' he barked, but didn't open the door. He only had a bath towel wrapped around his waist. Cesira would have seen the scratch on his left tit. Those prune-coloured nails of Sandra's were lethal.

'They didn't say,' Cesira whimpered.

Mayor Truini braced his hands against the washbasin and let out a sigh. She had to go. He really should get rid of her. He would have done it, too, if he could have kept the house. 'You can't kick a woman like Cesira out on to the street,' the party manager had warned him. 'You'd lose more votes than if you shot her in the main square. You have to seem to be the victim, Maurì. If she had a lover, for instance . . .'

The idea of Cesira having it off with someone made him want to laugh. She was the sort of woman every Trappist monk should have in his cell when he felt temptation coming on. She didn't drink, didn't smoke. She didn't even go to the bingo. She prayed first thing in the morning, last thing at night, went to Mass on Sundays and feast days. Could you kick a saint out on the street?

A saint?

Cesira stole from supermarkets. Packs of cheese, tubes of pâté, jars of mayonnaise. But he couldn't get shut of her for stuff like that. What would the voters say if he shopped his own wife for thieving? *Sure there's only one thief in the family?* They'd laugh at her for five minutes, then they'd crucify him.

He dropped the towel and wrapped himself in a black bathrobe, pulling it across his chest to cover his war wounds. Bloody Sandra!

His wife's nails rasped against the door again. 'Maurì?'

Truini pulled tight on the belt of his robe, then opened the door.

His wife peered up at him like a rabbit that knew it was on the lunch menu. She looked like a bit like a skinned rabbit, too. Long nose, no chin, large ears that lay flat against her skull.

'Where is it?' he growled.

Cesira raised her hand and showed him the mobile phone.

He grabbed it, closed the door in his wife's face, then sat down on the toilet seat.

'Good morning,' he said in a voice that was smooth but had an edge to it, as if he had been disturbed while doing something important. If they were calling on that number, it might be some big knob from the regional government, the local MP, or one of the national party coordinators.

'Did I wake you up, Truini?'

The mayor frowned. He didn't recall giving that number to Luigi Corbucci. In fact, he'd made a point of *not* giving him the number. And the question wasn't a question at all. It was more like a reprimand with no hint of an apology for disturbing him at home.

'I was having a shower.'

'Good for you, Truini. It's next to godliness, right? Just called to say that word's come through from the planning office. We won't have any trouble there. We're right on course with the building permits. It's time to start things rolling. Time for you to push the boat in the right direction. We're talking about the big one, understand?'

Was Corbucci pulling his leg?

'All the permits? That's impossible! What was it, a couple of months ago? You said you'd talk it over with the other partners . . .'

Truini recalled the conversation with Luigi Corbucci, but not in any detail. It had gone in one ear and straight out of the other. Nothing ever happened quickly in Italy, and Umbria was slower than most. Things dragged on for years and years. You had to have the right men in your pocket to get anything done in the countryside. The longer it took, the better, so far as he was concerned.

'Exactly. Three months back, Truini.'

Corbucci had to be taking the piss. You couldn't get approval for a project as big as that in a few months. Truini stood up from the toilet seat and closed the bathroom window. It wouldn't be the first time he had caught Cesira listening outside windows. He didn't give a bugger if she heard him chatting with Sandra, or one of the others, but not with Luigi Corbucci. There was too much at stake. The silly cow was capable of repeating every word she'd heard down at the hairdresser's, just to let them know how important her husband was.

'I'll have to call a council meeting . . .'

'The next one's scheduled for Friday.'

Did Corbucci realize what he was saying? They weren't in some one-street town in fucking Calabria. You needed to move like a deep-sea diver five miles down, wearing lead boots and a big brass helmet.

'I've issued the order of the day,' he said defiantly. 'The councillors know what they're supposed to be discussing. To be frank, I thought it would take a lot longer to approve this project. You'll have to break it to the investors. The people that we need to convince are the hardest nuts to crack.'

'What's got into you?' Corbucci's voice was as sharp as acid. 'They've already *been* convinced. They've *approved* the plan. All you've got to do is push it through the council, carry the vote with your majority, then leave it to the office johnnies for the rubber stamps and signatures. A piece of cake.'

Maurizio Truini pulled at the belt and his dressing-gown fell open. He was feeling hot and flustered. Corbucci was getting on his wick. First, he'd called up on the phone reserved for important official calls. Then, he'd practically told him what to do. Truini stood in front of the mirror and stared at the scratch on his chest.

'Why don't we wait a bit, then talk it over with the other partners?'

Corbucci's voice sliced through his own. 'We've talked it over, I told you. The next one off the ground's the housing estate. We'll set the others up according to the calendar. The shopping mall comes first, though.'

Truini was sweating now with anger and frustration. The shopping mall was a hand grenade, and Luigi Corbucci had just pulled out the pin. You couldn't plonk a concrete box of five thousand cubic metres anywhere you felt like. Everything inside the city walls was sacred. OK, you'd come out of the supermarket loaded down with carrier bags, and the view would take your breath away. But seen from the town, it would look as if the Martians had landed.

'It won't be easy . . .'

'Truini, you don't me need to tell you where all your votes came from. You wouldn't want me telling anyone else, I bet. We're counting on a mayor who isn't afraid to make the big decisions. Wasn't that the slogan for your election campaign? I'll be in touch.'

Fuck you! Truini's mind shrieked.

'I look forward to it,' he managed to say as the line went dead.

Cesira was waiting for him in the bedroom, looking as frightened as the condemned rabbit she reminded him of. He saw the question in her eyes, but he ignored it. What did he have to tell her? Who Luigi Corbucci was? What they'd been talking about?

'White jacket, pink jeans,' he ordered.

Cesira went to the wardrobe and laid the clothes he wanted on the bed, but that look would not go away.

'There's a funny smell in the garage,' she said as she passed him clean underwear and socks. 'It smells like drains, or something.'

'The neighbours,' he said dismissively, 'spreading manure on the tomatoes.'

Cesira shook her head. 'It doesn't smell like manure to me.'

Truini sprinkled on some D&G, finished dressing, then checked his appearance in the full-length mirror. That linen jacket was a work of art. A perfect fit, so long as he didn't button it over his gut. He knotted his tie – pink to match the jeans – then stretched his neck to the right. There was no sign of Sandra's nails. He pushed a large pink handkerchief loosely into his breast pocket, then left the house.

A couple of neighbours working in their gardens called 'good morning' as he walked down the ramp to the garage. He saw the way their eyes widened. The peasants seemed to think a mayor should dress in black like a cut-price undertaker. Dark blue or pearl grey was his choice for formal occasions; the rest of the time he could get away with just about anything.

He walked down the ramp and pulled up sharp in front of the garage door.

Cesira was right for once. That stink was not the usual smell of manure. He pushed the garage door, which rolled up automatically. The black 520D saloon was like a panther waiting to be let off the leash. He took a step inside the garage, punched the key and the locks tocked.

The smell seemed to be coming from the car itself.

Jesus Christ! If she'd had left a bag full of meat to rot in the boot he'd wring her bloody neck. You wouldn't get rid of a smell like that in a hurry. He pressed the button, and the boot clicked open with a noise like a mating grasshopper. He pressed on the boot lid and the baggage compartment yawned open on a spring-loaded mechanism. He stepped back coughing, as if a giant fist had come out of the boot and punched him in the guts.

He jerked to the right and coughed up his breakfast.

THIRTEEN

The same day

T he vast square outside the railway station was deserted.
Ragged election posters drooped and peeled from adver-
tising placards like forgotten laundry, the once radiant smile
of Mayor Truini washed-out and faded now. On top of the hill a
mile or so away, the town was hazy, out of focus, the lines of the
cathedral spire and the medieval castle shifting in the heat of
the midday sun.

The only sounds were the thrumming diesel engines of empty
buses waiting outside the station building and the hum of conversation from three dark-skinned boys who were huddling together under
a canopy outside the station bar, each one with a large canvas holdall.
They were waiting for the train which would carry them south. It
was a Friday, and they had come up for the weekly street market,
hoping to make a bit more money than usual as they wandered
around the small towns in the province, or stood outside the shops
and supermarkets offering Kleenex tissues, false Bic lighters, charm
bracelets and anything else that might tempt someone to stop and
buy. A lot of shoppers handed over a euro, then moved on without
bothering to look at the stuff they were selling. It was begging, and
they knew it. The good thing was that they rarely needed to replace
the stock. Other people, young kids for the most part, sometimes
stopped a little longer.

'Hey! Hey!' said one of the boys. 'We got us a fish, maybe.'

His eyes were fixed on a white car rolling on to the station forecourt, coming down from the town, though *white* was not the word
to describe the colour of the vehicle. The bodywork was an abstract
painting in distress. Rust had eaten away the bottom corners of the
doors and pocked the bodywork, while rings the colour of dry shit
encrusted the wheel arches.

'How much you unload today?' Malouf asked his friends.

'Two wraps,' Ahmoud grumbled.

'One,' the third boy said. 'Maybe these be good for four or five?'

'Six be better. Two for each of us.'

The car pulled up in the parking lot, but the doors stayed shut.

Two boys in their early twenties sat in the front seats, elbows resting on the open windows. The one in the driver's seat lit a cigarette and puffed smoke out into the air. The blue cloud rose in a vertical column, then got lost in the warm air. The passenger glanced towards the station, then turned and said something to the driver.

'They lookin' good,' Malouf said, propping his empty Coke bottle on the ground. He laughed and cupped his hands to his lips. 'Hey, man, we a-over here!'

It was a whisper, nothing more. A joke between friends. The boys in the old white car didn't hear the invitation. If they were interested, they would make a move when they were ready. If you went looking to make a sale, your sentence doubled. All three Africans had been in jail at least once. They didn't solicit for business on the streets of Italy any more. They showed themselves, then waited. People knew what they were selling. No one said a word, but they all lit cigarettes, moved to the edge of the pavement and stood there blowing out smoke signals. They were less than twenty yards from the boys in the car, who were sending out signals of their own, though they didn't know it.

If those Italian boys wanted snow, blow or Mary-Jane, they'd come looking for it.

'We've got ourselves a situation.'

The Watcher was speaking into a microphone that was activated by the asterisk symbol on his mobile phone. To all appearances, he was just an ordinary guy in a dark blue Lancia saloon car making a regular phonecall. The words of his supervisor sounded in the earpiece.

'What's going on?'

'Riccardo and Davide are sitting in the car outside the station. Three African dopeheads are giving them the come-on.'

'Take some pictures. If anyone spots you, drive away slowly. We've got taps on the vehicle now but we could fill the sound gaps with visuals. Buying drugs would look good on the report sheet . . .'

'They're getting out of the car.'

'And?'

'They're heading over towards the dealers.'

'Can you get a shot of them?' the supervisor asked.

The Watcher chuckled. 'I've just taken a couple. The money's in one, the baggies being handed over in the other.'

'Send them through by message mail. We'll put someone on the dealers' tails.'

'Someone?'

'There are two agents on the train, keeping an eye on our boy. They'll take care of the Africans. Don't bother following his mates into the station. Just stick behind their car and see where they take you, OK?'

'Zip.'

That was the closure code. The Watcher steadied the mobile phone on top of the steering wheel, as if he was reading a message. He zoomed in, then shot off three snaps of the drug dealers standing beneath the canopy. It wasn't easy to make out their features, but their clothes were distinctive enough: denim jackets, T-shirts, washed-out denims and worn-out trainers, each one carrying a big canvas hold-all. He would have bet that they were known faces.

Within a minute, he had sent the images off.

A tannoy announced the arrival of the train. A bell began to ring, a low, persistent, irritating tinkle that would go on clinking until the engine tripped a stop as it coasted up to the station platform.

The Africans slung their bags on their shoulders, then followed the boys into the station building. So far as the Watcher could see, there wasn't another person around. No one else was going to Rome so late in the day. There were no railway staff to be seen, no porters or station master. Like most railway stations in small Italian towns, everything was automatic now. You fed cash or a credit card into the right machine and the machine gave you tickets, guide maps, hot snacks, cold drinks, cigarettes, newspapers. There wasn't a vending machine for drugs yet, but it was only a matter of time.

At 14.15 the train pulled in.

By 14.18 the train pulled away again, taking the Africans south, but not home.

Depending on where they got off, they'd be arrested or followed. They might lead to bigger fish, of course, but they were small fry, probably not worth taking into custody. Six months free board in an overcrowded state prison and they'd be back on the streets again in another provincial town.

At 14.21 three boys walked out of the station.

The Watcher took a snap, then made a note on his timechart.

The two that he had been following, Riccardo Bucci and Davide Castrianni, plus the boy that they had gone to the station to meet. Lorenzo Micheli was the one that the Legend was interested in. The boy had a hold-all slung across his shoulder and was wearing a green military jacket, green camouflage pants and a pair of heavy Dr Martens boots. An anarchist according to the files, an activist and a protestor.

The Watcher opened his mobile phone again, pressed the gate symbol on the handset and held it to his ear. He could hear what the supervisor in the communications centre was hearing now. Doors opening, voices, doors slamming shut . . .

The rusty white Fiat Uno was bugged.

The voices often overlapped, but the Watcher recognized two of them. He knew who was saying what. Later, he would fill in the names on the transcript.

'How was the march, Lorè? I bet you didn't connect . . .'

There was an explosion of laughs and animal noises, and the car swerved violently as it left the station square fast.

'Watch the friggin' road, you asshole!'

'Asshole? Me? Let's hope you got your finger out, Lorè . . .'

'We shouldn't have let him go on his own . . .'

'Been hitting the bong, have you? That's all you lot are good for!'

'Talking of which, we got some stuff at the station – three Africans . . .'

'You call that brains? Jesus! Buying stuff on the street! The pigs'll—'

'What pigs? At two o'clock? They'll all be snoring after lunch!'

'Hey, Lorè? Did you meet them, then, or didn't you? I mean to say, if we're gonna organize something . . .'

The voices were lost as a CD came on, loud and booming.

'Turn that fucking rubbish down,' Lorenzo shouted. 'Turn it off!'

The music stopped as abruptly as it had started.

'They're a bunch of wankers. We need to make our voices heard.'

Two of the boys began to sing out loud, if you could call it singing.

'Come off it. Shite! We don't need anyone to tell us what to do. I've been giving it a bit of thought,' Lorenzo said. 'After the earth-quake, nothing here is ever gonna be the same again. And once the cash starts rolling in—'

'Let's hope there's some for me. I've got a leaking roof and walls full of cracks.'

'Listen up, I'm talking about a protest movement. Rebellion. They're gonna start building roads an' stuff, pouring concrete all over the place. We've got to fight, resist, do something that'll make a noise, you get me? We need to make a splash. Then the Block'll come rushing to help *us*. But *we* are the ones who have to start it. Like . . . Like the Sioux when the white men came. We'll . . .'

The car was full of whooping Indians now, like in the films.

Lorenzo Micheli joined in for a bit, then yelled at them: 'Shut the fuck up, will ya? We're gonna have to meet and work out a plan of action.'

'Tonight we hit the woods, Lorè, build a bonfire . . .'

'It's all sorted – roast sausages, beer, the dope we picked up from those Africans.'

'How does that sound for the start of a revolution?'

Lorenzo Micheli let out a sort of war cry, and the other two joined in.

FOURTEEN

Later that day

Corrado Formisano struck a match.

Down in the valley he saw the tiny black dot approach the first bend. It would take the car ten minutes to reach the farmhouse.

He lit the cigar then drew the harsh smoke deep down inside his lungs. He had picked up the habit in prison. Whenever he felt the four walls closing in, whenever he felt like slitting somebody's throat, he turned away and lit a cigar. Few of his cellmates knew how lucky they had been. Only one of them had ever made the mistake of moaning about the smell, and he never did it again. Not after having swallowed a lighted Garibaldi cigar. Word got around fast inside the maximum-security block.

Now, Corrado was smoking to calm his rage.

He caught sight of the car again as it went round a bend. The narrow road twisted and turned like a snake slithering to the top of the mountain, but the farmhouse was as good as a watchtower. If you saw someone coming up you had plenty of time to decide whether to hang around or take to the woods. He'd had been living there for over a year and hadn't had a visitor until Raniero Baretta had shown up one day a couple of months before.

Raniero had phoned him half an hour ago.

'I'm on my way, Corrà,' he said. 'Don't go walkies.'

He didn't say a word about Zì Luigi.

Raniero was one of Don Michele's boys. Corrado remembered him from way back. Raniero had a face like a weasel, a guarded smile and some hollow charm. He still recalled the look of awe on the kid's face the first time they'd met. Corrado had been Zì Luigi's shooter then. Had been? *Still was.* Now, Raniero was climbing the tree, it seemed, and Corrado didn't like him any better on that account.

Who the fuck did he think he was ordering about?

The Mercedes pulled into the farmhouse yard a few minutes later. The chickens scattered in a flurry before the wheels, flapping their wings, clucking aloud, resenting the intrusion. As the big car skidded to a halt and the motor cut out, the birds went back to their never-ending grind, pecking at the hard ground, fighting over a grain of corn.

Raniero called from the window. 'How you keeping, Dead-Eye?'

Corrado stiffened, flicked the cigar away. The nickname sounded like an insult on Raniero's lips. He walked down the stone staircase, getting ready to tell the fucker to watch his mouth and show respect, but as Raniero got out of the Merc the passenger door swung open and another punk climbed out as well. Shorter than Raniero, he was built like a tank. If Raniero was the brains, his mate was the muscle.

'Who's your friend?'

'Ettore,' Raniero said. 'He's a new recruit.'

Corrado nodded and the punk nodded back, his eyes two narrow slits.

A blue tattoo wound up the kid's throat and curled way behind his ear like a sick-looking creeper. Corrado pointed his finger at it. 'What's that you've got on your neck – some poxy birthmark?'

Ettore didn't say a word. He didn't look away, though.

Raniero spoke instead. 'That's a salamander, that is. Ain't never seen one, Corrà? They're all the fashion, these days. A lizard that walks through flames? You come through a gunfight, you've earned yourself the tattoo. Don't worry about Ettore. He knows how to handle himself. All my boys have got one. I'd show you mine,' he grinned, 'but I wouldn't want to make you blush, Corrà.'

All my boys?

How many men did Raniero have working under him? The announcement put him even more on his guard. There couldn't be more than half-a-dozen lieutenants Don Michele trusted that much.

Then another thought flitted through Corrado's mind.

Was that the lizard the park ranger had spotted at Soverato beach? One of Raniero's boys? Ettore, maybe?

Raniero tapped his fist against Corrado's clenched bicep.

'Nice place Zì Luigi found you, Corrà,' he said, his face cracking into another cheesy grin.

Ettore smiled when Raniero did, Corrado noticed.

'You're out of harm's way up here,' Raniero went on.

Corrado shrugged his shoulders. 'A man gets sick of talking to himself.'

'You need a bit of company, sure,' Raniero said. 'That's why—'

Corrado cut him short. 'Why didn't Zì Luì come up?'

Raniero took a step towards him, showing Ettore his back, blocking him out, as if he had something to say that wasn't meant for the punk to hear. 'Luigi's got things to do in town,' he said. 'Don Michele wants to pump the action up, but things ain't easy. We won't be on our own up here for long, Corrà. We've got to cover every base.'

Corrado took in what Raniero was saying. *Luigi?* Where was the respect in that? Luigi Corbucci was *Zì* Luigi, boss of the *comandamento,* the top dog in Umbria.

'What's that supposed to mean?'

Raniero raised his hand and mimed a pistol. 'No fireworks, Corrà. Not for the moment, anyway. You know the tale about the stick and the carrot. Mules, right? If it won't take the carrot, give it a wallop? We have to convince the locals to cooperate, not frighten them to death. The Light Infantry, let's say, which ties our hands. *'U capisc', no?*' He lit a cigarette, waved away the smoke. 'You nearly blew the lid off it, you did. Andrea Bonanni, right?'

Corrado's temper erupted. 'The fucker was spilling his guts to the law!'

'And you blew his brains out.' Raniero shook his head, then made a clicking sound with his tongue.

'Zì Luigi said to shut him up.'

'A quiet word. That's what he meant.' Raniero took a deep breath, let the air out slow. 'You're a shooter, Corrado. The best there is, and everyone knows it. But this is not the time for guns. We have to keep our heads down, only do what Don Michele tells us to do. When the time's right . . .'

Raniero let the promise hang.

Corrado felt something like a chill wind on the back of his neck. 'Where does that leave me? They want to ditch me, right? Is that why Zì Luigi never comes up?'

Raniero joined his hands in prayer, moving them back and forth like an admonishing priest. 'What the fuck has got into you? We need you more than ever, mate.' His voice dropped down a tone, turned serious. 'Just – don't – shoot – anyone, Corrà. Do what you're told, and nothing more. Another trick like Bonanni . . .'

Corrado felt a flood of sweat beneath his armpits, despite the cold.

'Is that what Zì Luigi sent you up here to tell me?'

'I'm here to tell you what we want you to do.'

Corrado felt the tension ease off inside his chest. They hadn't stitched him up, then. No shooting, that was the message. Not now, maybe later. There were other jobs that they wanted him to do. Probably more stupid stuff, like stinking up the mayor's car.

Raniero clapped his hands and smiled. 'What happened to your southern hospitality? Ain't you going to offer us a drop of vino, Corrà?'

It sounded like a request, but Corrado knew that it was an order. He felt like killing the pair of them with his bare hands, and he would have done it, too, if it hadn't been for Zì Luigi and Don Michele. They'd take it personally, and that would be the end of everything.

He went into the house to get a bottle of red and three glasses.

When he came back out, Raniero was sitting on one of the plastic chairs near the barn. Corrado often sat out there at night and smoked a cigar, watching the glimmering lights in the valley below. Ettore was standing behind Raniero's shoulder, which left one empty seat. Corrado had seen that set-up a hundred times before – prison chairs in prison interrogation rooms.

Raniero watched him come. 'It's secluded here,' he said. 'Maybe they could spot you from a plane. Have a seat, Corrà.'

Corrado gave them glasses, poured out the wine, then sat down.

Raniero crossed his long legs. 'Is it as quiet as it looks? That's what I'm thinking.'

Corrado took a sip of wine. 'I ain't got a woman, if that's what you mean.'

Raniero laughed as if he'd made a joke. 'Just like prison, eh? Still, we saw loads of working girls on the road coming up from the south. Black, but not that it matters. Do you bring them up here, then?'

'I come back on my own.'

Raniero nodded and took a drink. 'What about the neighbours?'

Corrado shrugged. 'The nearest farm's a mile away.'

'Get on well, do you?'

'They're peasants. What have we got to talk about?'

'So what's the score with the cops?'

'I go to town each Friday, sign on.'

'They ever come up here to roust you?'

'Why should they? I'm on parole, not under house arrest.' Corrado placed his glass on the ground, then turned to face Raniero. 'What's with all the questions?'

Raniero drained his glass, and Ettore did the same.

Corrado saw a butterfly tattoo on Ettore's wrist. Blue, smudged. A prison tattoo. Anything that could fly was popular when you were locked up day and night. Corrado had tattoos himself. Only two, though. Old style. No birds or bees, just dates. That lizard on the punk's neck, though. That was shouting out for recognition, that was.

Raniero clicked his tongue against his lips. 'This wine's piss, Corrà,' he said. 'What was the stuff that you were famous for?'

'Sassicaia.'

'The very best!' Raniero said.

'Zì Luigi always sent me a bottle when I had a job to do.'

Corrado hesitated for an instant, but he didn't ask the question that was plaguing him: Will he ever send me another one?

'We've got a got a job for you to to do,' said Raniero. 'An important job.'

'Like what?'

'We want you to take care of a guest.'

Corrado stared at him. He should have realized this was coming. They wanted him to shelter someone on the run. The farm was just about as remote as you could get. 'When's he coming?'

'He's here already.'

Instinctively, Corrado glanced towards the car.

Raniero smiled. 'He's in the boot,' he said.

Corrado felt his head begin to spin, and it wasn't the wine that was doing it. Raniero had shot someone. Or Zì Luigi had done it himself. Why hadn't they told *him* to do it? For a moment, Corrado found it hard to breathe.

'What happened?' he managed to say.

'He didn't keep his side of the bargain. He has to disappear.'

They had a job for him, all right: gravedigger.

'We need to take a look around,' Raniero told him.

Corrado stood up, but Raniero wasn't having it. 'Leave it to Ettore,' he said with a wave of his hand. 'Let's see what he's made of.'

Corrado's eyes followed Ettore as he opened the door and stepped inside the barn, acting like he owned the place. Corrado felt impotence welling up inside him. Anger, too. He wasn't armed, but Raniero was, he'd have bet on it. It was like when the guards walked in unannounced and turned your cell upside down.

He lit a cigar and held the smoke in his mouth, blowing it out very slowly.

'The man in the boot,' he said. 'Who was he?'

Raniero shrugged. 'A piece of shit.'

Ettore emerged from the barn and waved his finger. 'Nothing, Raniè,' he said.

'We can bury him in the woods,' Corrado suggested.

Raniero gave him a sharp look. 'Animals would dig him up in no time.'

Corrado crushed his fist tight, almost snapping the cigar in two. He couldn't stand being told what to do by a punk who would have shit himself rather than open his mouth not so many years before.

'There's one thing, though,' Ettore said, his eyes sparkling.

'A can of petrol?'

'Pigs, Raniero. Pigs.'

Raniero sat up straight. 'Will they do the job?'

'We'll need to give them a helping hand.' Ettore's blank eyes turned on Corrado. 'What's that dog you've got locked in the cage?'

Corrado spat. 'That ain't no dog. It's a wolf.'

Raniero tapped his ankle with the tip of his shoe. 'Keeping a zoo now, are you, Corrà?'

'It's just a cub,' Corrado said. 'I found it wandering on the mountainside a few months back. It was lost, maybe, or the pack had left it behind. They come round looking for food in winter.'

He had brought the cub back, fed it, kept it in the cage, watched it grow. There was something about a wolf that Corrado liked. The fierce independence, the sparkling eyes that didn't miss a thing. It would eat whatever he gave it, but it wasn't tame and never would be. A bit like himself, he sometimes thought.

'They're fucking eating machines,' Ettore said.

'Pigs are greedier,' Corrado shot back at him. He didn't want them touching the wolf. 'Pigs keep on eating till they burst. An' there's four of them.'

Raniero clicked his tongue against his teeth. 'You're the expert,' he said after a bit.

Ettore seemed to find the situation funny. 'A wolf might come in handy one of these days, Raniero, eh?'

Raniero gave a sigh. 'That's a thought . . . Come on, lads, there's work to be done. Corrado, you give Ettore a hand.'

Raniero didn't make a move. He sat there smoking, Don Michele's adjutant, waiting for Corrado Formisano to obey his orders, watching as Ettore opened the boot of the car.

'Don't you wanna see him?' Ettore pulled away a plastic sheet, then threw back a strip of dirty rain coat. Half the man's face was ghostly pale, as if it had been drained of blood. The other half looked like a block of mahogany, the side staved in, an eyeball hanging loose.

They hadn't shot him.

Corrado felt the tension lift. They'd given him a whack with something heavy. Maybe Raniero wasn't spinning him a line. When the time came, when Zì Luigi really did want someone shot, he'd send for Corrado, like he'd always done.

'You ready?' Ettore said.

Corrado let out a sigh, then grabbed the dead man's legs.

Once they got the body inside the barn, Raniero came to watch. There was an old boiler suit and a pair of wellies that Ettore could wear, Raniero decided. Ettore didn't ask any questions, never said a word. He did what Raniero told him to do, and seemed pleased at the thought of a bit of exercise.

'Needs to get his hands dirty,' Raniero said with a grin. 'The way we all did.'

It took less than an hour.

Ettore cut the body into bits with the diesel chainsaw, then began to feed the pieces into the pigsty. 'Those pigs must think it's Christmas,' Raniero said as he drained the last of the wine. 'Listen up, Corrà, we can't use pigs all the time. You'll need to collect all the bones and burn them. A barrel of nitric acid should do it next time. Drill a small hole in that concrete feeding trough and all the muck'll run off into the soil.'

'Will there be others, then?' Corrado asked him.

Raniero blew out his lips. 'Who can say?' He clicked his tongue as if he'd just remembered something else. 'There's one other thing,' he said, walking out of the barn towards the car, telling Ettore to finish up. He waited for Corrado, led him to the Mercedes and opened the rear door. A white pine box that looked a bit like a baby's coffin was resting on the back seat.

'A sign of our appreciation,' Raniero said, handing it over.

Who's we? Corrado thought. He recognized the box. It was similar to the ones that Zì Luigi used to send him. But Raniero had said no guns. *What the fuck was he playing at?*

Raniero led him back into the barn.

'You'll find an envelope inside the box,' he said. 'Next time you go to town, just drop it in the post, Corrà.' Then he turned to Ettore. 'You finished yet?'

Ettore unzipped the boiler suit and dropped it on the floor beside the chainsaw. 'All done,' he said.

Raniero walked to the far end of the barn, lit a cigarette and peered into the cage where the wolf was staring back at him from the farthest corner.

'Fuck me!' he said. 'I've never seen a wolf close up before.'

FIFTEEN

The same day, a different mountain

'Sip it slow, Brigadier, or you'll just feel worse.'

Brigadier Tonino Sustrico nodded gratefully and took another sip. Could anything be worse than what he had already seen that morning?

The farmer, Roberto Casini, had run back to his cottage for a bottle of wine when he saw the *carabiniere* officer collapse in a heap. The wine burned like vinegar in Sustrico's throat, but he felt a welcome tickle as it hit the lining of his stomach.

'I brewed it myself,' Casini was saying. 'It goes down like a trout swimming with the stream. Have another drop, Brigadier.'

Sustrico hadn't eaten anything that morning, that was the problem. He'd just had a cup of black coffee before leaving the house, his shift due to start at seven. As commander of the local *carabinieri* barracks, he was used to having his breakfast served up on his desk at nine o'clock – a capuccino and a hot honey-filled croissant.

But Roberto Casini had phoned before breakfast arrived.

Casini was a farmer, he said. He lived in the village of San Bartolomeo sul Monte. He had found something, though he wouldn't say exactly what it was at first, as if he thought the *carabiniere* might not be interested.

'You might want to take a glance,' he said vaguely, apologising almost, the way that mountain dwellers often did. 'If you've got the time, that is.'

'What have you found?' Sustrico insisted.

'A body,' Casini said at last.

Sustrico had driven up to San Bartolomeo sul Monte by the 'scenic route' as the tourist map called it, a narrow ungravelled road which wriggled its way up the top of the mountain like an earthworm. There was a breathtaking view of the valley on the left-hand side, picturesque medieval villages in rough stone clinging to craggy outcrops of rock, as if an artist had decided to put them there for the benefit of visitors.

Sustrico usually enjoyed a drive in the national park, but Special Constable Eugenio Falsetti had been at the wheel that morning.

A fast-track recruit in his mid-twenties, recently arrived from Milan, Falsetti had been seconded to the local force for three months to 'widen his professional experience'. The kid was a dogsbody, that was the truth of it, filling in for one of the regular officers who was away on sick leave. Falsetti hadn't been impressed by anything they'd seen – the amazing view, the dark green pines, the pretty villages – least of all, the human leg poking out of a crack in the rock at a place called Belvedere.

Sustrico's eyes had blanked the instant he saw it.

'From the knee down,' Roberto Casini had said, though 'from the knee up' was more correct. The skeletal leg was pointing straight up into the sky, like a flagpole flying bits of muscle and shreds of skin, as if some malign hand had pushed the body hard into the ground the way you might stub out a cigarette in an ashtray.

The thought of somebody doing that to you had made him black out.

Sustrico had seen just three corpses in his working life. They'd all been battered about a bit, but that was standard when they'd all been involved in motor accidents.

'You get used to it,' Eugenio Falsetti was saying, standing over him as he came round, folding his arms like a veteran. 'I threw up the second day on the job in Milan. A shoot-out in a Chinese sweat-shop. Six dead. A real bloodbath, that was.'

Twenty-two years of service, and Sustrico had fainted like a novice.

As he questioned Roberto Casini, Sustrico was careful to keep his back to the scene. The leg sticking up in the air like a leafless tree had made a lasting impression on him, but it didn't seem to bother the farmer. It didn't bother Falsetti, either. He made himself useful on the phone, calling up the doctor, telling him where they were and what they were doing, telling him to get a move on.

'Half an hour, Chief,' Falsetti announced, and lit a cigarette.

Sustrico didn't like that 'chief'. There was rank in it, but no respect.

'Until the doctor arrives,' Sustrico said, 'we don't touch anything.'

'Standard,' Falsetti said.

Which left Roberto Casini. Sustrico wondered whether the farmer might be able to tell him anything useful. In particular, he wanted to hear Casini's version of how he had stumbled across the body.

'It was just . . . there, wasn't it? Like it sprouted overnight. Didn't you feel the shock down in town? Eleven o'clock last night? A minor earthquake, they said on the telly this morning. I lost some tiles off the roof. It must have split the rock, or shifted it sideways, and it pushed that leg up out of the crack. As anyone can see.'

He kept pointing, but Sustrico was careful not to look again.

'If you ask me, they killed the beggar, shoved him in, then filled the crack with muck and leaves. The head should be . . . just about there.'

Casini seemed to be convinced that the body belonged to a murder victim.

'Why push someone into a crevice?'

Casini took another swig of wine. 'It's easier than digging,' he said. 'Then there's the scavengers. The woods round here are full of boar. Wolves, too. They'd have a hard time getting at it, see. The juicier bits were deep inside the rock. Whoever put him there didn't want him to be found.'

Logical and possible, though an accident was still the most likely explanation.

'Any idea who he might be?' Sustrico asked.

The farmer looked at him sharply. 'The killer?'

'The leg, the victim. Has anyone disappeared from the village in the past few months? They might have fallen into the hole by accident – left the house, went for a stroll and never came back.'

Casini shook his head. 'There's eleven of us up here in winter, Brigadier. Thirty or forty in summer when tourists rent out the empty cottages. I'd know if anyone was missing. If you ask me, that poor sod's been there for quite a bit.'

Doctor Sordini arrived a short while afterwards.

He confirmed what the farmer had said as soon as he saw the leg. 'It didn't happen yesterday,' the doctor said. 'It depends how well the rest of the body was covered up. The leg's been stripped of flesh, probably exposed to air and insects. We won't know about the rest until we see it.'

The doctor was happy to sample the wine when the farmer offered him the bottle.

'If I'm going to certify it,' Sordini said to Sustrico, 'you'll need to pull it out.'

As coroner, the doctor's job was simply to verify the fact that a death had occurred.

'Isn't a skeletal leg enough?'

'A leg is not a vital organ.'

Casini offered to bring a pick and spade from his farm, but he didn't offer to help them. That job fell to Sustrico and the special constable.

'Which "vital" organ are we looking for?' Falsetti asked the doctor with a snigger.

Sordini glared at him. 'Heart, lungs, kidneys . . .'

'You're lucky,' Casini chipped in. 'The earthquake's done the hard work. You just need to loosen the soil then pull him sideways out of the crack. I'll bring another bottle of wine. It's dry work, digging.'

Tonino Sustrico told him not to bother, but after ten minutes shifting soil that had fallen in a heap at the foot of the rock face, and some more minutes pulling bones and bits of clothing from the crack – handing them to the doctor, who laid the pieces out on a plastic sheet – the two policemen wiped their brows and reached for the bottle.

Doctor Sordini joined them. 'The evidence won't run away,' he said. 'I can safely assert that he . . . that *it* is a man. You can tell by the length of the thigh bone.'

'The partisans buried their dead up here during the war,' Casini was telling Falsetti, 'but I've never come across a skeleton before . . .'

As he was speaking, Falsetti pulled a skull out of the rock and held it up.

There was a hole in the centre of the forehead the size of a plum.

'You ever butchered a pig?' Casini asked. 'Shoot a bolt between its eyes, it doesn't feel a thing.' He pointed at the hole in the skull. 'Point-blank range, see? It doesn't mean he died straight off, though. Sometimes, those pigs just keep on squealing . . .'

'It's possible,' the doctor said quickly, cutting him off. 'With a head wound, it's often hard to say how soon the victim died, though it's usually instant. There'll be forensic evidence in the soil, of course. And if he was killed here, the bullet will be in there some-where, too. I think we must assume that he was murdered, Sustrico. We need to call in the experts to establish the crime scene and vacuum out the crevice.'

Falsetti hooked a biro through one of the eye-sockets and deposited the skull with the rest of the remains on the plastic sheet. They stood there like mourners at a wake, looking down at the body draped in decaying rags, hair still clinging to the skull, flaps of blackened skin like polished leather, rubbery-looking gristle which held the joints together. The back of the skull was missing but there were plenty of teeth, some loose, some still attached to the jaw. Falsetti showed an unhealthy interest in a dark flap of skin attached to the shoulder bone. 'There's a mark of some sort, though I can't make it out. You'd need to blow it up on a computer screen.'

'Is there anything that might identify him?' Sustrico said to Falsetti. 'Labels, bills, a driving licence?'

Falsetti was down on one knee next to the plastic sheet the farmer had provided. He looked up at Sustrico, then at the doctor and let out a groan. It was obvious who was going to have to do the dirty work.

'See if there's anything in his pockets,' Sustrico told him.

Falsetti pulled a face, but he went through the pockets of what remained of a jacket and trousers.

'Nothing,' he said.

'Have another look inside that crack in the rock.'

Falsetti glared at him. 'If the Regional Crime Squad . . .'

'Take a look!' Sustrico snapped. The sod was playing the know-all now, just because his commanding officer had fainted. 'That's an order.'

Falsetti leaned against the rock, moved his hand around inside, then said: 'What's this, then?' *This* turned out to be a rusty *Moretti* beer bottle top. 'If we're going to identify him, the pathologist's going to have to work some magic in the examining room,' he said, wiping the dirt from his hands, then rubbing his hands on his trousers.

'What do you think, Doctor?'

Doctor Sordini stroked his chin and looked perplexed. 'There isn't much to work on. Dental records might help, if they exist. I mean to say, if we don't know who *he* is, we don't who his dentist might be.'

He seemed to offer little hope of ever identifying the dead man.

'Let's wait for the Regional Crime Squad,' Sustrico said, putting an end to the discussion. The thing that worried him most was the

thought that he would end up with an unsolved case on his desk
– a dead man, an unidentified killer.

'Falsetti, make the call. Use the car radio. It'll be recorded
automatically.'

Falsetti opened his mouth to protest, then raised his arms in
surrender. As he walked towards the farm and the car, he stopped
and lit a cigarette. He didn't seem to be in a great hurry.

'Which hole did *he* crawl out of?' Sordini asked.

Sustrico smiled. 'He's a self-righteous little bugger, isn't he? A
temporary placement. Thank God he won't be here forever.'

The doctor nodded. 'After what he's seen today, he may ask to
go home earlier.'

Sustrico didn't bother to correct him. 'He's from Milan. A grad-
uate trainee. Came down here expecting a holiday in the country, I
imagine. He didn't think he'd have to get a bit of dirt on his hands.
That'll teach him!'

'I wasn't expecting it either,' the doctor complained. 'I haven't
been called to a murder scene in the last ten years. A husband who
blasted his wife with a twelve-bore shotgun. A hideous spectacle,
but nothing like this. A murderer is almost unheard of in Umbria,
I'd say.' He picked up the bottle of rosé. 'Another drop, Sustrico?
I hate to think of having to spend the rest of the week sorting
through the bones. Thank God for the RCS!'

When the ambulance and the Regional Crime Squad arrived, the
bottle was empty.

It wasn't such a bad wine, Tonino Sustrico decided.

Doctor Sordini had already ordered a dozen bottles from Roberto
Casini.

SIXTEEN

A week later, near Perugia

General Corsini pressed a button and the glass panel slid
down. 'Ease up, Gianfranco,' he said to his driver. 'There's
no hurry.'

The driver let the Alfa cruise down to fifty on the crowded

motorway. Cars and lorries started piling up behind them. No one was going to racc past a dark bluc saloon car with *Carabinieri* written on the flank in large white capital letters.

Corsini raised the glass panel.

If you got there early, a secretary would offer you a seat and ask you to wait. It was one of the games that political people played, especially in the smaller provinces. He could use the time more profitably in the comfort of his car, look through the documents, decide how much to tell her. The situation left no room for error. He wanted President Donatella Pignatti to understand that he had taken the trouble to come to her, but *not* to praise or flatter her. If you took the evidence at face value, she was no better than a house-maid that you couldn't trust. Let her roam around on her own and she'd steal the family silver.

The press didn't call her the 'Queen' for nothing, though the file his men had put together said a great deal more about the highest-ranking politician in the province. The new president of the county had got herself into a fix, shifting people about and making enemies, getting rid of some and filling the empty seats with people who would do her bidding. She knew there was an official investigation going on but she couldn't know how wide the net had been cast. Magistrates in Rome were digging up dirt on the construction company that the Queen was about to pass judgement on. Favourable judgement, obviously. Millions of euros were up for grabs. What the magistrates didn't know was who the construction company really belonged to.

Only General Corsini knew.

And the Queen, obviously. She was the key to the plan that was forming in his mind.

Had he been superstitious, a gypsy might have told him that a young woman with spiky red hair held his future in her hands. Then again, if the Queen had been offering her palm for a reading, the gypsy would have warned her to be on the lookout for an older man in a dark blue uniform who could pull her out from under an avalanche of serious accusations: abuse of power, corruption, specu-lation and a great deal more. And that was what he meant to do, of course. Save her and save himself. They would see eye to eye, he was convinced of it.

His telephone trilled the first five notes of a march by John Philip Souza.

'Corsini,' he said quietly into the mouthpiece.

A smooth voice wished him a very good morning, thanked him for all the trouble he was taking and hoped that the traffic wasn't too heavy. Finally, the voice asked him the question that he had been expecting.

General Corsini listened politely. 'Inform the president that I can't be there any earlier,' he said. 'I'll see her at eleven o'clock or shortly after, as we agreed.'

He snapped the phone shut and smiled. The Queen was nervous. She wanted to get the meeting over with. She couldn't wait to find out what it was all about. And if the tone of the secretary's voice told him anything at all, the Queen was running scared.

He lowered the dividing glass again. 'Pull in at the next service station, Gianfranco. They do an excellent espresso. We've got all the time in the world.'

Paolo Gualducci put the phone down.

'No chance. He must have another appointment lined up first.'

Donatella Pignatti – *Doctoressa* Pignatti, as everyone called her, making the effort to show respect for her academic background and lick her shapely backside at the same time – let fly a wrathful curse. 'They say that he's a shit. He's full of himself, apparently.'

If her private secretary had been the only person there, she would have said a great deal more, and with far more virulence. She signed the papers that the bald clerk was holding in front of her then waited until the door closed behind him. The clerk would carry the message around the building: 'Watch out, she's in a royal mood today.' As a rule, they dressed her temper up in brighter tinsel, saying what a tough pair of balls she had.

She sat back in her padded leather seat. 'What is this general *doing* here, Paolo? What's his game?'

Gualducci shrugged his shoulders. 'Someone in Rome might know.'

Donatella Pignatti ran her fingers lightly through her gelled hair, conjuring up the spikes.

'Ask *them*? You must be joking! It would be all over party headquarters in less time than it takes to . . .' She let out a sigh. 'Those bastards would be turning somersaults if they knew that he was on my tail. The question is which cards is he holding in his hand?'

'A pair of sevens, at least. He must have something worth betting on,' Gualducci said. 'Still, looking on the bright side, he isn't here officially. It is a courtesy visit.'

'Courtesy, my arse! I'll be quaking by the time he gets here. I can't even talk to my lawyer.' She stood up, walked to the window and looked down on the traffic in the square, the stream of people coming out of the building like a file of ants, all heading for the nearest bar. 'Last night I dreamt that a handsome stranger handed me a string of pearls,' she said.

'A gift's a good sign,' Paolo reassured her. 'A string of pearls. Wow!'

The Queen turned on him, her face dark with rage. Lipstick had bled at the corner of her mouth, but who had the courage to tell her?

'Bollocks, Paolo! Pearls mean tears. Don't you know that?' She ran her fingers through her hair again. 'Those horrid black uniforms – like giant bloody crows. You know what *they* bring. Shit, and more shit!'

Paolo Gualducci had only seen her once before in such a state: a party delegation had come up from Rome the month before, bringing news that they were thinking of backing a different candidate in the next regional election. Too many rumours were going around on her account, they said, and none of them were good. She had started off magnificently, showing the balls that everyone was always going on about, but then the mask had started to slip.

Today, he thought, she sounded like a housewife at the wrong time of the month.

SEVENTEEN

The same morning, Spoleto

Donna Tardioli had been the mayor's secretary for two months.

She'd been working in the registry office previously. She was still in the same building, but up on the top floor now, with more responsibility and a better salary. There had been a shorthand test and a personal interview with Mayor Truini, and Donna Tardioli had come out top of the list. The other girls were jealous, obviously. They called her Prima Donna, or Belladonna. It wasn't only on account of her office skills she'd been promoted, they said. That low-cut frock she'd worn to the interview had made the most of what she had to offer, but hadn't they all dressed up for the mayor that day? Now, word was going round that Mayor Truini had his eye on Sandra Panetti, and that Donna was heading for the chop. As a consequence, all the other secretaries – except Sandra, obviously – had warmed to her in the last couple of weeks. She was generous to a fault, they said, and she had one talent that nobody could deny: she could tell what the mayor was thinking just by looking at him.

She studied the way he parked his car in the forecourt, the way he walked into the town hall, the way that he dressed. She was as sharp as Jim the cabin boy in *Treasure Island*, someone said, always quick to let the whole staff know what to expect that day: *calm, changeable, stormy weather, strong gales*. She even used the right nautical terms when she warned them to *batten down the hatches, clear the decks* or *lower the mainsail*.

The mayor arrived that morning giving off the strangest signals.

Even Donna Tardioli couldn't make sense of them. He was dressed to kill, but his green shirttail was hanging out beneath the flap of his white linen jacket. In his summer clothes he handed out smiles and compliments as a rule, inviting councillors and visitors, the female ones especially, to join him later in his office for coffee.

As Donna stood up to greet him, he glared at her.

'Don't break my balls,' he said. 'Call Landini. Tell him to get here fast.'

He strode past her, barging into his office, and she noticed something else. He was wearing the blue leather moccasins that generally went so well with his pink jeans, green shirt and ivory-coloured linen jacket – they were *good weather* signs as a rule – but there was mud caked on the toes of his loafers, and traces of mud on his jeans as well. It was as if the mayor had been forced to trudge across a ploughed field or dig a hole for some reason.

Donna tried the bank, then rang the mayor on the inside line.

'Landini isn't in his office this morning.'

'Get me the manager, Franzetti, then,' the mayor snapped.

A couple of minutes later she had to call him back. '*Signor* Franzetti's at the swimming pool. He goes there every morning . . .'

The mayor exploded. 'Phone the pool and get him out of the water! I want him in my office inside fifteen minutes.'

The phone went dead in her hand.

Ruggero Franzetti was in the middle of his morning session.

As he breaststroked down the pool, eleven lengths already done, he saw one of the lifeguards standing there, hands on hips, muscles like Mister Universe popping out of his white string vest. The lifeguard raised his right hand and wiggled his forefinger, telling him to swim a bit faster.

Franzetti touched the edge of the pool, then started to tread water.

'Truini wants you in his office,' the lifeguard said, his tone imperative. 'Now!'

The lifeguard owed his job to the mayor, like a lot of other people in town.

Franzetti didn't have time for a hot shower. If Truini had sent for him so early in the day he must have a good reason. He pulled on his brushed cotton slacks, trying not to touch the damp tiles. The trousers had cost him a fortune from a tailor's shop in Jermyn Street, London. One leg trailed in a puddle.

Shit!

Ten minutes later, Franzetti was at the town hall.

'The mayor?' he asked, panting with the effort.

Whether it was the swimming or running up the stairs that had done it, Donna Tardioli couldn't say, but he did look a mess. She pointed to the closed door and watched the bank manager walk towards it. He looked so bedraggled, his hair uncombed, and the left leg of his trousers was wet. Some sort of emergency was up, she realized, as Franzetti knocked on the door and a voice boomed out: 'Come!'

Mayor Truini cut straight to business.

'Where the fuck's Landini?'

Ruggero Franzetti was the manager of the bank. Cosimo Landini was the director.

'I saw him the other day,' Franzetti began to say. 'He doesn't tell me when he is or isn't coming into the office . . .'

The mayor cut him off. 'A certain businessman . . . a mutual acquaintance. He called me up an hour ago.'

Franzetti knew at once who the mayor was talking about. Cosimo Landini had handled the negotiations, while Franzetti had drawn up all the contracts. 'What did he have to say?'

'They want to start building straight away.'

Franzetti blew out air. 'That's all we need, Maurizio,' he said. 'Does he have any idea how tricky it is to move all this cash around without alarm bells going off? Landini was telling me to slow things down as much as possible. I mean to say, if the Ministry of Finance were to latch on to it—'

'You both knew what you were getting into when you started doing business with Luigi Corbucci,' the mayor burst out, managing to keep his voice low, the veins standing out in his neck. 'Put your mind to it, Ruggero. You'll find a way to handle it. Tell Landini. He'll go along with it, I'm sure.'

Franzetti's face was white with fright. Then again, Truini thought, it probably matched the expression on his own face. He wondered whether somebody might have left a 'gift' in Franzetti's car boot, and whether Franzetti had been out digging holes, too, before he went to the swimming pool.

'We barely handle so much cash in a normal fiscal year,' the manager was saying. 'OK, we're handling a lot more money this year, what with the earthquake and the reconstruction, but we're talking about millions . . .'

Truini ran a hand through his hair. 'Didn't they teach you anything at that London School of Economics?'

'The Harvard Business School,' Franzetti corrected him.

'Wherever,' Truini snapped. 'We've got no choice in the matter. They're going ahead and I've got problems of my own. I'll have to put the proposal to the council next week. They'll approve it like a shot. It means work, jobs, future votes, a bulky envelope here and there. Then, Corbucci . . .' He stopped and lowered his voice. 'Then, *they'll* come looking for you and Landini. Invent something fast, that's my advice.'

Ruggero Franzetti let out a sigh and furrowed his brow. 'There is a way,' he said, 'but we'd need a lot of names.'

'What sort of names?'

'People who wouldn't know what the inside of a bank looks like.'

'Who, for instance?' Truini growled, his patience running out.

'OAPs, foreign residents, immigrants, vagrants. People who *could* open an account, technically anyway, but they don't have a cent, or they don't need an Italian bank account. People who would never even know if there was a bank account made out in their names. Dummy accounts that I can handle personally. That's what I need to set up.'

Truini was silent for a moment. 'How many names do you need?'

'The more, the better, so I can spread it around.'

'A hundred?'

'That would do it.'

'You'll have a list tomorrow.'

Franzetti's eyes gaped wide. 'Where will you find them?'

'Nursing homes, religious orders, orphanages, people who lost their homes in the earthquake, plus all the ones you mentioned before. How does that sound?'

'It sounds good,' Franzetti said, his voice brighter now.

'Let me know what Landini has to say, OK?'

Donna Tardioli noticed that the bank manager had smoothed his hair, and that he had more colour in his cheeks as he left the mayor's office that morning. She caught a glimpse of Mayor Truini, too, before Franzetti closed the door.

The expression on his face was as black and stormy as before. Maybe even blacker. It didn't sit well with his green shirt and pink jeans.

EIGHTEEN

The same morning, Perugia

'**G**eneral Corsini!'

The Queen raced forward to greet him.

'I've been looking forward to this moment – meeting you in person. It is such an unexpected honour!'

The general lifted the Queen's hand towards his lips and kissed air.

The only sound he made was the sharp click of his leather heels. The fact that he had chosen not to don his uniform that day made the scene less formal. He was wearing a light grey suit, impeccably cut. A slim black leather briefcase dangled from his left hand.

Donatella Pignatti felt a gripe deep down in her stomach. *Was that where the danger was lurking?* 'Shall we make ourselves comfortable?' she asked.

One corner of the large room was fitted out as a sitting room, with two padded Frau sofas and matching armchairs in smart red leather, and a coffee table in the centre laid out with a spread of national magazines. On two of them the face of Donatella Pignatti smiled out at the world. Her face might have been on all the other covers, too, and why not, after all? She had seemed to be going places: a woman who was young, attractive in an aggressive sort of way, a politician who had carved a place for herself in a galaxy that was dominated by grey-haired men.

Those magazines were a few years old, and Arturo Corsini knew it.

'I'll . . . er, leave you alone then.' Paolo Gualducci made a half-bow, hoping that one of them would invite him to stay.

Donatella Pignatti glanced at the general, who didn't say a word. 'I'll call you later, Paolo,' she said.

Gualducci closed the door and Donatella Pignatti sat back, hooked one leg over the other and smiled at the general, hoping that the smile didn't look as tense in the general's eyes as it felt on her face. 'How can I help you, General Corsini? I hardly expected a private visit from a man in your position.'

Corsini's mouth pulled tight at the corners.

If that was a smile, she thought, things were worse than she feared.

'The reason is in here,' Corsini said, laying his hand on the briefcase that he had placed beside him on the sofa.

The Queen felt her heart throb painfully, but she managed to smile back at him. Dampness flushed beneath her armpits. She prayed no stain would appear on the white cotton blouse she was wearing. She must not reveal a hint of the tension that was creeping over her like a paralysis.

She watched without a word as Corsini took a fountain pen from his pocket – a gold Mont Blanc Meisterstuck 84 – and wrote on a notepad in handwriting that was large and a trifle infantile: *Is there a room where we can speak?*

The Queen leaned forward and read what he had written, not quite sure what the sentence was supposed to mean. She looked at him with an expression of confusion on her face. When he raised his forefinger and twirled it in the air, she suddenly saw the light. In the same instant, she realized that General Corsini's visit might *not* be quite as menacing as she had feared.

She jumped up with a smile. 'May I offer you coffee? We have . . . well, it's only a vending machine. Down in the basement. But the coffee is surprisingly good.'

Corsini stood up, briefcase in hand. 'I'd be delighted,' he said. 'I didn't have time this morning.'

They walked down the corridor towards the lift, passing a number of employees as they went. All of them acknowledged the Queen with a deferential smile. General Corsini guessed that she kept them under her thumb by alternating moments of apparent joviality with explosions of controlled rage. Her underlings had the look of whipped dogs that dared not bite the hand that fed them.

'Congratulations on your presidency,' Corsini said. 'Finally, talented women are beginning to make their mark in a jungle run by alpha males.'

'The same cannot be said of military life,' the Queen joked back.

'It takes us a lot more time,' the general admitted. 'First we need to find a tailor who can cut an elegant uniform. Then again, a firm male hand on the rudder . . . It isn't such a bad thing. Especially if the captain knows which direction to take.'

'You may be right,' she conceded, wondering what he was hinting at.

They were walking past a door when Donatella Pignatti pulled up sharply, as if she had just remembered something. 'Would you care to see our new computer system? It's a recent investment of which I am extremely proud.'

The word *Archive* was written on a piece of A4 paper in blue marker pen.

She knocked on the frosted glass door. No one answered, which wasn't surprising, as nobody had yet been appointed to begin the digitalization of a massive handwritten day-by-day archive which recorded more than seven hundred years of local administrative history. Computer boffins were ten-a-penny, but it was hard to find one who could cope with the dog-Latin text that had been in use until the middle of the eighteenth century.

'This should do fine,' she murmured, raising her hand to her lips. It sounded more like a cough than a sentence.

General Corsini glanced up and down the corridor, then nodded.

'There are computers in here that anyone would envy,' she said out loud.

They stepped inside a room that was lined with shelves full of ancient folders and registers. The air was dry and dusty, heavy with the tang of leather and rotting unturned pages.

She closed the door and turned to face the general. 'You frightened me back there,' she said, her smile more relaxed and natural than before. 'If somebody is spying on us, I wish you'd tell me whether he's an enemy of yours or an enemy of mine.'

'Let's not talk of enemies,' Corsini said. 'The important thing is to provide no motive for anyone to see things in a different light. Don't tell me that there aren't hidden microphones in your office, because I won't believe you.'

'We don't record conversations . . .'

'I wasn't thinking of *your* office practice,' he said.

There was frequent talk of bugging in the building. Mostly it was joking, but there were people who took it seriously. 'What would they record?' she asked him. 'The gossip of secretaries, the rubbish that Mr X tells Mr Y, who passes it on to Mr Z?'

At the same time, she always spoke of business and politics as if there were unseen ears listening to every word she said. On that score, frequent swearing was guaranteed to enhance her reputation as a tough nut, if nothing else.

'Is that what you've come to tell me?' She put her hands flat on a desk and leaned close to a computer screen, as if she were reading data. Corsini placed one hand on top of the screen and inclined his head towards hers, as if he were reading the same thing on the same blank screen.

'We cannot stay here long without raising suspicion,' he said, 'so let me begin. There are investigations under way on your account regarding contracts you have signed in the last twelve months and others you are about to approve. At a guess, I'd say that you are looking at eight to ten years in prison and the end of a promising political career. Especially now that they have found the clincher.'

Donatella Pignatti could hardly breathe. 'Clincher?'

'A shell company that leads back to your husband and, thus, to you. A holding company that owns the land on which a certain university department is soon to be built, along with three halls of residence, a shopping centre, staff apartments, a sports centre, an Olympic-size swimming-pool . . . Do I need to go on?'

Donatella Pignatti turned on him with fire on her tongue, her eyes ablaze.

General Corsini held up his hand. 'Don't,' he warned her. 'I have copies of the documents in my briefcase. You may insist on seeing the evidence, but I am certain that you already know the details. So, let's be civil. You are safe until a magistrate decides to move on it. Or until you beat them to the punch.'

'I didn't know that we were living in a police state.'

Corsini smiled and clicked his tongue. 'You do me wrong,' he said. 'You know who I am. You know what I do. And this *is* Italy. Nothing regarding politics or politicians rests for very long in the hands of the magistrate who chances on the case. That is, if the news is permitted to circulate. That's why I am here. We must work together to ensure that it does not get out.'

'Will you put the cuffs on my wrists?' Her voice was brittle, though she managed a brave smile. 'You are famed for your high-profile performances, General Corsini. Live TV, bright lights, a show for the folks at home. The dashing hero who rushes in to rescue Italy – the poor damsel in dire distress.'

'Forgive me, President Pignatti,' he said. 'I do not think that your arrest would be prime-time watching. It wouldn't even make the headlines.' He pulled a wry, lopsided grin. 'You know as well as I do that, for the moment at least, you are just a large fish in a very small pond. Local news for the local papers. That means page twenty-two in *Corriere della Sera* or the national dailies. However, we can make the front page together . . .'

The door opened a fraction, and a head peeped into the room.

President Pignatti spoke up loudly: 'The archive will soon be available to the public, historians and researchers.'

'Oh, excuse me, President,' a voice said, 'I didn't realize—'

'This is not a place to smoke, I've told you before!' she shouted.

The door closed quietly and she bent close to Corsini again. 'But you *are* a national figure,' she said in a determined whisper, 'a high-ranking *carabiniere* officer who is often in the public eye. This small pond evidently means *something* to you. Let me ask you a question. Are you trying to blackmail me?'

Corsini stifled a laugh by feigning a cough.

'If I request to speak with you in private, and in a room where we will not be overheard, you must realize that I am not attempting to entrap you. Indeed, I am offering my hand to pull you out of the hole that you have dug for yourself. A very deep and dangerous hole, I would add. I also know that you have been the object of . . . unwanted attention, let's say: anonymous threats, things stuffed through your letterbox, or left in full view on your doorstep . . .'

'Is my private life an open book?' she said.

'You can be certain of it. You opened the door one day and found the body of a chicken without its head. You told your secretary. Ten days later, you opened the door again and found the body of a cat. You found the head, too. They were lying on the welcome mat a foot apart in a pool of blood. The next day, the phone calls started. It's all in here,' he said, indicating his briefcase. 'It would be hard to explain why you didn't report the situation to the authorities. You should have come to somebody like me. Still, I have taken it on myself to make sure that you don't get into similar scrapes. After all, we have your splendid political career to think of, don't we?'

'Why would you help me?' Donatella Pignatti threw a cocktail of a glance at him: equal shots of fear and hope, a cube of ice and a shot of bitters.

Corsini saw the victim's head on the block, waiting for the axe to fall. 'We need to confront an enemy together, President Pignatti.'

'Which enemy are you talking of?'

'An enemy that we can defeat. Our victory will warn the others that we are to be feared. It's an ancient strategy of war, dear lady. Find an opponent you can annihilate and the others will think twice before they attack again.'

'I don't know anything about military tactics, General Corsini. It's hard to apply them to the world of politics.'

'*The Art of War* by Sun Tzu is a book that every politician should read.'

The Queen arched her plucked eyebrows. 'I've never heard of it,' she said. Then she tried to bluff. 'To be honest, I've no idea what we are talking about.'

Corsini smiled, but not a trace of it appeared on his lips. 'I know what is happening in your region,' he said. 'A river of money is flowing through your office as a result of the earthquake. You will create an army of enemies who would give the world to lay their hands on the information in my briefcase . . .'

'Is that what you are doing?' she said. 'Using what you know to threaten me?'

'Don't misunderstand me,' he snapped. 'I don't care what you do, but you and I must work together on a project that I hold dear. There is a battle I must win. And you'll win, too, by helping me. I want your full cooperation. You'll put no obstacles in my way. The State must triumph. Always. You and I represent the State . . .'

'What are you asking me?'

'I am not asking, I'm telling you. Don't you want to be on the winning side?'

'Do I have a choice?'

General Corsini smiled. 'Would you believe me if I said you did? What I propose is a victorious collaboration which will be to the advantage of both of us. One day, when you have risen to the top of the ladder, I may presume to ask a favour, I hope?'

The Queen's face reminded Corsini of his six-year-old niece when he read her a fairytale and she asked him if he thought Prince Charming would save the Sleeping Beauty.

'What do I have to do?' the president asked.

As General Corsini took the lift down to the ground floor, Donatella Pignatti caught a glimpse of her own reflection in a plate-glass door. The visit had turned out better than she could have imagined. This stranger had brought her a string of pearls.

The fact that he wasn't handsome made no difference. *Pearls?*

Someone else would soon be shedding tears.

NINETEEN

Lunchtime, the same day

'False move, Seb.'

Cangio's fingers froze on her flesh. 'Eh?'

She raised herself on her elbows and looked him in the eye. 'Do you call that a caress? It may put me to sleep but it sure isn't going to turn me on. What's bugging you? We're in *bed* together!'

Cangio opened his mouth to speak, but he knew that she was right.

'You called *me*,' she protested. 'What a romantic tryst this turned out to be!'

He had phoned her that morning, halfway through his patrol of the western perimeter of the park. 'I'll be home for lunch, if you fancy stopping by.'

'Lunch?' she'd said with a wry laugh. They met during her lunchbreak whenever they could manage it. The supermarket closed at one o'clock, and it opened again at four. 'What have you got in the fridge?'

There was stale bread, and not much else.

Loredana had laughed. 'Stocked up for seduction, as usual! I'll bring the groceries, but you'd better make it worth my while. Lunch sounds fine, but I fancy something a bit . . . you know, *spicier* to finish off with.'

He had played dumb. 'Ice cream?'

He'd been thinking about her all morning, eager for lunch and even keener for the dessert, but Marzio Diamante had phoned him the minute he got home. Marzio had been patrolling the other side of the park that morning, up on the mountains overlooking the town.

A body had been found outside the village of San Bartolomeo sul Monte.

Two minutes later, Loredana had come bustling into the kitchen, armed to the teeth with a farmhouse loaf, a bag of San Marzano tomatoes, two mozzarella cheeses the size of cannonballs, a bottle of Farchioni extra-virgin olive oil and a bottle of Trebbiano white wine.

'Let's get lunch out of the way,' she'd said with a grin.

She'd set to work with a sharp knife, sliced the cheese and tomatoes, laid them out in two tiers, red on white, added a sprinkle of salt and pepper, a sprig of fresh basil that she crushed with her fingers, then finished it off with a generous lashing of Farchioni's finest olive oil.

'God's gift to the working girl!' she'd said as she laid lunch on the table.

The Caprese salad had been delicious enough to distract him for five minutes. But then he'd started to think again about what Marzio had told him.

The body had been pushed into the cleft of a rock . . .

'Hey, cowboy!' Loredana's lips had pressed against his. A trace of olive was there, and he'd licked at it. 'It's time for dessert.'

'Mm, that oil is tasty!'

Three minutes later, they were naked in bed. He'd lost himself inside her, and the time flew by. They dozed for a while – she'd been working flat out all morning – then she'd woken him up, they'd kissed, and it had started all over again. At a certain point, she'd skipped out of bed. 'I've got an idea,' she'd said. A minute later, she'd returned with the bottle of olive oil. 'This stuff is amazing on your skin,' she'd said, dribbling a few drops into the palm of her hand and rubbing it into his chest, moving slowly downwards.

Another five minutes had gone by.

'Now, it's your turn,' she'd said, rolling on to her front.

That was when she'd pulled him up on his caress, and his hand had stopped moving.

Now she rolled back on her shoulder and looked at him. 'Want to tell me about it?'

He took a lock of her hair and wound it around his finger. 'There was an earthquake last night. Did you feel it?'

'It couldn't have been very big,' she said. 'I slept like a log. But everyone was talking about it in the store this morning. So what? This is Umbria. Earthquakes happen here all the time.'

'At San Bartolomeo sul Monte. It was big enough to spew a man out of a rock.'

Her brown eyes opened wide. 'A man? Out of a what?'

'The remains of a man . . .'

'Oooh, spooky!' she said.

'Marzio spoke to a farmer up there. It was quite a sight, apparently. A body jammed deep into a crevice, a skeletal leg sticking up in the air. The *carabinieri* were there.'

Loredana frowned at him. 'Do they know who he is?'

Cangio shrugged. 'Not yet . . .' He leant close and kissed her. 'He'd been shot in the head, Marzio said. A big gun at close quarters, by the sound of it.'

Then he caught one of her nipples between his lips and sucked on it gently.

'Hey, lunch is over!' she said, but she didn't pull away, instead leaning closer, her hand sliding down to the pit of his stomach, moving gently, making the most of the olive oil that remained. 'I've never heard of anyone being killed around here before,' she murmured.

'Has anyone gone missing?'

She pulled a face at him. 'Do we have to talk about bodies?'

Cangio wasn't listening. 'They should find out who he was from the DNA.'

'Why are you so interested?' she said. 'You've got this body to work on . . .'

'A man shot through the forehead, then they push him down a hole? In Umbria?' he said. 'As if . . .' He hesitated. Did he need to unload his worries on to her?

'As if what?' she pushed him.

'Where I come from,' he said, 'people often disappear.'

Cangio saw the look of impatience on her face. 'That's Calabria,' she said. 'This is Umbria. Um-bri-a! Things like that don't happen up here.'

'But it did happen,' he said. 'It happened in San Bartolomeo.'

'And you start thinking straight away about the Mafia.'

Cangio smiled. 'The Mafia's from Sicily. In Calabria we have the 'Ndrangheta. The 'Ndrangheta are much more dangerous . . .'

'You sound sexy when you say it like that.' She laughed, trying to imitate him, growling out, ''Ndrangheta, 'Ndrangheta.'

He could never have imagined telling any of the girls in London about the 'Ndrangheta. They weren't interested in what you were thinking. They were interested in one thing only: what you had inside your pants.

'There's nothing sexy about a criminal organization that murders people,' he said. 'They make an estimated forty billion euros tax-free every year out of drugs, slot-machines, violence and prostitution. And now they are going legit, ploughing their dirty money into business and investments all over the country. Nobody says no to easy money, especially when they point a pistol in your face.'

Loredana laid a hand on his shoulder and pulled him towards her. 'Is that what happened to you, Seb? Did they stick a pistol in your face?'

He stared into her eyes. 'I saw them kill a man, Loredana. I was a witness. That's why I ran away to London. Which makes me a coward, I guess.'

'Forty billion euros,' Loredana whispered. 'What do they do with it? I mean to say, you can't just walk into the Post Office and say you'd like to deposit forty billion euros.'

'Forget the Post Office,' he said. 'There are banks in difficulty, businesses in trouble – they never refuse a helping hand, a much-needed investment. They don't ask where the money comes from. The 'Ndrangheta never stops making cash, and they need somewhere to hide it. There are plenty of people who are willing to help them.'

Would she think he was trying to explain away his cowardice by telling her how powerful the mobsters were, and how weak he and others like him really were?

'Who owns the supermarket where you work?' he asked her.

'I've no idea,' she said. 'The chain's head office is in Bologna. They've got big stores all over the place. Are you trying to tell me that the Mafia . . . the 'Ndrangheta, is running the whole of Italy?'

'Forty billion euros is more than a rich African state makes in a year,' he said. 'I bet you've never been to Crotone. It's a small town down in Calabria. They found a man one day, and the police discovered that he had seven million euros in the bank. The money wasn't his, though. He probably knew nothing about it.'

Loredana's eyes were wide open, staring at him. 'You're kidding?'

'He was a dummy, a name. He could have bought the best hotel in town, yet he was sleeping under bridges, the richest tramp in the province. Nobody knew until the police ran his name through the computer and came across his deposits and withdrawals.'

Loredana cupped her head in her hand. 'Have you ever checked the banks to see how rich you might be?'

Cangio laughed. 'I haven't, and I hope I'm not!'

'Why not?'

'The tramp was dead when they found him. Maybe he'd discovered what was going on and they'd cut his throat.'

'What about the money?'

Cangio shrugged his shoulders. 'The account had been emptied out. They'd found another frontman, probably. A kid in primary school, or one of those people you see working in the fields collecting tomatoes – an immigrant worker with a residence permit. They always have a long list of names . . .'

'Is that what he was, the man they killed and buried in San Bartolomeo? A frontman? Is that what you're worried about?'

Cangio pulled her close. 'When I go for a stroll in Umbria, I want to find truffles, mushrooms, wild asparagus, olives,' he said. 'Not corpses with bullets through their brains. Speaking of olives,' he said, kissing the tip of her nose, 'how much oil is left in that bottle?'

TWENTY

Later that day, Spoleto

The door opened and a face appeared.

Tonino Sustrico swallowed a curse. Special Constable Falsetti was the last person he felt like humouring at the end of a hectic day.

'Can I trouble you, Brigadier?'

'Try not to,' Sustrico warned him, tidying a desk that was already neat.

He had just printed out his case report regarding the discovery of the corpse in San Bartolomeo sul Monte. A phone call to the local monitoring station on Monte Pettino had helped a bit. The epicentre of the earthquake had been recorded on the seismograph at less than a mile from the village: 3.4 on the Richter scale, an undulating wave which had faded after 8.7 seconds. Not so large, the seismologist commented. There had been no damage to buildings, but the 'upsurge' effect had been intensified by the fact that the shudder had been less than four miles beneath the earth's crust and that it had rumbled on for so long. Long enough to spew the body out of the ground.

It sounded good as explanations went.

Experience had taught Sustrico that there was nothing like scientific data and numbers with decimal points to add a touch of authenticity to whatever rubbish you were obliged to write. The problem was that there was nothing more he could say about it. He had summed up the accidental finding of the body by Roberto Casini, but had been unable to suggest which lines of enquiry the investigation should take. The identity of the victim still remained a mystery. And as for who had killed him, they weren't even on the starting block. The Regional Forensic Laboratory thought the teeth might lead to an eventual match, but that could take weeks or months. Then again, it might lead nowhere.

Cause of death: a .38 calibre shot through the forehead.

Who had fired the fatal shot? Unless somebody came forward and confessed, they were a long way from ever finding out.

'I thought you'd gone home,' Sustrico said. 'Didn't your shift end at four?'

Falsetti closed the door but didn't sit down. 'I'll be going in a bit,' he said. 'I've been busy. In fact, I think I may be able to put a name to the body.'

Sustrico shuffled the papers on his desk. 'Is that so?'

'I'm not one hundred per cent certain. Eighty per cent, let's say. Do you recall the skin on the shoulder blade?'

Sustrico nodded, remembering one of the photographs in the lab report.

'It was the only bit of skin that hadn't rotted. There was a tattoo . . .'

'More like a stain,' Sustrico corrected him.

Falsetti ignored him. 'I thought I'd check it out. I may have been lucky, let's say.'

Sustrico smiled. 'Lucky means clever, I take it.'

He didn't want the little shit to think he was a bumpkin. 'Lucky,' Falsetti said again. 'There's a tattoo shop in town, and they're on the Internet. I compared the lab's jpeg with the patterns shown on their website, then I phoned them up and asked some questions. The tattoo that we saw . . . The artist keeps records. That's what I meant when I said *lucky*. He checked his books and he says he's used that pattern only five times in the last two years, and – hear this! – he keeps the names of all his customers. He won't do a tattoo unless you show an identity card. We know one of the names on his list, Brigadier Sustrico. He's got a criminal record. Does the name Andrea Bonanni ring any bells?'

Tonino Sustrico sat back in his seat and laid the report flat on the desk. He had never heard the name, but he knew from the grin on Falsetti's face that he was going to have to rewrite his report before he went home. A wasted afternoon. *Jesus!* Next time they asked him to take a trainee copper from the north to cover for holiday absentees he was going to say no. It was better to muddle along without help. Less than a year spent working in a big city and smart-arsed characters like Eugenio Falsetti had seen it all and done it all. They seemed to know everything there was to know about policing.

'Five names, you said.'

Falsetti nodded. 'True, but Andrea Bonanni's the only one who's ever been in the local maximum-security prison. He served three years of an eleven-year sentence for drug trafficking. Originally he's from the town of Crotone down in Calabria. He got himself a tattoo to celebrate the week he was released. But there's something else . . .'

Sustrico didn't bother to ask, just waited out the melodramatic pause.

'I called the prison. There's a guy who works there – a mate of mine from Milan, as a matter of fact. We sometimes grab a beer together. He checked the prison archive. While Andrea Bonanni was banged up inside he asked to speak with Magistrate Catapanni. They met on four occasions.'

'Calisto Catapanni?'

'That's him.'

'He's attached to the local procurator's office. What makes you think it's important? Magistrates speak with criminals all the time.'

Falsetti arched his eyebrows as if to say, *Are you really stupid, or just pretending?* 'Why?' he said. 'This is a clan killing, Chief. The Calabrian 'Ndrangheta, to be precise. The name comes from the Greek word for a brave and honourable man. Bonanni was brave, all right, but he wasn't honourable. He spoke with Magistrate Catapanni and the clan didn't like it. That's my take on it. It's a typical mafia-type MO. They wiped him out with a bullet between the eyes. That's what they do to anyone who rats on them.'

Boom! How Sustrico hated people from Milan. Everything that happened to them was big, important, super, mega. Silvio Berlusconi was only one of the hated millions. The Milanesi were full of themselves. Fast-tracked Special Constable Eugenio Falsetti goes off on a holiday placement to a country town where they stopped robbing hens just the day before yesterday and straight away, there you go: the Mafia did it!

'That's what *who* does?' Sustrico said sarcastically.

'I told you, Chief. The 'Ndrangheta . . .'

'I've seen the same films you've seen,' Sustrico said. 'I watch the news as well. But let me remind you, Falsetti, this is *not* the deep south. This isn't Naples or Palermo. Up here things are different.'

Falsetti wasn't phased. 'Maybe so, but somebody with the same tattoo Bonanni had was found with a bullet in his head. Bonanni's disappeared, and he was collaborating with a magistrate. It sounds like Naples or Palermo, or Catanzaro in Calabria to me. That farmer on the hill was right about one thing: they didn't want that body to be found. We wouldn't have found it at all if it hadn't been for Mother Nature.'

Tonino Sustrico let out a rasping sigh. 'If you like to read in bed, Falsetti, I suggest you catch up on the latest crime statistics for the province. We've got the lowest murder rate in the nation. No violent crime. Some drug consumption but it's under control. Not a single reported case of criminal extortion. What would the 'Ndrangheta be doing up here? Boring themselves to death? Or maybe they like a decent glass of wine with their salami sausages—'

'They're national, Chief, mobile,' Falsetti interrupted him. 'Milan's overrun with mafiosi. They're taking over the country. Not the way it happens in the films, of course. These people are businessmen. They're on the look-out for new investment opportunities. Especially in a quiet place like this, where nobody would suspect what's going on—'

Sustrico interrupted him. 'Let me tell you how I see it, Falsetti. That is *not* Andrea Bonanni. I've no idea who he is, I admit, but it hardly matters. A travelling salesman or a railway worker, maybe. He was visiting town and he met a woman. The woman's husband killed him in a fit of jealousy and he knew where to get rid of the corpse. A crevice up in the mountains? That's local knowledge, that is.'

'But . . .'

'If you want a tale a bit more colourful,' Sustrico continued, 'let's say that drugs come into it. A local dealer, a customer who doesn't pay. The dealer shoots him then gets rid of the body. No corpse, no crime. It might be as simple as that, don't you think?'

'Let's hope so.'

Sustrico breathed out loudly through his nostrils. 'Thanks for trying, Falsetti. It's been a tough day but you've been a great help.'

As soon as Falsetti closed the door, Sustrico pulled the document up on to the computer screen again and added a note at the end of his report: *We await the results of dental evidence in the hope that the teeth may throw light on the possible identity of the corpse.*

He printed out the corrected page, threw the old one into the rubbish bin, then phoned the courthouse. The court was closed for the day, a woman's voice replied, but when Sustrico told her who he was and who he was looking for, he got the answer he was after.

'I've got his home number if you want it, Brigadier,' the woman said.

Sustrico wanted it, and made a note of it.

He thanked the woman, put the phone down, then picked it up again and called the new number. It rang and rang for quite some time. He was almost on the point of giving up when he heard a click and a voice whispered gently in his ear: 'Yes?'

'Magistrate Catapanni?'

'Who is that?' the voice asked, sharply now.

Sustrico identified himself and explained why he was calling. He had met the magistrate a number of times in the exercise of his duties, though he had never been able to work up much sympathy for the man. Calisto Catapanni was always cold and distant, a cut above the rest of humanity, it seemed, though everyone knew he'd been stuck in the same job in the same small town for almost twenty years.

'Andrea Bonanni?' the magistrate repeated. 'But you can't be certain of it. Well, Brigadier, the wisest thing would be to wait for the outcome of the forensic tests, don't you agree? Let's see what the experts have to say . . . rather than muddy the waters any further.'

'That's just what I was thinking, sir,' Sustrico said.

The line went dead without a word of goodbye, or even thanks.

Bugger you! thought Sustrico as he reached for his jacket.

TWENTY-ONE

Two weeks later, Spoleto

Three of the boys were stretched out on the steps of a fountain.

It didn't look as though they'd had much sleep, and they were wearing the clothes they'd worn the day before, the creases showing. The lanky one called Riccardo Bucci was making short work of an ice-cream cone, while the other two popped cans of beer they had bought from the general store on the corner.

Hair of the dog, the Watcher decided, given what they'd put away the night before.

Between sips, the drinkers let their beer cans rest inside the overflowing basin of the ornamental fountain. The water flowed from one of the mountain springs which had made the town a sort of primitive spa. He had picked up a pamphlet from the hotel desk which claimed that the Romans had colonized the town a couple of thousand years before because the water was so cold; there were the remains of the ancient Roman baths to prove it.

He sipped his coffee and took another glance.

They were messing around, splashing each other with water, the noise they were making turning heads in the square. A vegetable market was going on, and there were quite a few people about, so he had no chance of overhearing what they might be talking about. Still, he had a pretty good idea. He hadn't been out of his room the night before. Instead of reading or watching TV he had tuned in on the signal coming from the bugged car, then switched over to the frequency used by the long-distance surveillance team that had been trailing them out in the woods after dark.

Now he knew precisely what they had been doing.

First, they'd driven out of the town and into the hills, where they'd spent the early part of the night roasting sausages, drinking beer and smoking things they shouldn't have been smoking. Shortly after two a.m. they had called it a night, making one short – pre-planned? – stop in town before they all went home to sleep it off.

He had listened to the recording again that morning. Summing it up, there'd been a barbeque in the woods. The four boys who made up the band, plus the sister of one of them, and a couple of her girlfriends. When it was time to pack up and go home, Lorenzo Micheli had loaded the girls into the sister's car and taken them home, while the other three lads had piled into Lorenzo's car, the one that was fitted with the bug.

When they had got back to town, the cars had gone in different directions.

The recording of the conversation in the car was a mess. To make a readable transcript of what had taken place would not be easy. There'd been plenty of high-pitched shouting and wild enthusiasm before the event, self-congratulation and noisy celebrations afterwards. Now, of course, it was as clear as a bell what they'd been up to. He sat at a table beneath a sunshade in the open-air café, one eye on the suspects, the other on the mobile phone in his hand, and the article which had appeared that morning on a local website.

VANDALS AT WORK

Police were called to a work site on the northern edge of town where the new flyover is being built. Construction workers arriving at 6.30 this morning found the main gates broken open, according to the site foreman, Aldo Cuccia. 'A lot of damage has been caused to plant and machinery,' he said.

The windscreen and the headlights of a company van had been shattered, while all four tyres of a dumper truck had been spiked with nails. The intruders also wrote insulting phrases on a wall with spray paint.

There has been public opposition to the building project in recent months from local environmentalist groups, including Legambiente, Italia Nostra and the WWF, as the new flyover rises in front of the façade of the church of San Caterina, which is widely held to be one of the finest examples of early Renaissance architecture in central Italy.

A police spokesman issued a short statement. 'Judging from the amount of wilful damage, we believe that the delinquents made a lot of noise. We entreat local residents, or anyone passing the site last night, to get in touch with us. They may have seen a car drive in or out, and might be able to help us clear up the time at which the aggression took place.'

The article closed by promising '*more details before the day is out*'.

What the article did not know, and what the police had refused to reveal, was that the vandals had gone one step further before they went home. The Watcher had been lying on his hotel bed, smoking one cigarette after another, following the situation as it began to unfold. Maybe 'unwind' was a better way of describing it. It was all there on the tape, and he had heard it as it happened. As a witness on behalf of the prosecution, he would be lethal.

Or would he?

'At 02.47 I heard a loud crash as the suspect's car smashed through the gate . . .'

'Objection!' The defence lawyer would jump up, appealing to the judge with supplicating hands. 'This loathsome snitch may say he heard my client's car crash into something last night, but there is no way of knowing *what* the car may have crashed into, nor of saying with any precision *where* the crash took place. If, indeed, it *did* take place.'

'Objection sustained.'

A judge had a vested interest in dragging out a case, of course. Even so, no judge in his right mind would deny the other damning bit of evidence. There'd been almost fifteen minutes of silence, broken only by an occasional whoop of excitement or the crash of glass as it broke. They had been inside the compound, causing damage to vehicles and building equipment, pissing into the fuel tank of a bulldozer. Then, one of the boys had returned to the car, taken something from the boot, then sat inside the bugged car and made a phone call. This was Federico Donati, the one who studied art and fancied himself as the Italian Keith Haring. He had taken a spray can from the boot, grabbed his phone and called the fourth member of the gang, Lorenzo Micheli, the one who had taken the girls home.

The transcript read as follows:

Federico: *Are you in bed, Lorenzo? Who with?*

Lorenzo replied, but the microphone didn't pick up what he was saying, not that it made the slightest bit of difference.

Federico: *We've almost finished here. You're missing all the fun. There's this big blank wall . . . it's fresh cement. Like a big, empty canvas. I was going to spray a psychedelic dick on it, but . . . Yeah, that's what I thought. A real waste . . . So, what shall I write?'*

Lorenzo had told him, and Federico had repeated the slogan, and that was what the workers found on the blank cement wall of the flyover-to-be. The *carabinieri* had taken photographs before it was painted out, of course.

An exploding cartoon cloud of a bomb, and the word *BOOM!*

'That'll put the shits up them,' Lorenzo had said.

The Watcher smiled to himself, seeing in his mind's eye the gobsmacked defence lawyer trying to crawl his way out of that deep hole.

But then his smile clouded over.

He watched Riccardo Bucci go into the shop on the corner and return with three more cans of beer. He chucked them into the fountain, splashing the other two boys, who yelled at him and splashed him back until someone shouted at them, telling them to stop behaving like a bunch of kids or he'd call the coppers.

That was the problem. It wasn't just the fact that they behaved like kids – big kids, oversized kids, bored kids, who were old enough to buy beer – the truth was that was exactly what they *were*. A bunch of kids with no responsibilities, nothing to do, nowhere to go, and it didn't look as though things would change much in the near future. OK, a couple of them were students working part-time through the summer vacation. They were only working for the beer money. Come autumn they'd stick their noses back in their books again. The other two had no qualifications, and one of them was unemployed. Only a miracle would save them. The Watcher might be gone within the month when the students went back to school, but the other two boys might be emptying cans of beer beside the fountain every day for the next fifty years.

That was what bothered him.

There was an aspect to the 'investigation' – he used the inverted commas mentally – that he hadn't been able to put his finger on from the start. He had been watching them for three weeks now and the tapes and photographs were piling up. There was bound to be fingerprint evidence, too. If the surveillance team was putting together a dossier against the boys, they had more than enough to bring charges.

But what 'charges'?

He had spoken with his supervisor that morning, telling him about the material he had recorded the night before. You could hear them, he'd said, calling each other by name as they smashed their way into the building site, laughing as they chucked bricks and broke glass, joking as they smashed things up. But what did it amount to? Acts of vandalism, a heavy fine, a tiny blot on their record sheets, a statutory conditional sentence as first-time offenders? They were just a gang of kids letting off steam in a tiny town where nothing exciting ever happened.

Kids.

A burly copper on the doorstep would frighten the life out them and their parents. A quiet word, a serious warning, and that would be the end of the story.

'I feel like a babysitter,' he had said to his supervisor.

'And that's what you are,' the supervisor had replied. 'So shut up, sit tight and watch the fucking baby.'

He had said a lot more, too. The Legend was running things. The Legend knew what was behind it all. The Legend was never wrong. Et cetera.

The Watcher watched the babies pop their cans, guzzle beer, smoke cigarettes.

What the hell was *dangerous* about them?

TWENTY-TWO

The same day, Perugia

C alisto Catapanni had only been there once before.

It had been at the very start of his career, one of the first cases he had handled as a junior magistrate when he was appointed to the court. It hadn't been necessary for him to go there on that occasion either, but he had gone all the same.

'Just for the experience,' as he had said at the time.

It had turned out to be a very unpleasant experience.

He hadn't been able to imagine what would happen to a body when it hit the ground after falling three hundred feet from the medieval bridge that spanned a gorge outside the town.

Still, this one was a body that he *had* to see.

He hadn't been called to San Bartolomeo sul Monte. The *carabinieri* had brought in the Regional Crime Squad, which meant that there would be no official inquest until after the post-mortem had been performed. But Sustrico's telephone call had worried him. If that corpse belonged to Andrea Bonanni, the informer he had had released from prison then lost track of, his own future as an investigating magistrate would be at risk. *At risk?* His career would be finished.

He had driven to Perugia to attend the autopsy.

Doctor Petrillo would be doing the post-mortem examination at eleven o'clock, he had been told by the receptionist. It was almost half past eleven now, and Doctor Petrillo had still not arrived.

'Is he always late?' he asked the woman behind the reception desk.

He was scheduled to be in court that afternoon, and he was cutting things close.

'It depends,' she said, though she didn't say what it depended on.

Twenty minutes later, a man in a white medical overall arrived, spoke for some moments to the receptionist then came over to where the magistrate was sitting.

'Giovanni Petrillo,' he said, holding out his hand. 'Magistrate Catapanni, thank you for coming. Is this case yours?'

There was an air of playful levity about the doctor.

Calisto Catapanni stood up and shook the man's hand with a degree of embarrassment. 'Not exactly,' he said, 'but I am interested in trying to find out who this man might be.'

'Do you have somebody in mind?' Doctor Petrillo asked.

Catapanni nodded. 'A criminal who was recently released from prison,' he said. 'An informer who was working with me.'

'And you think that this may be your man?'

Catapanni asked himself how far he might be able to help the doctor come to the right conclusion.

'I don't believe so. It's just . . . Well, it's a shot in the dark. The news that I have suggests . . . that is, it *seems* to suggest, that he may have disappeared abroad.'

Doctor Petrillo waved his hand towards the swinging doors as though he might be inviting the magistrate to have a coffee in a bar. 'Let's get started then. Just give me a couple of minutes to change, will you?'

Five minutes later, dressed in a dark green smock and a white face mask, the pathologist pulled away the rubber sheet and exposed what Calisto Catapanni had driven to Perugia to see. What remained of the corpse was naked now, a collection of body parts on a metal table. The skull was detached from the sagging mass of the blackened skin and dirt-stained bones. One of the legs was a withered black branch. The other one was a chocolate-brown skeleton. But the first thing the magistrate noted was a large blue stain on the upper right arm of the man that he had seen one day in prison wearing a sleeveless vest. He couldn't be certain, but it was very similar to the tattoo on Andrea Bonanni's right arm. If nothing else, it was in the right place.

'Do you recognize anything?' the doctor said, pulling the mask up over his face.

Catapanni shook his head and wished that he'd been wearing a mask, but Doctor Petrillo was already at work and gave no sign of noticing his uneasiness.

'In such a state,' Catapanni said, 'I really couldn't say. I wonder how you hope to go about it. There's . . . well, there's so little on which to work, I mean.'

The pathologist picked up the skull and held it in his rubber-gloved hands.

'The cause of death is unequivocal. A single bullet to the brain. How old was your man?'

Catapanni hesitated. 'I'm not too sure,' he said. 'Late thirties, early forties?'

'We can determine certain aspects of age by examining the cranial platelets,' the pathologist went on, turning the head in his hands as if it were a basketball, 'where the separate elements of the skull have conjoined. Here, as you can see, the joints are almost invisible, which means that he – we're talking about a male – is at least twenty-five or twenty-six years old.'

Catapanni shrank back as the doctor held the skull out. It's Andrea Bonanni, he thought with a sinking feeling.

'Physical examination does not provide conclusive evidence. We know that he is no younger than twenty-five, though he could be sixty, seventy, or even older.'

Catapanni breathed more easily. 'Can science be no more precise?'

'Well, there's always the tongue test,' Doctor Petrillo said. 'But I won't be doing that!'

'Why not?'

'You have to lick the bone.' The doctor laughed. 'If your tongue sticks to it, you send for a forensic anthropologist. A bone historian, let's call him. Otherwise, it all comes down to chemistry. The laboratory tests will take at least three weeks.'

He looked at Catapanni as if to say, what's next?

'The man I took under my wing almost certainly had a drug habit; cocaine, perhaps. I wonder whether that might help?'

'Again, it all ends up in the laboratory, I'm afraid. They'll need to cut his hair into short sections then analyse each piece to identify which drug or drugs he was using, and to estimate over how long a period he was using them. Hair grows at about half an inch per month, so we have quite a wide spectrum to work on.'

'What about colour? Of the hair, I mean.'

'It will need to be washed, leached and dried before we can establish that, Doctor Catapanni. What remains of the hair is filthy, as you can see . . .'

'Surely the teeth will tell you something?'

Petrillo pursed his lips, then smiled. 'If we had his medical records, his dental profile, we'd know already who he is. I'm sorry I can't be any more helpful at the moment. You'll have to wait for the results of the tests, I'm afraid.'

'Whoever killed him didn't want him to be recognized, I suppose,' Calisto Catapanni concluded.

'So it would seem,' Doctor Petrillo agreed. 'I'll probably end up writing something along those lines in my report.'

The trip had been worthwhile, then, Catapanni considered.

There was no immediate need to alter what he had written in his most recent request for promotion and a transfer to the north: he was still working with an important member of an 'Ndrangheta clan regarding drug trafficking in Milan and Lombardy.

At least, until the test results came through.

TWENTY-THREE

A few days later

Corrado Formisano placed the gun on the table next to the bottle of fizzy wine.

The Force 99 was a work of art. So was the bottle of Sassicaia that Zì Luigi always sent him when he blasted someone.

But this time Raniero had given him a bottle of piss, and a different job to do.

Things were sliding downhill fast.

Gravedigger first, then messenger boy,

Was he the fucking postman now?

Raniero wanted to humiliate him, take him down. And that was how Corrado felt: humiliated.

The fury was building up inside him.

Raniero had stepped into Zì Luigi's snakeskin shoes. He was making all the moves in Umbria, calling all the shots. A star like Raniero moving up wouldn't let Zì Luigi stand in his way.

And if the Zì was up for the chop, Corrado knew that he was next in line.

Unless Raniero got the chop first . . .

He'd been expecting a bottle of Sassicaia when he blasted Bonanni. Zì Luigì had told him to shut Bonanni up, and that was what he'd done. That was what he always did, and Zì Luigi should have known it. Instead, the boss had lost his rag and put the blame on him, telling him he'd put the business in Umbria at risk. Now he was reduced to this.

A five-year-old kid could post a fucking envelope!

He recognized the address. He had been there a few weeks back and left a dead cat on the doorstep, the way Raniero had told him. The woman hadn't taken the warning, hadn't done what she was supposed to do. Not if Raniero needed to send her a reminder.

Corrado knew what he would have done.

He'd have told her to kiss the hot end of the Force 99. She'd have got the message, and so would anyone who stepped into her shoes.

But Don Michele wasn't having it. *No more shooting*, Raniero had said. The fuckers knew what needed doing, but they lacked the imagination. If you wanted someone to do something, you had to send the right message to the right place.

And that was what Corrado had done.

He weighed the pistol in his hand, sighted down the barrel. The Force 99 corto was the latest version of a pistol he had always loved. It fired .38s but it took other calibres, too. You could make as much or as little damage as you wanted to make. A *condition 1* gun, 'cocked and locked', you could carry it around with a slug already in the chamber, the hammer drawn back. All you had to do was flick off the safety, then squeeze.

He flicked off the safety, squeezed the trigger.

Click . . .

Instant death, and no fuck-ups.

He ought to have dumped it after doing Bonanni, but he couldn't chuck the Force 99 into a river. It sat so sweet in the palm of his hand. It was chunky, but light as a feather with a polymer frame. Matt black, no silvery bits to flash in the dark. Lisa had brought it up the day they let him out of jail. She had known what would make her baby brother happy after twelve years without one. The gun was what he had missed the most in prison.

The gun, the job, and Zì Luigi.

Zì Luigi told you what he wanted, then he left you to work out the details: how to do it, when to do it, where to do it. A name became a face. You hunted it down, closed in for the kill, showed the mark the gun, then you let him have it. You saw the fear in his eyes, felt the kickback in your hand, the smell of his shit, the rush of pride, then the taste of the Sassicaia afterwards.

That life was finished.

Chin! Chin! Salute!

He took a slug of wine from the bottle, then spat it out.

He pushed the loaded clip into the Force 99.

Out through the door, a rabbit was nibbling grass in the backyard. He fixed the rabbit in his sights and his shirt button scuffed the table. The rabbit pulled back and disappeared from view, but Corrado didn't move. It would soon come back. The victim always did. Frightened once, they stepped into the firing line more boldly the second time, thinking it was safe.

He saw the wet black nose come peeping around the doorframe.

He aimed the Force 99 at the gap between its ears and flicked the safety off.

Did a rabbit have a brain? he wondered, gently squeezing the trigger. The rabbit dropped on the doorstep. The slug had gone in through its left eye and out behind the right ear, the rear sight a millimetre off. He set it a fraction to the left, then stood up, crossed the room and stepped over the tiny corpse, his heart pumping steady now.

It was the sight of blood that did it.

He stood in the yard and closed his eyes, feeling the breeze on his face.

The dull *thud* of the Force 99 always did that to him. It gave him a new lease of life while it took some other fucker's life away. He stood there without moving for some time. Night was the time that he liked the best. In or out of prison, lights out, a creature of the night.

Like that kid who drove by every night in his noisy old Land Rover, the park ranger, the one from Calabria who was watching the wolves up on the ridge. Night after night.

Corrado felt the bulk of the Force 99 in his hand. He pulled the hammer back and a .38 clicked into the breach.

TWENTY-FOUR

That night, in the national park

Cangio watched the kids through the night-scope binoculars.
The male had gone hunting as soon as the noise started
up, while the she-wolf had retreated into the den, pushing
the four cubs inside with her muzzle. There was something almost
human about it: the male goes out on the prowl, the female puts
the kids to bed, then watches over them.

It was the same group of kids he had seen there three nights
before. They were doing the same things, too, dancing around a
bonfire on the other side of the valley, letting out whoops and howls
like kids on a school vacation without a teacher to keep them in
line.

He could smell the weed across the half mile that separated them.
He could hear the music, too.

They had parked their cars on the edge of a clearing. The doors
of one car were wide open, the stereo on full blast, churning out
grunge or techno, or whatever they called music these days with a
heavy churning bass and not much else. That car was pale fluorescent
green seen through the night glasses, though he knew that it was
old and white, the bodywork spotted with rust.

The last time, they'd been partying, too. There were four boys
and three girls tonight, so someone would be going home empty-
handed. Not that they seemed to be bothered by the maths. They'd
been roasting sausages over the fire, emptying bottles of wine and
beer before the dope came out. Shortly afterwards they had started
acting funny.

He wasn't sure what the excitement was all about, but he had to
laugh when they all dropped down on their stomachs, ears to the
ground like a tribe of Apaches listening for the hoof-beats of
the Fifth Cavalry.

'The cavalry's already here,' he murmured to himself. 'One false
move and I'll encircle the lot of you.'

He had been there half an hour, keeping an eye on the wolves.

Whatever the kids were doing flat on their stomachs, it didn't last long. They gathered around the campfire again, reefers burning, beer bottles clinking, music blasting the night apart. If there'd been any more of them you'd have called it a rave party, like some of the ones he'd been to in London. The flames of the fire were white in the night-scope, and he felt the nip in the air. At least they had that in common, him and them. They liked the outdoors, the scent of the trees and grass, the perfume of wood smoke and sausages rather than being cooped up in a bar or a disco somewhere. He wouldn't have swapped a single night on the mountains for all the nights he had wasted in London pubs, where stale beer and stale piss were the order of the night.

He smiled to himself, remembering how the evening had started out: a pizza with Loredana, then she had suggested a night in a disco which had opened recently in Perugia. 'Why don't we go for a drive in the woods?' he'd suggested. They had tossed a coin, and he had won. Cheating, obviously. He wanted to keep an eye on the wolves. The first weeks were crucial. Loredana may have guessed what he was thinking, but she hadn't objected. Her plan that night had been to let him see the brand-new flesh-coloured bra and panties she had on – eagerly expecting him to peel them off at the first opportunity.

He had run his hands over the Chinese silk that gave off static, then said, 'I prefer the real thing,' unhooking the bra clip and helping her out of the frilly knickers while they lay on a blanket together beneath the stars in a spot that he knew well.

She was down-to-earth and had a sense of humour. He hadn't complained when she asked him to take her home. She was on the first shift starting at 6 a.m., she'd said, supervising the cleaners, chivvying the warehousemen and the staff that came in early to stock the shelves.

He had left her at her door, then headed for the hills again. A perfect evening, all in all: Loredana from eight to eleven, then a couple of hours with the wolves and their cubs.

Until the kids had arrived and the party had kicked off.

He watched them through the binoculars. They were picking up the empty bottles, collecting the plastic bags they'd brought the food in, stashing the rubbish in the boot of the old jalopy. Then they turned their attention to the campfire, unzipping their jeans, pissing on the flames, stamping the ashes. OK, they were regular partygoers, but they turned out the lights and picked up the rubbish when it was time to go home.

He checked his watch. *00.55*. The same as last time, more or less.

As he heard the slam of doors and the motors roar into life, he turned his attention to the serious business of the night. Once peace settled on the park again, he knew that the she-wolf would bring up the cubs for a breath of fresh air.

TWENTY-FIVE

The same night, in town

The signal improved when the car stereo was switched off. Finally, he could hear them speaking. Lorenzo Micheli was telling his sister to take her unidentified girlfriends home while he climbed into the bugged Fiat Uno in the company of Riccardo Bucci, Federico Donati and Davide Castrianni.

The Watcher sat up in bed and raised the volume. He had been recording them since they headed out of town at 22.20, and he wondered what the Legend would make of the music. In his opinion, it was crap.

'So, what's cooking tonight after the sausages and hash?' he murmured, a cigarette clenched between his teeth. 'Give me something to work on, lads, then we can all go home to our own beds.'

The motor of the Fiat Uno coughed back to life, like a terminal lung cancer patient coming out of a coma. There was an exchange of shouts between the two cars, grunting and groaning noises from the bugged car, then Lorenzo voice telling the others to 'Shut the fuck up!' with all the volume he could muster, and Riccardo Bucci saying, 'I heard a wild boar, I'm telling you.'

'Wild boar, my arse!' Davide told him. 'That was Federico farting after all the sausages and shit he shovelled down.'

'I bet you were a pig in another life.'

It sounded suddenly as if the car was full of grunting pigs, but the voice of Lorenzo Micheli was still as clear as a bell.

'We heard the cry of rebellion from the centre of the . . .'

'It was an earthquake, Lorè. Not a big one, but . . .'

They started cheering, as if an earthquake was something to get worked up about.

'That's right,' Lorenzo went on. 'It came from the core of the Earth. That's where everything started, Mother Nature fighting back, telling us she doesn't like what's going on, warning the fuckers that are too deaf to hear. We heard her, though, didn't we? *Didn't we?*' he shouted again. Then, like a battle cry, he shouted: '*Parvis e glandibus quercus!*'

'What's that supposed to mean?' Federico asked him.

'It's Latin. "Great oaks from tiny acorns grow".'

Riccardo laughed. 'Why didn't you say so? Y'know, keep it simple.'

Davide was giggling. 'Lorenzo's a poet! Lorenzo's a poet!'

Federico yawned. 'It's obvious, ain't it?' he said. 'Trees grow. They grow from acorns, right? So fucking what?'

The only one who wasn't laughing was Lorenzo Micheli.

He sounded deadly serious. 'It means that big things start from little things, you fucking idiot. It means you've got to start somewhere. Tonight we heard the voice of Mother Nature—'

'That was Federico burping!'

'She told us, didn't she? Anything that tries to put her down will be destroyed. Concrete, new buildings, all that stuff. That earthquake was a little one, a message for us, announcing what will come, sooner rather than later. The big one—'

Only Davide Castrianni objected. 'Come off it, Lorenzo! We've had our fill of earthquakes. My grandma's house got fucking bull-dozed, didn't it? That stuff we smoked is going to your head. You're having visions of the Apocalypse.'

'We have to *start* the Apocalypse!'

Shouts and screams drowned out the rest of what Lorenzo Micheli was saying. Once he got going, he sounded like the Pope, the Watcher thought. And the other boys seemed to agree with him.

'Sometimes you're a fucking asshole, Lorenzo,' Federico was saying.

'Sometimes?'

'Always,' the Watcher said, but no one in the car could hear him.

They were young, doped up, ready for fun. The night hadn't started yet. They didn't sound so much like rebels as a bunch of idiots, and Lorenzo Micheli was the worst of them, full of himself and half-baked radical ideas.

The Watcher lay back on his hotel bed and lit another cigarette.

Federico was right. Lorenzo *was* an asshole. He took himself so seriously. The others didn't seem to give a monkey's but they went along for the ride. It was the same damned thing every night: drinking, smoking, hanging out in the woods. He was sick of listening to them. They weren't going anywhere. The operation was turning into a washout. God only knew what had got into the Legend's head. There was no promotion coming out of this lot.

'Hey, I've got an idea!' Lorenzo was saying again.

The Watcher frowned. Were they going to prove him wrong?

There was a lot of oohing and aahing, then the car screeched to a halt and the doors swung open.

He couldn't make out what was going on, but he heard the noises.

It was 01.47 when he phoned his supervisor.

'Are you awake?'

The supervisor groaned. 'I am now.'

'They're smashing up one of the building sites. If we call out the local cops it shouldn't be too hard to catch them red-handed.'

The supervisor laughed. 'Relax,' he said. 'Leave them to dig their own graves.'

The phone clicked; the line went dead.

As the Watcher was cleaning his teeth, getting ready for bed, he stared at his face in the mirror of the hotel bathroom.

Whose graves were the boys supposed to be digging?

TWENTY-SIX

Later that night

A lump the size of a squirrel surged into his throat. Cangio swallowed hard and tried to hold it down, then he gasped for breath and vomit came hurtling out of his mouth.

As he was turning the Land Rover into the final bend near the summit, heading for the ranger hut on the other side of the mountain, the headlights had picked out something for an instant. It was dangling from a sign which told tourists that they were 976 metres above sea level. He'd braked hard, and the ancient crate had skidded to a halt. He'd left the motor idling, headlights on, and gone back down the hill on foot, flashlight in hand, to take a closer look. One glance had been enough. His stomach had reacted faster than his brain.

A wolf.

A young wolf, but not *his* wolf. It was something to be grateful for, but not much. Some bastard had hacked the animal's head off, hooked a piece of wire through one of its ears then left the trophy hanging from the altitude marker. Saliva hung in sticky strands from its jaw. Blood had dribbled halfway down the metal pole.

Cangio spat to clean out his mouth, wiped his lips on the sleeve of his shirt then began to root through his pockets, looking for something to cover his hand with. In his breast pocket he found the soft rag he used to clean the lenses of the binoculars. It wasn't the blood that he was worried about so much as the saliva. A wolf in the wild might be carrying rabies.

He twirled the rag around his finger, jabbed at a spot where the blood had clotted on the sign pole. He felt the clot give beneath the pressure. When he pulled the cloth away, he saw the smear that his touch had left. The animal had been butchered in the last half hour or so, he guessed.

He shone the torch on the wolf's gaping jaw. The teeth were long and still white. None were missing or broken. A young wolf, and a healthy one, too. No sign of mange or scabies. No scratches either, so it hadn't been part of a pack. Not part of a pack? That wasn't possible . . . Its dead eyes glistened in the powerful beam of yellow light. The head had been hacked from the body with a hunting knife by the look of it, the incision jagged, as if it was the first time for whoever had committed the atrocity.

So where is the rest of the wolf?

He stood back and shone the flashlight on the ground. A wide semicircle of bloody drips had sprinkled on the dry dirt road. There was no sign of the carcass.

Those damned kids?

Maybe they weren't the harmless nature lovers that he'd taken them for. He ought to have have nailed them the first night he'd caught them roasting sausages over an open fire. If he'd charged them with lighting fires in a restricted area this might never have happened. They would have steered well clear of the park, the wolves and him.

No, he thought, it wasn't the kids. Would they have been capable of catching and killing a wolf?

He flashed his torch on the ground again.

There was a single footprint in the dust, and no sign of tyre tracks except his own. Whoever the killer was he hadn't used a vehicle. Cangio followed the spots of blood across the track. Someone had cut across country from the ridge above, leaving a trail of blood that he might be able to follow.

Someone who lived on the mountain, then. Or a poacher . . .

There had been reports of poachers in the last few weeks and signs of their passage: discarded shell-casings, roughly-made 'hides', the remains of a boar which had been shot but had managed to get away before it bled to death. Even inside a national park, poaching was inevitable. Boar meat was tasty. Deer meat, too.

But who would eat a wolf?

And if you were looking for trophies, it was the head you would keep. Which left the craziest idea of them all . . .

Marzio had told him about the weirdoes who sometimes celebrated black masses in the abandoned churches scattered over the park. A couple of months earlier they had found a crow on an outcrop of rock, its breast splattered open, its wings spread wide as if it had been crucified. Marzio had started raving about devil-worship, though the lab results stated that the crow had eaten a rat that had been poisoned. It had dropped out of the sky and been smashed to smithereens on the rocks. But Marzio preferred his own satanic version of what had happened.

The head of a young but fully-grown wolf hanging from a road sign in the middle of nowhere was certainly weird, but was it satanic?

He tried to stick with the facts.

There might be a simpler explanation. A shepherd who had lost lambs to a hungry wolf perhaps taking revenge, exhibiting the head to catch the attention of the authorities, a silent protest about the fact that the area was so vast and there were only two park rangers to keep an eye on everything. But there had been been no reports of a wolf or wolves attacking dogs or sheep.

The trees and bushes rustled in the breeze, the wind picking up. At the summit, the mountain flattened out into a sort of grassy ridge where wandering shepherds brought their flocks to graze in summer.

There was a hilly bump on the northern flank where a couple of farmhouses and shepherds' huts were strung out on the lee side to avoid the savage winds of winter. That was the place to start looking.

He ought to call Marzio. Never go after poachers alone – that was the first rule. They were usually armed to the teeth. But Marzio was celebrating his grandson's first birthday and Cangio had insisted on doing the last sweep. Knowing that Marzio liked his drink, Cangio had offered to do the first tour of the park the next morning as well. Marzio had given him a mock salute.

'I'll pay you back,' he promised. 'But if anything comes up, make sure you call me.'

Marzio was thinking of a forest fire, but setting fires was a daytime thing, sun on glass, or herders burning off the woods to make more grazing land for their sheep, blaming the damage on picnickers and day-trippers. That night had been as calm and untroubled as all the other nights he had been working there. Since leaving London, he felt as though he had ended up with a paid job in paradise.

Now, paradise seemed a sinister place.

Someone was close by, burying the carcass under cover of darkness. He had to catch the culprit and secure evidence that would lead to his conviction. You couldn't just cut the head off a healthy specimen of a protected species.

He walked back to the Land Rover, grabbed a heavy-duty rubbish bag from the rear cabin then let out a contented growl. Marzio had jammed his work gloves in beside the spare wheel. They were old, worn and smeared with grease. Marzio never went out on patrol without them.

'Try changing a tyre in winter when it's wet,' he said. 'Handling a python's easier.'

Cangio put the gloves on, then carried the plastic sack back to the altitude marker. He stretched up on his toes and began to pull at the wolf's head. He felt like being sick again at the sound it made, the blood stuck like superglue to the metal post. The flesh came away like a rubber sucker on glass. He got the head inside the mouth of the rubbish bag, edged it in with his boot, then hauled it over his shoulder and carried it back to the Land Rover. He hadn't expected it to be so heavy – he was panting by the time he had finished.

As he put the vehicle into gear, he felt a surge of anger. He wanted to kick the bastard who'd done this in the balls. Anyone who killed a young wolf was worse than scum.

Five minutes later he cut the motor, took the Beretta pistol from the glovebox, checked that it was loaded, clipped the holster on to his belt, slipped a pair of handcuffs in his top pocket, grabbed his flashlight and set off on foot across the ridge. He had never had to play the policeman before but that's what a park ranger was, whether he liked it or not.

He headed towards the nearest farm.

If he saw any blood near the farmhouse, he'd call Marzio.

He didn't bother with the torch, just followed the track, keeping his eyes on the ground, knowing that his pale face would shine brighter than the half-moon above him. He dropped down behind the curtain wall as soon as he reached it. Far away he heard the rattle of a train down in the valley four miles away. The silence magnified the sound, reminding him how vulnerable he was. If he made the slightest noise, it would be heard.

A sheep let out a bleat. It was like a shotgun going off, and his heart skipped a beat.

Another sheep took up the cry, then silence settled on the place again.

He should have called Marzio from the radio in the Land Rover when he had the chance. If he were to use his mobile phone, his voice would be heard a mile away. Marzio might have known who lived there, but now it was too late to ask him.

And what if there really were devil-worshippers about? They might have left the wolf's head on show to lure him into their circle.

The chosen victim . . .

He smiled at himself. It was hard to imagine a devil so demanding it could only be placated by the blood of a twenty-seven-year-old park ranger with sallow skin, dark hair and coal-black eyes. He glanced at the luminous dial of his watch. Two a.m. The witching hour was long gone.

He clasped the pistol close to his chest and got ready to move.

The sheep bleated again, and he dropped down behind the stone wall.

'Coward!' he murmured, forcing himself to stand up. All he had to do was look around, see if there was any sign of blood. If there was, he would run back to the Land Rover, call Marzio over the short-wave radio and tell him to bring the *carabinieri*.

He didn't need to confront anyone.

He doubled over and went in through the gate like Chuck Berry doing the Duck Walk, crossing the yard in front of the house and making for the barn, a low stone building with a double wooden door.

The barn door was secured with a nail and a loop of wire. He slipped the loop off the nail, pushed open the door and stepped inside, pointing the gun and his torch in the same direction, catching his breath against the stench of the animals closed inside for the night.

The barn was bigger than he had imagined, divided in two sections by a stone arch. The beam of light lit up the gleaming eyes of half-a-dozen sheep closed inside a wicker pen. Next to the pen was a brick wall enclosing three or four pigs in a sty. One of them grunted out loud then shied away from the light. A cow was tethered to a manger against the far wall. It shifted and a chain clinked gently. Then it lifted its tail and let go a pat that must have weighed a couple of pounds.

He stepped beneath the arch.

That half of the barn was empty, except for a large wire cage that might have served as a kennel. Whatever it was, it was empty. If the farmer had dogs they might be guarding the farmhouse.

No, he corrected himself. One dog only.

There was a chain and a collar lying on the ground inside the cage. Did they let the dog loose on the hillside at night?

He turned to the right and the squirrel surged into his throat again. He swallowed hard to hold it down. There was a dark damp stain on the dry earth floor. The wolf had probably been butchered there. But that was not what had made him feel ill.

There was a feeding trough made of cement.

Next to it, two large glass jars bound with wicker work. On the neck of one of the jars was a yellow label with a large black skull and crossbones: *Nitric Acid – Danger!*

He glanced into the trough and his stomach clawed up into his throat again.

The park and paradise disappeared in a flash. All he could see was the bloody mess in the trough, while his nose burned with the reek of acid.

He heard a noise and spun round, his pistol pointing at the heart of a man who stood there in the beam of the torch.

The man held up his hands. 'Don't shoot,' he said. 'I'm not armed.'

Cangio recognized him straight away. It was the man who had crept up behind him the week before while he had been watching the wolves digging their den. The man from the south who wouldn't say where he was from that day they'd met in Enrico's bar.

'I thought you might pass by tonight,' the Calabrian said.

TWENTY-SEVEN

The same night

Cesira didn't need a light to find Maurizio's trousers.

When the mayor came home late, he slipped his clothes off in the living room, carried them into the bedroom and left them on the chair in the corner, where he expected to find his pyjamas waiting for him. Usually he woke her up when he switched on the bedside light to hang his watch on the silver stand the jeweller had made for him. His Rolex was the last thing he took off each night and the first thing he put on each morning after taking his shower. He needed a shot of Rolex more than he needed a shot of coffee, he often said.

Tonight he hadn't bothered with the light.

Cesira had often thought of hiding the Rolex Oyster where he'd never find it, but she knew she'd never get away with it. Maurizio would know straight off where the watch had gone, and he wouldn't have hesitated to give her a slap until he got it back.

She concentrated on small things now, things he would never miss.

There was a lot of pleasure to be gained from it. She'd watch him rooting through his pockets looking for a pen, small change or some other trifle, and only she knew where the thing was hidden.

She kept her souvenirs in her Fendi bag, the big blue bag she used whenever she visited the local supermarket. She had half-a-dozen plastic lighters and a silver ballpoint pen that one of his fancy women must have given him. He hadn't given a toss when that went missing; she supposed he must have ditched the girl by then. There were a couple of keyrings – the sort they gave you for free in petrol stations, but no keys, of course. Keys were asking for trouble. She'd been tempted by a small key once, but Maurì had kicked up such a fuss when that went missing, she'd 'found' it for him straight away. A couple of times she'd lifted notebooks from his jacket. The nice red leather address book had been empty, but there were names and telephone numbers written in the black one.

Maurizio had searched for the black one for a day or two, then he'd given up, so she reckoned he must have had the names and addresses duplicated on his phone or computer.

Her bare feet edged across the floor towards the pile of clothes. She was careful not to make a sound, not wanting to wake him up.

Maurì was breathing regularly, the rhythm broken now and then by a murmur or a sigh. The radio alarm clock on his bedside table had a digital dial with bright red numbers. *02.54*. He'd come in half an hour before and had had a shower before getting into bed, a sure sign he'd been giving it to one of his town-hall floozies. He'd fallen asleep in two seconds flat, which meant he'd been out wining and dining, and that it had all gone off the way he'd wanted it to go.

She stretched her hands out like a sleepwalker, touched the padded shoulder of his linen jacket hanging on the back of the chair. Versace, he'd said, though he'd bought it from a discount warehouse. If he lost a few pounds, he'd said, he'd look like Richard Gere. She reached her hand down into the nearest pocket, had a feel around, then reached for the pocket on other side.

If you thought of it as fishing, it was a disappointing catch.

Two paper clips, a rolled-up paper hankie and a three-pack of johnnies. There was only one condom left in the pack but she took it anyway, then put the empty packet back in his pocket.

As she turned away, her bare shin brushed against cold leather. His briefcase. The Bridge. Eight hundred and thirty euros. She'd checked it out on the Internet. He had gone all the way to Rome to buy it in Via Frattina. 'A celebration gift,' was the way he'd explained it, though the elections had still been more than a month away.

What was his briefcase doing in the bedroom?

He must be drunk, she thought. As a rule, he left it out in the hallway. She was ready to bet there was something in there she could filch, something that he wouldn't notice. And if he did start moaning, she could slip it back into his jacket or trousers without him catching on.

She bent down, turned the clasp, raised the flap and slipped her hand inside.

It was papers for the most part, and cardboard folders. A bunch of keys, but she couldn't take those. There wasn't a single pen or pencil – not even an elastic band. She pushed right down to the bottom and touched the plastic cover of his iPad. She was tempted, but she fought the temptation off. Then her fingernail snagged on something underneath it – an envelope, as it turned out. It couldn't be important if it was buried down there. Just to be sure, she opened it, took out a piece of paper that was folded in four, then put the envelope back where it came from. He'd be in for a surprise if he ever got round to opening the envelope.

She'd make him pay for his nights on the town. Even if he didn't know it, he'd been robbed. She stuffed the meagre loot inside her Fendi bag, then got back into bed.

Tomorrow she'd make up for it at the supermarket.

TWENTY-EIGHT

Three hours later

'What did he tell you?'

Brigadier Sustrico rubbed his eyes. His twelve-hour shift was coming to an end and tiredness showed on his lined face. The *carabiniere* glanced at the paper he was holding in his hand. 'What did you expect him to say?'

'Why he killed the wolf, for instance.'

Sustrico yawned. 'Oh, right. The wolf,' he said, not sounding very convinced.

The prisoner hadn't said a word as Cangio was driving him into town. Nor had he mentioned the fact they had spoken that day in the bar, or that they had met again out on the mountainside.

The *carabiniere* had locked him in the interview room, then typed his name into the computer system.

'Christ Almighty, you've hooked a big one,' he said, then shook his finger at Cangio as if he had committed a crime by arresting the man. 'Born in a place called San Sostene, province of Catanzaro, Calabria, on the second of July, 1959. A suspected hitman. They had him up on a multiple murder charge but he got away with manslaughter. You're lucky he didn't blow your head off, son. They had him locked up in the 41-bis block. That's Mafia, that is. He's out on parole after twelve years in the can, it says here.'

Cangio must have turned pale.

'You're as white as a ghost,' the policeman said. 'You sure he didn't shoot you? Arrest a man like him, you're taking a risk.'

'I thought he was a farmer.'

The *carabiniere* clicked his tongue against the roof of his mouth, then took off his cap and ran a hand through his thinning hair. 'He doesn't know a thing about this wolf you're so worked up about.'

Cangio rolled his eyes at the ceiling. 'I've got the head in the Land Rover! There was wolf hair in the cage, and the carcass was in an acid bath.'

The *carabiniere* lit a cigarette. 'A sick dog, he said. He didn't mention a wolf . . .'

'He had it locked up in a cage.'

'Come off it,' the *carabiniere* snapped. 'Anyone could have killed that wolf. It's happened so many times around here in the past. A wolf takes a bite out of a sheep's arse, the farmer grabs his shotgun and goes out hunting. He knows the park rangers – you lot – won't kill a wolf. Protected species, right? So he does the job himself. Amen.'

Amen?

As if anyone had the right to kill a wolf.

'Did you get anything out of him?' Cangio asked.

Brigadier Sustrico fanned himself with the two-page statement Corrado Formisano had made. 'Like what?'

'Like what he's doing here in Umbria.'

Sustrico stared at the papers in his hand as if he didn't know what to do with them.

'This is his declaration,' he said. 'I didn't have to force it out of him. He kept a sheepdog in a cage in the barn, the dog fell ill and then it died. He had to dispose of the body. That's his story.'

'Why use acid? Why didn't he bury it?'

Cangio must have raised his voice because the *carabiniere* made a gesture, inviting him to calm down. 'I asked him that,' he said.

'And?'

'He couldn't bury it. Wild boar would have dug up the body.' Sustrico squeezed the tip of his thumb against the tips of his fingers to form a tulip, then shook the tulip slowly at Cangio. A common gesture of impatience. *What more do you want?* He slapped the statement down on the table.

'Did he say what he's doing in that farmhouse?'

Sustrico looked at him as if he was mad. 'What's it to you? They let him out of jail – the poor sod has to live somewhere. He can live wherever he likes, I suppose, if his parole officer okays it. Maybe he's always fancied being a farmer.'

The brigadier was a local man, you could tell by his accent. An old-time country copper who'd probably never worked outside the area. He'd certainly never been posted to the south of Italy, had never seen the things that went on there. But could he believe that a man like Corrado Formisano was telling the truth?

'Then you turned up and stuck a pistol in his face,' the *carabiniere* went on. 'He says you didn't give him a chance to explain.'

'The wolf is a protected species. Under articles 544 and 727 of the penal code he's looking at a prison sentence,' Cangio said. 'And if he's out on parole, sentence suspended, they'll sentence him for this and make him serve the rest of his time as well.'

The *carabiniere* laid his hand flat on top of the papers. 'The judge will decide. He'll hear two different accounts of the facts and make up his own mind,' he said, as if he wasn't inclined to favour either version.

Cangio couldn't believe what he was hearing. 'Can I have a word with him?' he said.

'You had your chance when you arrested him,' Sustrico said with a sigh. Then he glanced at the clock on the wall. It was a quarter to six, the sun was already up. 'How long will it take you?'

'Ten or fifteen minutes.'

Brigadier Sustrico nodded. 'You've got ten. The van should be here by then. We'll be taking him into town. The magistrates are sitting this morning.' He pointed towards the interview room and let out a loud sigh.

The first thing Cangio noticed was how calm the prisoner looked.

Corrado Formisano was sitting at a metal table that was painted green, the neon light bright above his head, his large hands loosely clasped on the scarred tabletop. He looked wide awake, though he hadn't slept all night. Formisano glanced up at him and smiled. Thinking back, Cangio realized, Formisano had been smiling since the moment he had let himself be handcuffed to the roll bar in the back of the Land Rover.

Cangio wanted to know what a convicted killer from Calabria was doing in Umbria, while the *carabiniere* officer just wanted to ship him off to court and pass the responsibility on to someone else. Marzio had shit bricks when Cangio had phoned and told him what had happened. He should have been on duty, and knew that he would probably end up copping an official reprimand.

Everyone seemed to be worried, except for Corrado Formisano. The prospect of ending up in prison again didn't seem to bother him at all. It wasn't normal.

Cangio sat down on the chair which the brigadier had vacated.

'Another interrogation?' Formisano asked him.

'That's the *carabiniere*'s job,' Cangio said. 'Mine was to catch you.'

'You working together now?' Formisano grinned. 'I thought the different branches of the filth couldn't stand each others' guts?'

The prisoner had a small tattoo in the triangle of skin between his thumb and his forefinger – a snake with numbers written on its back. When he flexed his thumb, and he often did so, the snake's tail twitched.

'You *wanted* me to catch you,' Cangio said.

'Me, help a copper? Forget it.'

'You beheaded a wolf and left a trail of blood behind you. You knew that I'd be driving up that track. No one else goes past at that time of night. You knew that a ranger couldn't ignore a thing like that. You didn't try to get away, didn't try to resist when I put the handcuffs on you. And you've been telling that *carabiniere* fairytales. We both come from Calabria, *cumparu miu. 'U capisc' u grecu?'*

Cangio paused for a moment, giving him the chance to reply.

If the room had been wired they could have talked in the Calabrian dialect – *u grecu* – and no one would have understood a word that they were saying.

Corrado Formisano sat there, staring at his hand, moving his thumb, making the snake's tail twitch. He gave no sign of having heard a word, just stared at the smudgy blue figures which had impregnated his skin.

'What's the date for?' Cangio asked him.

Formisano clenched his fist. 'The day I went to jail the first time.'

'I bet you've got another one somewhere for the day they let you out.'

Formisano sat there like a statue.

'The way I heard it,' Cangio said, 'the second one means you hope you won't go back.'

Formisano looked up at him. 'No one wants to go back.'

'You do,' Cangio snapped. 'So, what's this all about?'

They sat there in silence, staring at each other.

Once he had been handsome, Cangio thought. The Calabrian's face had the hard lines, sharp nose and high cheekbones of the farmers and shepherds you sometimes met in the Sila and Aspromonte mountains, their skin baked brown by the sun, their muscles taut with labour, hands gnarled by hard work in the woods and the fields. But this man was no peasant farmer. He might live like one and smell like one, but he had spent his life cutting throats, not corn. This shepherd thinned the flock rather than increasing it.

Cangio broke the silence in the end. 'That was *your* wolf,' he said, leaning across the table. 'You kept it in a cage. Why won't you admit it?'

Formisano glared back at him: a cold, hypnotic stare.

The eyes of a killer, according to the *carabiniere*. What would have happened, Cangio wondered, if Corrado Formisano had decided that he didn't want to be arrested?

'That cage was where I kept my *dog*,' he said slowly.

He didn't seem to care if you knew he was lying through his teeth.

'There was a ball of wolf hair near the water bowl and blood on the ground. You cut its head off. I saw the carcass in the acid bath. You were getting rid of the evidence, the way they do at home in Calabria.'

Silence.

'What was the message?'

The silence went on and on.

'Who was it meant for?'

Cangio sat there watching him. Had leaving London been a mistake? he asked himself. Had he walked back into the trap that he had tried so hard to put behind him?

'*They* are here, aren't they?'

Formisano lips curled down at the corners. 'They?' he said. 'Who's they?'

Was Formisano taunting him?

If he'd had the pistol in his hand, Cangio would have shot him. To avenge the wolf, if nothing else. Instead, he leant over the table again.

'The 'Ndrangheta is here in Umbria. OK, I've got the message, Formisano. Now, listen to me. I've got a message for you. This is *not* Calabria. Things are different here in Umbria. And I'll do all I can to make sure that it stays that way. *'U capisc', cumparu?* You get it? Tell that to your clan!'

By the time he finished, he was shouting.

The door opened and Brigadier Sustrico walked in.

'Is everything all right?' he asked. When neither of the men spoke he stood there, looking at them. 'The van's arrived to take him to court,' he said.

Formisano let out a sigh of relief. 'Peace at last,' he said.

'Shouldn't he have a lawyer?' Cangio asked, his nerves on edge.

Two minutes before he would have shot the bastard; now he was worrying that the man might not have a lawyer to defend him.

'They'll give him one before he goes in the dock,' Sustrico said. He winked at Cangio. 'He'll soon be sleeping with all the other big bad wolves.'

Cangio turned the place upside down looking for the phone number.

He went through all his notebooks, the wolf-den diaries, all the prep and lesson notes he had accumulated at the university. He remembered having jotted down the name and the number, but he couldn't remember where. That was the problem back in the old days when mobile phones were just coming in, back in the days when he couldn't afford one. You made a note of a name or a number on whatever bit of paper came to hand.

Then, logic clicked in.

They'd been in the same organic chemistry class. The guy had failed the chemistry module, he recalled, but someone had mentioned that he was making a name for himself in the Special Operations squad of the *carabinieri* in Rome. The name and telephone number were scribbled inside the back cover of his old OC exercise book.

Giulio Brazzini.

He tried the number, but nobody answered. He tried a lot of times that day, and finally got through that evening.

Guilio remembered him, too. 'You bored the pants off me with those wolves of yours!' he said with a laugh.

He nearly had a heart attack when Cangio told him what he wanted. An hour later, it was Cangio's heart that almost stopped.

Giulio Brazzini called him back. 'You won't believe this,' he said. 'He said that he'll see you tomorrow morning. I told him you're a ranger, and that you work in Umbria.'

'Maybe he's interested in Calabrian wolves,' Cangio said.

TWENTY-NINE

Later that morning

Elena Brilli came at twenty past nine.

The postwoman seemed to be in a bit of a huff, which was unusual for her.

'Morning, Elena. What's up with you, my love?'

She looked at the early porter, Sandro Gioli, blew out her lips, shook her head then plonked two sacks of mail on the reception counter. She slapped a receipt down, waited for him to check the details and sign it.

'Two sacks. That's right, Elena. There you are, my love.'

'One of the kids is in hospital, Sandro.'

'What's up?'

'Appendix. They rushed him in last night. They'll take it out this morning. Soon as I finish the round I'll be up there like a shot.'

'Not to worry,' the porter reassured her. 'It'll be over in ten minutes. Chin up!'

When she was gone he cut the string on the first sack with a penknife, let half the mail dribble out on to the reception desk then started to sort it by department, laying the envelopes and packages out across the desk from left to right. It took him twenty minutes, and he finished by tying up each departmental bundle with an elastic band. While doing the job he managed to unload a couple of piles on to people passing through the reception area. No one complained if you asked them to take up mail for their department. It saved them having to explain where they had been. They could say they were waiting for an important letter. As a rule, they'd been out of the office for coffee or a cigarette, sometimes both.

He loaded the remaining bundles on a little cart, then took the lift to the top floor.

The president's secretary, Paolo Gualducci, was working on the computer.

'Morning, Sandro. What have you got for us today?'

There wasn't very much. Six letters with handwritten addresses in small, expensive envelopes embossed with the titles of the senders, or the names and symbols of the towns that had sent them. Those would be invitations to official events. There was a flimsy oversized white envelope that might have contained a report or papers.

'And then there's this,' said the porter, holding up a padded yellow envelope which seemed to be heavy at one end and light at the other.

Paolo Gualducci looked up. 'What is it?' he asked, taking the envelope from the porter and weighing it in his hand. The address was written in capital letters and red ink – a leaking biro by the look of it. The writing seemed to slant to the left, as if whoever had written it was no great expert with a pen. Gualducci turned the envelope over, looking for the address of the sender which was generally written on the back in case the letter got lost or couldn't be delivered for some reason. The back of the envelope was blank. He laid it down flat on his blotter.

'Thanks, Sandro,' he said, telling him to get lost, more or less.

As Sandro Gioli went out of the door, he heard Gualducci pick up the telephone and say one word: 'Security.'

Sandro Gioli was back behind the reception desk when a large black van with a flashing blue light pulled up outside the Regional Government building five minutes later. He held the door open as four uniformed men charged into the building, each carrying two large black canvas bags which were stamped with the letters R.B.D.S. He'd never seen officers like those in the building before. They didn't say a word to him or to each other. They commandeered the lift, passing the bags from one man to the next like a human chain, then they all piled in and pressed the button. The door closed and Sandro watched as the floors lit up on the panel, stopping on the top floor. The red light started flashing off and on, off and on. Evidently they had blocked the doors to the lift, which meant that both the lifts were out of action.

'You'll have to take the stairs,' he said as two girls came in from their coffee break.

'We're on the fourth bloody floor!' one of them protested.

While they were standing there, trying to decide what to do –

wait for the lift or climb the stairs – a voice came over the public announcement system.

'For your safety, you are advised to evacuate the building imme-diately. Leave all personal belongings behind you. Please, do not run. Use the stairs in an orderly fashion. The lifts are out of action. Go at once to your designated assembly point and identify yourself to your appointed safety officer.'

That was when the scramble started. The two girls were hardly out of the door before the stampede caught up with them.

'Don't panic!' Sandro Gioli shouted, holding open the door to the street as people went charging out. 'No pushing, please.'

Sirens sounded and two squad cars screeched to a halt in front of the entrance.

The policemen didn't enter the building. They took positions outside the main door instead, guarding it the way the Securicor men used to guard it, hands on pistols, in the old days when salaries and cheques had been delivered on the last Friday of every month.

Within three minutes, the building was empty.

As far as Sandro Gioli knew, the only people who remained inside were the president, the president's secretary, the four police officers and . . .

'Oi, you!' A policeman came running up the steps from the street. 'What the fuck are you doing in there? This place could go up at any minute.'

Next thing, Sandro Gioli found himself standing alone in the street. He had no idea where to go or what to do. He was the early porter. No one had ever told him where his designated assembly point was, or who his safety officer might be.

'What's up?' he asked the policeman.

'A bomb scare,' the man snarled. 'Now, get out of here!'

It wasn't a bomb.

Sandro Gioli heard the details on the six o'clock news that night.

Members of the Regional Bomb Disposal Squad had been called to the office. They had opened an envelope, the newsman said, *'which had been carelessly passed from hand to hand. No one seemed to be aware of the danger to which top staff and manage-ment had been exposed'*.

The report had cut to an interview with a high-ranking police officer. '*Incidents like this one,*' he said, '*often result in serious injury, and sometimes even death.*'

And yet, it wasn't a bomb. The bomb disposal experts had found three unexploded bullets. There was a shot of the Queen as well.

'I will not be intimidated,' she said defiantly, looking straight into the camera, as if she knew who might have sent her those bullets.

What a pair of balls she has, thought Sandro Gioli.

THIRTY

That evening

I t took him a moment to identify the voice.

The Queen sounded even more agitated than she had the day they had met.

'President Pignatti, I am so pleased to—'

She didn't let him finish. 'Correct me if I'm wrong, General Corsini. I seem to remember you saying that you had the situation under control.' Her voice was taut with anger. She didn't swear, but it required an effort.

General Corsini frowned and the nerve in his eyebrow began to throb.

'Has something happened, dear lady?'

She let out a snarl. 'Three bullets. Three of them! That's what I'm talking about. In an envelope addressed to me. It will be on the news at any minute. My bloody secretary called in the bomb squad! Are you quite *certain* that you have everything under control, General Corsini?'

He heard the sarcasm in her voice, but he didn't respond to it. 'The envelope was addressed specifically to you?' he asked.

'Haven't I just told you? Three big, shiny bullets!'

Corsini didn't say anything. He was thinking.

'Did you hear me, General?'

Corsini sat down behind his desk, his thumb nail jammed between his teeth.

'General Corsini, for Christ's sake!'

Corsini grabbed the bull by the horns. 'This means that I was right, President Pignatti. These people are very dangerous indeed, and it is time for us to act. They have decided to raise the stakes, it seems. But we can beat them at their own game—'

'*Game*, General Corsini? Which *game* are we talking about? My life is in danger, and you talk of games? You're joking, I hope.'

General Corsini took a deep breath. 'Listen to me,' he said, 'and listen carefully. Thanks to those bullets . . . thanks to *me*, you will be sitting in Parliament before too long. Do you understand me? All you have to do is follow my instructions to the letter . . .'

When he put the phone down some minutes later, General Corsini sank back in his padded chair and closed his eyes. Three unexploded bullets in an unsigned envelope. What was it that Sun Tzu had said?

'Take full advantage of new horizons as they open up.
Exploit the vulnerability of human nature.'

THIRTY-ONE

The next day

Maurizio Truini pulled up in the supermarket car park.

It was Thursday afternoon, so the place wasn't full. Then again, it wasn't empty either, as people started stocking up on stuff for the weekend. As he strode towards the entrance, heads began to turn his way.

He was wearing a pencil-striped seersucker blazer over a yellow shirt and straw-coloured trousers, a red tie and a matching breast-pocket handkerchief. But it wasn't only the flamboyant clothes that caught the shoppers' eyes – it was the state of the mayor's face that pulled them up sharp. Bright red cheeks, lips pursed, eyes narrowed, a look of stern determination clouding his features.

'*Ciao, Maurizio!*' someone called across the parking lot.

The mayor ignored them and kept on walking, straight in through the automatic doors.

A woman coming out with a loaded trolley and two young kids was forced to one side as he rocketed past her. There were six checkout counters, young girls in orange overalls 'manning' three of the tills and half-a-dozen shoppers queuing up to pay. About twenty witnesses, if you thought of it that way, but Maurizio Truini

just saw faces that lit up for an instant as they recognized him –
ooh, you'll never guess who *we* saw today! – then looked away
when they realized that he wasn't in a vote-seeking mood.

'Where's the manager?' he barked at one of the cashiers.

The girl at the checkout blushed bright red and pointed at a door
with a ground glass window on which the word *private* was written.

Truini turned away without a word. He didn't see the looks he
left behind, didn't hear the whispered comments. 'He's in a proper
state. Did you see the way he was scowling?'

'Someone's in for a right old rollicking,' the checkout girl
murmured as she dealt out change.

Mayor Truini didn't knock on the door marked *private*, didn't
wait to be invited in. He pushed the door, walked straight into the
office then slammed the door hard behind him.

A young woman was sitting behind a desk. Blonde hair tied up
in a ponytail, a pretty face, nice tits. At any other time he might
have tried it on. But Cesira was sitting in front of her.

'What the fuck's going on?' Mayor Truini growled.

Cesira whimpered something that he didn't catch.

'I'm sorry to say . . .' the girl began, but Maurizio Truini wasn't
having it.

'What the *fuck* is going on?' he repeated, separating the words,
one from another.

'The lady here—'

Truini stopped her. 'You know who the "lady" is, I presume?'

The young woman in the white cotton blouse opened her mouth
to speak, but the mayor got there first. 'And who the hell are you?'

The girl pinched a plastic nameplate on her shirt with her finger
and thumb. 'I'm the assistant manager, Loredana Salvini. I . . .'

'Where's Rodolfo?' the mayor insisted.

A trace of a smile seemed to grace the girl's lips for an instant.
'The manager's in hospital in Corfu. Food poisoning, I believe.
Rotten lobster. For the moment, I'm in charge here.'

Maurizio Truini's face snapped into a smile that was as stiff and
humourless as a wooden puppet's. 'Just remember who you're
talking to,' he said, 'or you mightn't be in charge for long.'

The girl stared back at him, abashed but not subdued. 'I'll try to
remember that, sir,' she said, as if she had a hard life dealing with
difficult customers on a regular basis. 'The lady here was caught
trying to leave the store with goods she hadn't paid for.'

'Goods?' Truini repeated. 'Which "goods" are we talking about?'

The assistant manager waved her hand over a tube of toothpaste and a little green box containing a pair of tights. 'These,' she said.

Maurizio Truini groaned out loud. He should have known they'd catch her sooner or later. Cesira's little habit. She had this thing about nicking stuff. 'How much are we talking about?' he said, pulling open his jacket and reaching for his inside pocket, his hand poised.

'Not a lot,' the assistant manager said with a conciliatory smile. 'The toothpaste's €1.35. Three or four euros, I suppose . . . I'm not really sure of the price of the tights. But the thing is, *Signore* Truini . . .'

'*Mayor* Truini,' the mayor reminded her.

'As I was about to say, Mayor Truini, this is *not* the first time. We have filmed your wife shoplifting quite a few times. I've discussed the matter on a number of occasions with the manager . . .'

'Rodolfo Venturini,' the mayor said, as if the name made a difference.

'We know who the lady is, of course. We know who you are, too. We have overlooked the matter previously. But it really does have to stop . . .'

'This will stop it for today,' Truini said, whipping out a €100 note from his wallet and dropping it on the desk in front of her. He took his wife by the arm and pulled her roughly to her feet. 'Grab your purchases,' he said. He turned to Loredana Salvini again. 'Keep the change,' he said. 'It will cover the next twenty visits.'

The assistant manager was on her feet now, too. 'We hope there won't be any more visits, Mayor Truini. Indeed, we . . . *I* would be most grateful if your wife took her business elsewhere.'

While the assistant manager was speaking, Cesira picked up her ill-gotten trifles and stuffed them back inside her handbag.

'I'll talk to Rodolfo when he gets back from Corfu,' Maurizio Truini said. 'You can bet your life that we'll be talking about you. Take my advice, love – start looking for a new job!'

As the couple left the office and the door slammed hard again, Loredana Salvini noticed the folded piece of paper that Cesira Truini had left behind on the desk. She picked it up and would have followed them out of the store and given it back to her, except for the fact that the mayor, her husband, had been so rude.

What should she do with it?

It might be nothing more than a shopping list, something of no importance. If that were the case she would drop it in the wastebin and forget about it. On the other hand, it might be something important. In that event, she thought, the mayor or his wife would be back for it. Loredana took an envelope from a drawer, wrote the manager's name on the front, then placed the €100 banknote inside it. Let Rodolfo sort it out when he got back.

She went into the shop and had a word with the girl on the nearest checkout. 'How much are the striped Golden Lady tights?' she asked.

'Two-forty nine,' the girl said.

'Ring up a damaged goods sale for €3.84,' Loredana told her.

Back in the office, she unfolded the sheet of paper and read what was written there. A list of names. There must have been a hundred of them. What had Cangio told her the other day about lists of names?

She folded the paper into four and put it in her handbag.

Maurì was in a right mood.

He gave her 'what for' all the way home.

'One of these days I'll wring your bloody neck,' he said as the car pulled up in front of the house. 'I won't be in for dinner tonight.'

Cesira was frightened, shocked. She had almost been arrested for shoplifting and all Maurizio could think of was his job at the town hall, his position in society, what people would say if the news got out that his wife was a thief.

She didn't have the courage to tell him about the piece of paper she'd taken from his briefcase the night before. She'd seen it lying on the assistant manager's desk, but Maurì was dragging her out of the supermarket door by then. What if it really was important?

She could tell him that she'd found it lying on the floor, then put it away in her bag, meaning to give it to him the minute he got home . . .

The blow caught her completely by surprise, a back-hander that split her lip and caused her nose to bleed.

'Don't ever do anything like that again!' he snarled.

As blood dripped on to her best pink blouse, she reached inside her blue Fendi bag for a paper tissue and decided to tell him nothing. It would serve him bloody right!

THIRTY-TWO

The next morning

He looks like Mister Nobody.

The idea popped into Cangio's head as General Corsini came striding down the corridor towards him, the spitting image of his maths teacher at secondary school. Cangio couldn't remember the teacher's name, but the nickname had stuck forever. The general wore the same sort of glasses, too – round metal frames with blue-tinged lenses that had a way of reflecting the light back into your eyes.

General Corsini and *Mister Nobody* might have been twin brothers.

The similarity ended there, of course. General Corsini wasn't the sort of man who would take kindly to fun at his expense. His had been a 'meteoric career', as more than one journalist had described it, making him, at fifty-one, the youngest ever head of the national Carbinieri Special Forces.

Cangio stood a head taller than the general, but his heart leapt into his mouth as the small man stopped before him. His legs were quaking as he snapped to attention and stiffly returned the general's military salute. He had been standing out in the corridor for almost an hour by then.

'You must be the ranger from Umbria,' the general said.

'Sebastiano Cangio, sir.'

'Have you been waiting long?'

'I didn't expect a reply so soon, sir.'

The general smiled. 'That wasn't what I meant, Cangio. Have you been waiting here in the corridor for long?' As he spoke, he took out a key and unlocked the office door.

Cangio saluted again. 'Not long, sir.'

'Good.' Corsini nodded, waving him in through the door like a policeman directing traffic. 'Let's waste no more of your time then,' he said. 'We need to clear this situation up.'

The office was empty. No secretary, no junior officers. No one but themselves.

Why had he been summoned so quickly? Was Corsini going to tell him that he had reported Cangio to his superiors for contacting an officer from a separate branch of the police force?

His heart was racing faster now. He felt a bead of sweat form on his forehead.

He had seen the general on television, read about him in the newspapers. The Legend, as the journalists called him, was the head of the Special Operations squad, an officer who had led daring raids against the Mafia, international terrorists, drug-runners, arms dealers and slave traders. Cangio wondered whether he had made a mistake which might cost him dearly.

It was summer outside the window but the office felt chilly. The sparseness of the furnishings made it seem even colder. A set of grey metal filing cabinets took up one side of the large room. A street map of Rome filled the wall above it. There was an L-shaped wedge of desks: one large, one smaller, each with a computer on them. A scanner and printer took up a corner next to the wide picture window.

General Corsini waved him to a chair in front of the desk then sat himself down at the smaller of the two desks inside the L, facing a computer screen.

'Do you mind if I take notes?' he asked. 'We won't involve anyone else for the moment, Cangio. Your fellow officers might not look kindly on the fact that you have chosen to approach me. Private's best, I think. Don't you agree?'

Cangio opened his mouth to speak, but managed nothing better than a grunt.

'Do I take that to be a yes?' Corsini asked him, looking directly into his eyes. The indefinable sadness in General Corsini's gaze watered down any suggestion of superiority or arrogance. It was as if he had seen far more than he cared to tell you, yet wished to spare you the painful details.

Cangio nodded. 'I stepped out of line, sir, contacting you. I realize now that I might get into trouble.'

'Trouble?' the general echoed, a thin smile tightening his narrow lips. 'Sometimes rules are made to be broken, Cangio. You did the right thing coming straight to me. Now, tell me about this wolf that lost its head.'

It didn't take Cangio long to tell the tale, nor give his opinion of what he had seen in Corrado Formisano's barn.

'There must be many wolves in the park, I suppose?' Corsini concluded.

'They keep out of sight as a rule, sir. Except when food is scarce. In winter they sometimes scavenge through village rubbish tips. But never in the spring or summer. They avoid people when the cubs are born—'

'A farmer might lose patience with a wolf that was robbing him of profit.'

Cangio shifted uncomfortably in his seat. 'That wolf belonged to him, General. He kept it a cage and fed it like a pet. Yet the same man hacked its head off, sir.'

'As you told your *carabiniere* friend, you've only got a ball of hair to go on. And he does keep other animals in his barn.'

'Corrado Formisano isn't a farmer,' Cangio said. 'He's a known member of an 'Ndrangheta clan.'

'Can you be so sure, Cangio? Perhaps this man is trying to put his criminal past behind him. Indeed, it may well be the reason why he chose to settle in Umbria, so far away from his home.'

Cangio ran his hand over his thigh, drying the sweat on the leg of his trousers. 'He left that wolf's head where he knew that I would find it, sir.'

Corsini settled the glasses more comfortably on his nose. 'Why would he do a thing like that?'

'He wanted to be caught, sir. There's no other explanation.'

'That does sound odd, don't you think?'

'I . . . I suppose it does, sir.'

General Corsini stared at him for some time, the bluish light from the computer screen reflecting off his glasses. It was impossible to see his eyes or guess what he was thinking. He didn't look like *Mister Nobody* now. The small, neat features of his face were mild no longer. He was waiting in silence, expecting Cangio to fill the void.

'I . . .' Cangio hesitated. 'I think it was a message, sir. Something he wanted *everyone* to know about.'

General Corsini whipped off his glasses and peered at him myopically.

'*What* would he want everyone to know, Cangio?'

Cangio cleared his throat again. 'That the 'Ndrangheta is in Umbria, sir.'

Corsini's fingers danced across the keyboard, then he sat back in his seat and folded his arms. 'The 'Ndrangheta? A traitor to his clan? Is that what you are saying?'

Cangio felt the heat of his hand through the damp material on his thigh.

'I . . . I can't say for sure. But as soon as I entered his barn I had the feeling that I was back in Calabria again. There are farms down there, sir. They call them factories – isolated places with concrete baths and acid . . . like the one that Formisano had. They say they use them to dispose of animal remains, but . . . well, sir, those baths can be used for getting rid of . . . well, other things, too. Enemies, rivals . . .'

'You certainly have a fertile imagination,' General Corsini said, replacing his glasses. He pursed his lips then cocked his head to one side. 'And you could be wrong. Formisano may be a better farmer than you give him credit for. He could have been using the acid to rid himself of rotten meat, infected carcasses. Or, as he claims, what was left of his dog . . .'

'But it wasn't a dog, as I told you, sir.'

'I've worked in the south myself,' the general went on. 'I've seen those things, too. But you may have read the signs incorrectly. We're talking about Umbria, Cangio. Why, it's one of the most crime-free areas in the whole country . . .'

Cangio couldn't stop himself. 'A body was found just the other day, sir, shot through the head at point-blank range . . .'

Corsini raised a forefinger to halt the flow. 'A corpse?'

'A skeleton, more or less, sir.'

'I read a brief report from the local *carabinieri*,' the general said. 'We need more evidence to go on before we come to any conclusions.' He tapped a button and the computer closed down. With the light gone, his grey eyes were visible again, as mild and patient as before. He joined his hands on the desk and said: 'What were you expecting from this meeting, Cangio?'

Cangio thought of the operations that the general had led: helicopters whirling overhead, screaming police cars encircling the criminals, armed masked men in uniform – *that* uniform, the one the general was wearing – handcuffing the wrongdoers, driving them off to jail, reassuring the world that the State was in control no matter what.

'I was hoping you would come the way you always do, sir. With an army of men. Even the most remote and isolated places are up for grabs when organized crime moves in. Umbria won't remain remote and isolated if *they* are interested.'

'The way I always do? Ha, I like that.' He peered intently at Cangio. 'What makes you think that we aren't *already* keeping tabs on the situation?'

Cangio gulped hard. His throat hurt, as if he had tried to swallow sand.

'I . . . I apologise, sir. I've put my foot in it, I can see that now. Are you going to report me to my superiors, sir?'

Corsini shook his head. 'I'd have done the same thing in your shoes.'

Cangio wiped his hand on his trousers again. 'I ought to have reported my suspicions to the regional parks commission commander, sir.'

'No, no,' the general said. 'Keep on reporting directly to me. You are a valuable asset, Cangio. You work in a position that we could never hope to fill. You see things that my officers would probably never notice. Let us say for the moment that the situation is under control. There has been no significant criminal infiltration in Umbria.'

General Corsini took a printed card from a box and handed it to Cangio. 'You can contact me at this number at any time of the day or night,' he said as he stood up. 'Keep me informed of anything that may arouse your suspicion. *Me*. Not your superiors.'

Corsini came around the desk, holding out his hand. Cangio leapt to attention, and felt like dying on the spot. *Mister Nobody* wanted to shake his sweaty paw.

THIRTY-THREE

Lunchtime, the same day

Tonino Sustrico was eating a *porchetta* roll when the telephone rang.

He picked up the receiver, held it to his ear and carried on chewing. The bread was crusty, the roast pork dry and salty. It clogged his tongue as he attempted to speak. Of course, it did no harm to sound a bit gruff and busy when the phone rang. The public shouldn't be encouraged to ring the *carabinieri* directly over any old thing.

'Yes?' he managed to mumble.

'That *is* that the local brigade of the *carabinieri*?'

'Hm . . . mm.'

'I asked to be put through to the senior officer.'

'Mm . . . that's me.'

Sustrico nearly choked as the caller announced his name and rank. He shot to attention, watching in horror as an overturned can of Fanta flowed in a tidal wave across the paper-covered surface of his desk. He gulped hard and the roast pork roll went down in a solid lump.

'Brigadier Tonino . . . Antonio Sustrico, sir. At your service!'

He pulled a tissue from his pocket, wiped his mouth then dropped the rag in the Fanta puddle, watching it transform from snowy white to soggy orange as the voice said calmly over the phone: 'I need some information, Sustrico. The head of a wolf was found in your area two nights ago, I believe.'

Sustrico's hand frantically brushed the crumbs from his uniform. 'A wolf's head, sir?'

'Exactly, Sustrico. What can you tell me about it?'

The Legend might have been standing there, staring at him. It wasn't such a farfetched notion. *How did he know about the bloody wolf?* The mayor had phoned the day before, ordering him *not* to release any news of the atrocity. 'We don't want to frighten the tourists, Sustrico. I've told the newspapers to play the story down. If anyone asks, just tell them it's a rumour that's going around.'

You couldn't spin a tale like that to the Legend.

'We arrested a man named Corrado Formisano . . .' he began to say.

'So I believe. A park ranger, wasn't it?'

Next thing, Sustrico was telling him about the crazy ranger who had walked into the *Questura* in the middle of the night with a prisoner in handcuffs. A man who had been identified as – or rather, a man who had identified *himself* as Corrado Formisano.

'A record as long as the Bible, sir. Brought in like a poultry thief.'

The Legend seemed to find the description amusing – not quite a laugh, more of a grunt than a chuckle emerged from his throat. 'And did this "poultry thief" make a full confession, Brigadier?'

Tonino Sustrico cleared his throat. 'Not as such, sir. He wasn't saying much at all. That ranger held on like a ferret chasing rats, sir. He wouldn't let it go. And anyway, he had the evidence with him . . . the head of the wolf, sir. It was safe in the back of his Land Rover. He insisted on pressing charges, said that he was ready to testify. Of course, we – *I* would have—'

The Legend cut him off, as if he had no time to waste. 'I'm sure you would, Sustrico. Now, listen to me carefully. I want you to fax me a copy of the statement that Formisano made, and I want to see a copy of the charges that Sebastiano Cangio brought against him. Faxes of the originals, do you understand? *Not* email copies. Send them directly to my office number. Is that clear?'

Sebastiano Cangio?

Sustrico saw black. The Legend knew Cangio's name, though Sustrico hadn't mentioned it. He knew a great deal more than he was letting on. What the hell was it all about? Was the Legend investigating how the local *carabinieri* station was run, his pen hovering over an order that would despatch Brigadier Antonio Sustrico immediately to Pantelleria, the southern-most island of the Italian peninsula, for the rest of his working life?

Sustrico saluted the empty room. 'I'll do it immediately, sir.'

'I know you will,' said the voice at the other end of the line.

A minute more, and it would be too late. '*Signore* . . .'

'What is it, Sustrico?'

Sustrico took a deep breath. 'There's . . . well, there is another thing that may interest you, sir. A corpse was discovered some days ago. In the strangest circumstances, a skeletal leg sticking out . . .'

'The body in San Bartolomeo sul Monte?' the Legend interrupted. 'Who is he?'

'It's too early to say yet,' Sustrico reported. 'The preliminary forensic assessment arrived an hour ago. I thought you'd want to know, sir, seeing as how . . .'

Sustrico finished the sentence in his head. *Seeing as you probably know already!*

'A bullet through the brain, I believe.'

'Calibre .38, sir. There's no match on the record, sir.'

Sustrico swallowed hard. The Legend was testing him, verifying what he knew against what he was being told. Any divergence, Sustrico thought, and he'd be packing his bags for Pantelleria at the very least, though early retirement on half-pay was another possibility.

'What about Cosimo Landini, the director of the local bank? He's missing, I believe.'

Sustrico felt as though he might be going to faint. *The Legend knew about Landini, too.*

'We are checking out all the possibilities, sir. Landini disappeared some time ago, but another man has gone missing more recently. Andrea Bonanni was released from prison a short time ago after collaborating with a magistrate.'

'And there's nothing in the autopsy to indicate which one of them it might be? If they have the names and the medical records, it should be easy . . . Unless, of course, that corpse belongs to someone else.'

'In which case, it will take more time, sir.'

The general was silent for some moments.

'Which magistrate was Bonanni collaborating with?' he said at last.

'Calisto Catapanni, sir.'

'Send me those faxes, Sustrico, and be quick about it!'

The telephone line went dead without a goodbye or a thank you.

Tonino gasped for air like a deep-sea diver breaking the surface after his oxygen tank had run out. His legs gave way and he sat down heavily in his padded leather chair.

What the hell was happening in Umbria? Earthquakes, unidentified corpses, missing persons, and now . . . the Legend.

The sun, the moon and the stars had changed trajectory.

It was time to think of taking early retirement.

THIRTY-FOUR

The next day

Something wasn't right.

Zì Luigi came storming out of the bank manager's office, his mug blacker than the ace of spades. Raniero reached to take his briefcase, but the Zì shrugged him off.

'We need to talk, Raniè,' he snapped. 'Remember that *trattoria* down by the river?'

'The one with the ducks?'

'That's the place.'

A crowd of bank employees were standing outside the main door, chattering and smoking, blocking the way. Raniero strode straight through them, inches taller than the guys and gals in the crappy grey suits. He turned back when he realized Zì Luigi wasn't keeping pace with him. The clerks and secretaries were eyeballing him resentfully as he pushed his way past them. Short and heavily built, he might have been a farmer who'd put on his best suit and gone to town to beg a loan off the bank manager. They might smirk now, Raniero thought, but they wouldn't have dared to mess with Zì Luigi when Corrado Formisano was standing at his elbow.

Raniero waited for him by the car.

'What the fuck are you grinning at?'

Raniero didn't answer him, just held the car door open, closing it gently before he walked round to the driver's side. He fired up the Mercedes and joined the traffic that was building up as the lunch-hour rush for home began.

Zì Luigi sat staring out of the window, the corners of his mouth drooping down like a poxy dick. Someone had fucked his day up good and proper. Raniero didn't say a word. He knew that Luigi would tell him once he got his brain in working order.

'You'd think the chequered flag had dropped.' Zì Luigi let his hand fall with a heavy slap on his knee. 'Vroom, vroom, vroom! Stupid fuckers fighting over a bit of road, then queuing up at the next set of traffic lights.'

Raniero was tempted to laugh. A bit of road? Zì Luigi had come through a dozen wars with hundreds of victims and all for the sake of a few square feet of territory. Was he trying to be funny, or was he being serious?

They drove for another mile, and still Zì Luigi didn't say a word.

Fuck a duck, Raniero thought. 'How'd it go this morning, Zì?' he asked. 'You seem a touch pissed off.'

That snapped Zì Luigi out of his mood. He liked it when you tried to guess what he was thinking. 'That director,' he said. 'The *new* one.'

'What did he want?'

'He's started talking like Landini.' Zì Luigi's voice went up a scale, took on a whining tone like a nagging wife. 'We need to slow things down, *Signor* Corbucci. We're treading on thin ice, *Signor*

Corbucci. These bullets somebody sent to President Pignatti . . . the coppers'll be swarming all over the place like flies on a fresh turd.'

Luigi pulled out a white linen handkerchief, his monogram stitched in blue, and wiped his mouth.

'Fucking Corrado! You gave him the message, didn't you? Send them to her home. And what does he go and do? He sends the bullets to her office instead of leaving them on her doorstep! She'd have kept her gob shut and done what I wanted. Now the papers are full of it. The nationals, too. Franzetti had them lined up on his desk.'

'Corrado's lost it, Zì Luì. He ain't sane no more.'

Zì Luigi gave no sign of having heard him. 'There I was, trying to help that piece of shit, trying to get him back on his feet for old times' sake.' He made a dismissive gesture with his hand, as if he were swatting flies. 'Jesus Christ, who told him to go and fucking improvise? Didn't I always give him what he deserved?'

Zì Luigi liked the old ways, the big symbolic gestures. A gold watch for your first blood, a St Christopher medal if you had to go abroad, a bottle of Sassicaia if you knocked someone off. He seemed to think that things would never change, that business would go on the way it had always done. He was living in cloud cuckoo land. Raniero had had a quick word with Don Michele while Zì Luigi was in the office chatting with the bank manager. As soon as he'd opened *Corriere dell'Umbria* and read the news.

'Let Luigi run with the ball,' the don had told him over the phone. 'If he runs the right way, fine. If not, Raniè . . .'

'Them bullets aren't the end of it,' Zì Luigi growled. 'He chops the head off a fucking wolf and gets himself arrested! Where the fuck did Corrado find a wolf?'

Raniero remembered the wolf Corrado had kept in the barn. 'A wolf?' he said, playing dumb. 'That's really pushing it.'

Zì Luigi wasn't listening. 'That Franzetti was pissing his knickers. The coppers'll put two and two together, he reckons, and come up four.' He blew out noisily through his nose. 'We need to get this sorted, Raniè.'

Raniero eased his foot on the accelerator as they approached the restaurant. 'If you want me to take care of him . . .'

Zì Luigi cut him off quick. 'Lunch, Raniè. First, we eat, then we talk.'

Il Vecchio Mulino sat on the banks of a shallow trout stream that ran through the valley, wood-covered mountains on both sides. If you looked out of the picture window you could see a fish swim past occasionally. If it was a private chat you wanted, you took a table in one of the corners away from the window.

It was quiet that day, only half-a-dozen customers in for lunch, all watching out for the live trout that would make their day. Raniero had been there a couple of times before with Zì Luigi, the first time watching fish, the other time talking business.

The Zì didn't wait for the waiter or the maître d' to welcome them in, he just plopped himself down at the table furthest away from the water.

'Sorted? How?' Raniero reminded him, but a waitress appeared.

A pretty kid, seventeen or eighteen, Raniero reckoned. Cherry ripe and ready for it. She smiled at him, then said, 'What can I—'

Zì Luì didn't give her a look or let her finish her spiel. 'I want that homemade pasta with the truffles,' he said.

'*Strangozzi . . .*'

'No mean portions, mind. And give me a truffled trout to follow. With er . . .' Zì Luigi picked up the menu, gave it a glance. The girl grinned at Raniero, her green eyes flashing at Zì Luigi, then back at him. '. . . roast potatoes and this stuff here, what is it . . . *agretti*?'

'It's a bit like wild spinach, sir.'

'That'll do. You, Raniè?'

Raniero didn't bother playing around. 'Give me the same,' he said, and watched her go – white cotton blouse, tight black skirt, fishnet tights. He knew she was giving her bum that extra little sideways push for him. When business was sorted, he would definitely be coming back here.

He turned to Zì Luigi. 'You want me to take out *this* manager, as well?'

Luigi shook his head. 'Franzetti learns fast, Raniè. All he needs is a whiff of this.' He rubbed his thumb and fingertip together like a bankteller. 'We have to clear the way for him, that's all.'

Raniero nodded. 'I thought you said he wanted to put the blocks on?'

Zì Luigi opened his mouth to speak but the waitress appeared again with a bottle of wine and a plate of ham, cheese and melon. Before she left them to it, Zì Luigi started in with his fingers.

'Tasty ham,' he said, wiping his mouth with the back of his hand. 'Give me a bit of bread, Raniè.'

Raniero sat back in silence and watched him clean the plate. 'You were saying . . . about the bank manager,' Raniero reminded Zì Luigi, but the waitress was back by then, asking if they liked the ham and carrying away the empty plates.

A minute later she was back again with the pasta. As she laid the plates on the table – the pasta looked like a pile of tape-worms in a slimy black sauce – she glanced at Raniero, held his gaze and said, 'I told the chef to treat you like family.'

That made Zì Luigi laugh. 'That's what we *are*!' he said as he grabbed his fork and tucked in. 'Hmm, delicious!' he said, his eyes closed and mouth full, a string of pasta dangling from the side of his gob leaving a trail of olive oil like snail slime.

The waitress smiled at Raniero. 'Enjoy!' Going back to the kitchen, she moved even slower this time.

Zì Luigi cleared a third of his plate without a word. 'He's right, though. Franzetti, I mean. Bullets all over the place, the papers bursting with them, dead wolves and Corrado locked up in the jug. I should have gone up there to see him myself instead of sending you and Ettore. He took the message wrong, and that's a fact! So now we've got a problem.'

Raniero ignored the insult, Zì Luigi implying that he hadn't handled Corrado right. To be honest he did blame himself a bit, though wasn't going to admit it. He'd seen the tension building up in Corrado but he hadn't read the situation. They'd let Corrado out on parole but they hadn't let him go home. Stuck up on the mountain top alone he'd been like that nuclear plant in Japan, temperature rising, bound to blow sky high. It hadn't taken much to get Corrado going, that was for sure. Still, it was Zì Luigi who'd fucked it up. He should have left Corrado where he was and let the cops and social workers keep an eye on him. The best thing would have been to blow him away, but the cops had been too close to risk something like that.

'Things have taken a turn for the worse,' Zì Luigi was saying, mopping up the last of the truffle sauce from his plate with a bit of bread. 'Jesus, I could eat another plate of that!' He wiped his mouth with his napkin, then stared at Raniero. 'I want you to fix it, Raniè. The quicker the better.'

Raniero put down his fork. He'd had enough. He didn't like the grub they served in the country. Back home it was all fish – real fish, fish from the sea – not mouldy old truffles, farmed trout and fried lumps of grass.

'Fix what, Zì Luì?' he said, playing dumb again, stringing the old man along.

Luigi didn't answer him directly. 'Not what, Ranié. *Who* . . . Corrado. You've got the connections.' He rolled a lump of bread into a dough ball then popped it into his mouth. 'I ain't been inside for over twenty years. Is this what getting old means?'

Raniero didn't know how to take the question. 'You did your best by Corrado,' he said. 'There's nothing left to do, Zì Luì.'

'You'll handle it, then?'

Raniero raised his glass and held it up to the light. 'This ain't Sassicaia,' he said with a smile.

Zì Luigi smiled back at him. 'I know the bubbly is more to your taste. Just get it done and you'll be drinking some of that Pol Roger Winston Churchill. How does that sound?'

Raniero nodded, wondering what the Don would give him. Don Michele was worlds apart from men like Zì Luigi. He was younger for a start, only five or six years older than Raniero. He knew a Philippe Patek from an Oyster Perpetual.

Zì Luigi jumped up suddenly. 'I need to take a piss.'

'Consider it fixed,' Raniero assured him. 'A phonecall's all it takes.'

The lines around Zì Luigi's eyes relaxed, then he toddled off to the loo.

The old man's prostrate was playing him up again.

THIRTY-FIVE

The next day

General Corsini closed the slim file.

Calisto Catapanni was forty-two years old and he had spent his entire career in a small provincial town where nothing much ever happened. Perhaps his wife had held him back. Catapanni had married Elena de Bonis within a year of arriving from Milan to take up his first appointment as an investigating magistrate, and de Bonis was a well-known name in town. Her father, Aldo, had been a judge on the local circuit; two of her brothers ran a successful law firm which handled divorce and slander cases for the most part. The de Bonis family owned a splendid, once-noble palace in the oldest part of town, and they all had apartments there. Calisto and Elena Catapanni had been living in the building since the day of their marriage.

And yet, Magistrate Catapanni wasn't happy with life in the provinces.

He seemed to harbour ambitions – dreams of escape, dreams of glory, as General Corsini saw them. On a couple of occasions he had tried to make a name for himself and earn promotion, though neither attempt had come to much. Particularly the most recent one.

In search of something which would bring him into the public eye, Catapanni had begun to take a special interest in the local maximum-security prison. Career magistrates were always keen on such places. They were full of criminals desperate to get out and not at all concerned about the means they used to do so. Catapanni had chanced on a prisoner named Andrea Bonanni. Bonanni had served less than three years of a ten-year sentence on charges connected with drug-trafficking and extortion, but he wasn't cut out for prison. He was small fry, relatively speaking, a foot soldier from one of the strongest 'Ndrangheta clans in Catanzaro. Catapanni had spoken privately with him on four separate occasions, then secured his release and admission to a collaborators' protection programme when the man declared that he was willing to 'reveal important information regarding the importation of cocaine and heroin from Venezuela and Colombia'.

Within three weeks of his release, Bonanni had disappeared.

If the corpse that the earthquake had disgorged at San Bartolomeo sul Monte – just five miles from the magnificent palace where Calisto Catapanni was living – turned out to be the corpse of Andrea Bonanni, it was a fair bet that the magistrate would be stuck in the provinces until the day they decided to pension him off.

Would any desperate prisoner entrust him with their lives again? On paper, Calisto Catapanni was the man that he was looking for. General Corsini picked up the telephone and called the number.

A voice answered, though not immediately. A female voice, a

woman who identified herself as a clerk to the court, announced that Procurator Catapanni was 'not in his office at the moment'.

General Corsini told her who he was and she put him through immediately. 'Procurator Catapanni,' Corsini began, 'I apologise for disturbing you. You're busy, I imagine, but there is something that I wish to discuss with you. I was hoping to come up from Rome to see you personally, but . . .' he paused for a moment, '. . . I'm pretty busy, too, as you can imagine.'

'I fully understand, General Corsini. I was writing up a case report . . . a case of no great urgency, I do assure you. How can I help you?' The man's voice sounded diffident, yet curious at the same time. Corsini thought he could hear the dialogue going on inside the magistrate's head: *Friend? Or foe?*

'I'll get straight to the point,' Corsini said. 'It concerns an investigation on which I am working. If I may steal a few minutes of your time, I'll fill you in on the details.'

Five minutes later Corsini stopped speaking and waited for the magistrate to react.

Calisto Catapanni was silent for some moments, and when he did speak up, he seemed even more reserved and measured than before.

'I've been working in this part of the world for . . . well, for almost fifteen years now, General.'

'Fourteen years, seven months and a week or two,' Corsini informed him.

'You seem to be informed of the facts,' Catapanni said, and he might have been forcing himself to smile as he said it. 'What I really meant to say was that . . . well, I'm surprised, truly surprised. In all the time I've been here I have never heard the slightest mention of anything so serious as what you are suggesting.'

'I can understand that, Doctor Catapanni.'

Corsini using the formal expression, *dottore*, a term of little meaning which many magistrates seemed to love.

'The thought of such things happening here in Umbria,' Catapanni said. 'The green heart of Italy, as the poet, Carducci, once—'

'A magnificent image,' General Corsini pounced, 'but dated and rhetorical, don't you agree? The earthquake knocked the "green heart" for six, and things are bound to get worse before they get any better. The reconstruction of the province will have the gravest consequences, as I told you, with money pouring in from Bruxelles.

Umbria will never be the same again, I fear. The important thing is to strike, and strike quickly.'

The general needed a magistrate's signature to authorize his operation, while the magistrate in question seemed to be hedging his bets, nervous about what he might be letting himself in for.

'An emergency situation,' the magistrate said.

'An emergency which can be averted,' Corsini shot back at him.

'And you can document everything you've told me so far?'

'Everything.'

The general paused for a moment, letting the message sink in.

'A corpse has come to light in Umbria in the last few days,' he went on. 'I have read the *carabinieri* reports. So have you, I imagine. The body has not been identified as yet, but if it does turn out to be the man whom you released from prison . . . well, I'm sure you don't need me to elaborate any further. It would be a serious blow to your career. I advise you to take the opportunity that I am offering. It may never come your way again, and will turn your colleagues green with envy. I do not wish to sound rude, Procurator Catapanni, but really . . . you ask me if *my* investigation is watertight? If you would rather place your hopes in the Andrea Bonannis of this world, just tell me and I'll look elsewhere for help. You are not the only magistrate in Umbria.'

Moments passed in silence, then the magistrate spoke. 'What do you want from me, General Corsini?'

'For the moment, I need authorisation to put my men in place in the area under your jurisdiction. All the risk, if that's what you want to call it, will be on my head. But you and I will share the glory.'

'I can have the papers on your desk tomorrow morning,' Catapanni said.

A minute later General Corsini put the phone down, opened the bottom drawer of his desk and took out three things: a green carboard box stamped with the face of Giuseppe Garibaldi, a slim Prometheus lighter made of solid silver, and a cheap metal ashtray which advertised Cynar. He smoked a *toscano* cigar only four or five times a year – when he needed to concentrate, or when he had something to celebrate.

This time, it was a combination of the two.

THIRTY-SIX

One hour later

The Watcher was glad to be back home in Rome, his mission over.

He killed the jet of hot water and heard the phone ringing. The voice of his supervisor was quivering with a rage he could barely contain. 'Where the fuck were you? Why didn't you answer the phone?'

Am I supposed to shove it up my arse to keep it dry? he thought.

'I was in the shower,' he said instead. 'I wasn't expecting any calls. Not after handing in the final report—'

Another curse cut him off. 'All leave's cancelled. You're back on duty.'

Clearly, there was a problem. Equally clear was the fact that he was going to be a part of the solution.

'The Legend wants to see you, pronto. Given that you're as clean as a baby's bum I'll tell him to expect you straight away.'

'What's up?'

'Someone's sent some bullets through the post to the President of Umbria. The Legend wants to know what's going on. You were up there . . .'

'Wasting my time, minding those bloody kids!'

'Following orders,' the supervisor reminded him. 'And here's another one. Get down here double quick!'

'I'll be twenty minutes, depending on the traffic.'

'Make it ten, or you'll be in trouble.'

The Watcher snapped his mobile phone shut then reached for his underpants. Jesus Christ! If the Legend had lost interest in those kids he could say goodbye to the promotion he'd been counting on, and the office job that went with it.

'Shit!'

THIRTY-SEVEN

18 September, 18.03

The green light blinked on.

A moment later, the cablegram machine began to spew out a message.

It was a rare occurrence, and Brigadier Tonino Sustrico just happened to be in the operations room at the time. He picked up the sheet of paper, read it once, then read it out loud to his three subordinates.

ALL RANKS RECALLED TO ACTIVE DUTY – STOP – IMMEDIATE MOBILISATION – STOP – FURTHER INSTRUCTIONS FOLLOW ON – END OF MESSAGE.

Mario Pulenti, the radio operator, stared up at him. 'What's going on then, Brigadier?' He and Sustrico would have been going off duty at eight o'clock.

'I have no idea,' Sustrico admitted. It might be anything from the whim of some high-ranking officer who happened to be passing through town to the announcement of a full-blown coup d'état. 'You'd better start making the calls. I want everyone here asap. *Now*,' he added, before Pulenti could ask him what he meant.

By the time the clock struck seven, the twelve *carabinieri* who manned the station were crowded into the operations room, staring at the cablegram machine. Nothing more had come through after the first message. Three minutes later, the green light blinked on and another sheet of paper came rolling into the collection tray, like a snake uncoiling.

'Their clock's slow,' Pulenti said.

SPEC OPS COORDINATOR ARRIVAL IMMINENT – STOP – ALL RANKS CONFINED TO BARRACKS – STOP – RADIO SILENCE IMMEDIATE – END OF MESSAGE.

Sustrico passed the sheet of paper to the others.

'Special Operations Coordinator?' Carosio asked him. 'What's the operation?'

'I know as much as you do,' Sustrico replied.

Mario Pulenti was in a proper state. 'You'd think they frigging owned us! I'm supposed to bc taking the missus to her mother's for dinner. She'll go bloody nuts, she will!'

Fifteen minutes later, everyone was busy on their mobile phones, calling family or friends, trying to explain that there was an emergency without having any idea of what the situation was. Carosio was saying that he wouldn't be home that night, asking his father to pick up his son from catechism lesson. Luisella Tonelli, the only female, was cancelling the pizza she had arranged with her friends. Tonino Sustrico was telling his wife for the fourth time: 'You *know* how it is, love. We're a paramilitary police force. If an order comes in, it has to be obeyed. Do you want me to lose my pension?'

At that moment, the special operations coordinator walked in.

'Shut those phones!' he snapped.

'The situation is simple,' the coordinator was saying.

They were in the conference room, the eight officers who had worked the day shift and the four who would have been on-duty that night. Everyone was sitting down, except for him. He laid his hands flat on the table, leaned forward, then fixed his eyes on each of them in turn.

'You call me Coordinator,' he said. 'You don't need to know my name or rank, which is, I assure you, superior to the rank of any man or woman in this room. You are all on duty until I say that you are free to go home. Is that clear?'

Pulenti pressed his lips together, but still the words came out.

'Have we been kidnapped?'

A thin smile appeared on the coordinator's lips. 'You might call it that,' he said. 'Just be glad that you'll be released quite soon.'

Everyone knew who he was. Everyone had seen him on the television or read about him in the newspapers. No one had ever thought they would meet him face-to-face.

Tonino Sustrico would have preferred to keep his mouth shut, but he was the senior officer in the room – after General Corsini, obviously. Everyone turned to him, expecting him to speak up for them.

'Excuse me, sir. You said that something important is going to happen. Will we be told what this is all about? And will we be taking an active role in the operation?'

'You will all be a part of what is about to happen. From a logistical point of view, only at the beginning. First, I want everyone to understand that this is a matter of national importance.' General Corsini stopped short. 'Any questions?'

Sustrico turned down the corners of his mouth, raised his chin in the air and looked around the table. His gesture expressed more clearly than words what he wanted to say: *What the hell is going on?*

General Corsini's glasses flashed beneath the neon lights overhead. His fist fell gently on the papers spread out before him. 'Let's make the most of the time that remains before my men and the magistrate arrive, and this operation kicks off in earnest.'

Pulenti was sitting next to Sustrico. '*His* men? What's he talking about?'

Fortunately, only Sustrico heard him.

22.35

Generale Corsini was shut up in the communications room. No one had seen him since nine o'clock.

Sustrico and the others remained in the conference room. They'd talked the situation over for a bit, then Sustrico had laid his head on his arms and fallen asleep. The last thing he remembered saying was that it reminded him of the night his youngest had been born. 'Fourteen hours of passion. On my feet all bloody night.'

The next thing, he was woken up by an argument that was going on.

Eugenio Falsetti was the youngest officer in the station. 'Just 'cause I'm the lowest in rank, why should I have to do the cooking?'

It was getting late, and everyone was hungry. No one had been at home for dinner. There were three packets of spaghetti, half a bottle of olive oil, a can of tomatoes and a jar of dried red peppers left over in the larder. As a rule, whoever was on the night shift kept the cupboard stocked up for an early morning *spaghettata*. No one had come prepared that night, and there were more of them than usual.

Sustrico looked at Falsetti. 'Do it!' he said.

Falsetti's pasta was overcooked, they all agreed, but everyone tucked in and made the most of it. The *spaghetti alla diavola* was served on plastic plates left over from the time a lorry had been stopped on its way from Serbia to Rome packed with illegally imported cats and dogs that were nearly dead of thirst.

Falsetti had knocked on General Corsini's door, asking if he was hungry.

The Legend didn't even look up at him.

'Bring me a large black coffee,' he said. 'Make it strong.'

02.30

Everyone was sleeping, more or less.

Michele Carosio was alone at the reception desk when a sharp rap woke him up. General Corsini was standing in front of him.

'My men will be here at any moment,' he warned. 'Let them in without delay.'

Five minutes later, the buzzer sounded from the door down in the street.

At that time of night it seemed lower in tone and more sinister than usual. Then again, everything seemed strange and menacing that night. Not just the pale, drawn face of Magistrate Catapanni – Carosio had seen him occasionally when he escorted a prisoner to the local court in the centre of town – but also the three tall men who walked in through the swing doors at the magistrate's back. Each one wore a black assault uniform, a black bulletproof jacket, a black balaclava, and carried a Beretta PM 12 machine gun.

They didn't even look at Carosio.

General Corsini was standing outside the fax room.

'Magistrate Catapanni, gentlemen,' he called. 'I've been expecting you. In here, please. We need to run through the final details.'

THIRTY-EIGHT

19 September, 03.01

It was dark on D wing.

Even darker than he had expected. The night lights glimmered like pale mushrooms growing on the ceiling. Moonlight, coming in through the windows on the right, cut pale diamonds on the rubber-tiled floor, the slanting bars like shallow incisions in pure crystalline carbon. Along the left-hand side of the corridor the isolation cells were marked off by steel doors at intervals of twenty feet.

He counted them until he came to the sixth door. There, he stopped and listened.

A maximum-security prison is never silent. Even so, there was an uneasy sort of peace. He could hear the sound of muffled snores, the stifled voices of prisoners talking in their sleep, living out their dreams, the pounding of a steel door closing somewhere far off. He had passed through two barred gates already, and no one had tried to stop him. Nobody was supposed to stop him. No one was supposed to see him. Some poor bastard of an underpaid prison guard had been there with the pass-key minutes before, opening the gates and doors, preparing the way.

Still, it paid to be careful.

It wouldn't be the first time a man in his position had been betrayed by the people he was supposed to be working for. Before he did the job, he needed to be sure that he wasn't being set up. Life was life, but two consecutive life sentences would be pushing it. There'd be no remission for another killing. Once he was in the cell it would be child's play to lock him inside with the victim. No amount of explaining would get you out of a fix like that. Not when you were supposed to be locked up in your own cell fast asleep.

Further ahead, through three more sets of closed barred gates, he could see the dim lights in the palisade area at the far end of the corridor. That was where the prisoners were brought each morning for security checks and handcuffing before being taken off to court or transferred to another prison. Returning prisoners and new inmates were forced to wait there until the cuffs and the restraining belts had been removed and they were escorted to their cells. He felt an incredible sense of freedom in being able to move through the prison unchained and unguarded. The neon light of a snacks-and-drinks machine flashed on and off in the palisade like an irregular stroboscope. The bulb was fading but no one would change it until it popped.

He looked back over his shoulder. Darkness, silence, unrestricted space.

He had left the barricade gates wide open in case he had to run. He could say that he'd been trying to escape if they caught him in the corridor. Trying to get out of jail was legitimate. Six months in solitary and that would be the end of it.

But what he was doing now . . .

He laid his hand on the door of cell number eighteen, then pushed it open.

The heavy steel door swung back, resisting slightly, and he stepped quickly into the narrow room. It might have been his own home from home. There was a narrow window-slit in the far wall, a metal toilet bowl beneath it, a metal washbasin in the corner and a narrow bed pressed up against the right-hand wall. On the left, a slim-line plasma TV had been secured high up on the wall near the ceiling, a single bookshelf suspended below it, a metal desk and a metal chair that served as a table where you ate your meals and read your mail. His own cell was identical, except for two things: the mess on the table and the man on the bed.

Moonlight shone in through the slit and fell on the table.

There was a plastic plate, a plastic knife, a plastic fork, a plastic mug and a half-empty plastic bottle of mineral water. The prisoner hadn't had the time to wash up after the special dinner he'd been served that night. He'd scoffed the lot then gone straight to bed. The ketamine and diamorphine had knocked him out, as it was meant to do.

The fish had been pumped full of it.

He glanced at the dirty plate, the scaly skin, the big bones of the sea bream.

The prisoner was lying on his back, snoring loudly, his mouth wide open. He didn't seem to be dreaming, his eyelids heavy, motionless, like those of a corpse that a mortician had finished making up for a funeral; a stocky, dark-skinned man in his mid-fifties, whose curly black hair had a light grey frosting. A man he had never seen before, and hoped he would never see again.

He paused, and listened again. This was the moment of greatest danger.

If the prisoner woke up now, if the guard with the key had second thoughts, if one of the other guards came wandering through D wing and saw the open gates and the unlocked door, then he was in the shit. Not that any of guards would want to get involved. 'Do it any way you like,' Raniero had told him. 'Just make it look like an accident.'

He looked around the cell. There was a lot of stuff he could have used. Pillow, shoelaces, towel – you could throttle a drugged man with any of those. But he'd seen something better the instant he entered the cell. He went over to the table, picked up the fish skeleton by its tail, moved close to the bed then sat down heavily on the man's chest.

The sleeper's mouth gaped open. He was too far gone to react or make a sound. Out cold, even with fourteen stones of criminal malice sitting on top of him.

He slid the fish into the prisoner's open mouth, then he stood up.

There was a *swoosh* as the man on the bed gasped for breath. A gurgle as he tried to swallow, and the bones slid deeper into his throat. His eyelids fluttered, but he didn't wake up. He choked and gagged, tried to retch, his throat muscles fighting instinctively to eject the bones, trying to cough them up and out.

He pinched the man's nose between his thumb and forefinger, pressed his left hand over the man's mouth and held it there, crushing the fish bones further into the gaping hole. He felt warm vomit hit the palm of his hand, a smell of fish and lemons in the air.

He pressed down harder.

It was over in less than a minute.

The body bucked a couple of times, then the head sank back lifeless on the pillow.

A cardiac arrest, maybe, or pseudo-anaphylaxis. That was the medical term for it. A bad reaction to fish, or the fish bones wedged in his gullet. That was what the coroner would be told to say. The official announcement wouldn't change a thing. The prisoner in cell eighteen was dead, whoever he was.

He caught hold of the fish by the tail fin, pulled hard and the skeleton came sliding easily out of the dead man's mouth. The muscles in his throat were limp now, offering no resistance. He rinsed the vomit off beneath the tap, then dropped the fish skeleton back on the plastic plate where he had found it.

He stood by the door for a moment, then peered out into the corridor.

All was silent. The coast was clear.

Two minutes later he was back in his own cell, stretched out on the cot.

He heard the sound of footsteps coming slowly down the corridor. They stopped outside his door. Nothing happened for some moments, then a key turned in the lock. The footsteps moved away, and he heard a clang as the steel gate closed. Some moments later, further off, the second gate closed.

The guard was going to lock the dead man in his cell.

The killer didn't hear the sound of the key in the lock. He was fast asleep by then.

Someone said next morning that Corrado Formisano was dead.

THIRTY-NINE

19 September, 05.15

I t started as a rumble far away to the south.

Distant thunder, you might have thought, though there wasn't a cloud in the sky.

Then four black dots appeared above the hills, four helicopters flying north in a tight formation. People who were awake that early wondered what was going on as the rotor blades began to pulse and beat like a single throbbing heart, changing rhythm as the aircraft broke away in different directions, covering the four points of the compass, hovering over the four gates that led in and out of the old town centre.

People getting ready for a hard day's work in factories, quarries and building sites cursed and swore, imagining that some bigwig from the government had decided to stop off in town for breakfast before flying on to wherever he or she was going for lunch at the taxpayers' expense.

Other people wondered whether some sort of military exercise was taking place. It was odd, they thought, because helicopters had never been seen around the town before.

And did they need to make such a god-awful noise?

Many people turned over and went back to sleep despite the racket. Others just put the coffee-pot on the stove and turned the radio up a bit.

05.25

A man was working in his allotment close to the southern gate.

He leant on his spade, shading his eyes against the first bright rays of the sun. A hundred yards away a helicopter was hovering thirty feet above the houses. Black lines suddenly uncoiled from the helicopter, then men came sliding down the ropes, landing on one of the roofs or maybe sliding further down into the street.

He didn't know what to make of it.

He had seen such things on television.

But that was television . . .

05.27

Lorenzo Micheli was aware of a flitting shadow through his half-closed eyes.

Then something cold and metallic dug hard into his right temple. A hand crushed down against the side of his face and pushed his head into the pillow, a voice exploding in his ear.

'Where are the bullets?'

Lorenzo opened his eyes and tried to move his head.

He saw himself reflected in the wardrobe mirror. A man in a black assault outfit and ski mask was pointing a pistol at his head, bending low, shouting in his ear: 'Where the fuck have you hidden the guns?'

It was hard to answer, his mouth pushed into the pillow. 'What guns?'

'Where are they?'

The man in the mask was not alone. Lorenzo heard other people moving around inside his bedroom. A table, chairs and other furniture screeched as they were pushed aside. Books hit the floor, then a stack of CDs crashed on to the tiles in their plastic covers. A cup or a plate was smashed to bits.

The voice next to Lorenzo's ear cancelled out the other sounds. 'Get up slowly. I want to see your hands at all times. This pistol's loaded.'

Three minutes later, dressed but unwashed, hands cuffed behind his back, Lorenzo Micheli was hustled down the steep staircase. On the way out he counted eight masked men with machine guns guarding all the doors and the windows.

Outside, it was chaos. More masked men, more guns, a helicopter hovering low in the sky, a big black van with *Carabinieri* written on the flank in large white letters, the pale faces of people who were peering out of all the windows.

The narrow street was full of armed men.

Twenty? Thirty?

As they pushed him into the back of the van, Lorenzo wondered whether the police had come to arrest him alone, or were they rounding up every single person who lived in the neighbourhood?

The double doors slammed shut and the wailing siren drowned out the noise of the helicopter.

05.28

His mother burst into his bedroom and switched on the light.

'Wake up, Davide! Something's going on outside.'

A heavy sleeper, it took him a few moments to pull himself together. His mother was standing by the window, pulling back the curtain, looking down into the back garden.

The danger was out there, it seemed.

He jumped up, moved to her side, terrified by what he saw outside. Seven or eight masked men in black uniforms were encircling the house. Each man held a machine gun at the ready. Wide awake, he turned towards the door but his mother held him back, a sob breaking from her lips.

'Who are they? What do they want?'

He grabbed his phone from the bedside table and dialled a number that everyone knew: 112.

A deep bass voice answered at once: '*Carabinieri*. Who's speaking?'

'Davide . . . Castrianni. A gang of men. In my back garden. With guns,' he managed to say.

At the other end of the line, the voice said calmly: 'That's us, Davide. Just open the door and come out with your hands up!'

05.32

Signora Donati wasn't alarmed when she heard the doorbell ring.

She was waiting for Sauro, the male nurse, who gave her husband his injections. Sauro had told her that was on the first shift at the hospital that day, so he would be coming early. She had got up on purpose.

She opened the door and a man pointed a pistol in her face.

A man?

The face was covered in black, except for two round eyeholes and a larger hole which showed his mouth.

'*Carabinieri!*' the mouth hissed. 'Where's Federico?'

Signora Donati fainted, but it couldn't have been for long. She opened her eyes, struggled to her feet and pushed her way towards Federico's bedroom through the crush of men in black who were blocking the narrow hallway. A figure was standing over her son, holding a pistol next to Federico's cheek. The boy was crushed against the wall, his face pushed out of shape by the gun. Two men were tapping the walls like doctors tapping her husband's chest and back, while others were pulling out drawers and opening cupboards, throwing everything into a heap on the floor.

She heard a crash in the living room as a mirror or a picture hit the tiles. She looked in the direction of her own bedroom. Her husband was holding on to the doorpost like a drowning man, his face pale and drawn, as if his heart was acting up. Then she was hustled aside as Federico was taken out in pyjamas and bare feet, a man shouting into his ear, 'Where are the guns? Where've you hidden them?'

Federico shouted back: 'What guns? What the fuck is this?'

Before she blacked out again, *Signora* Donati saw her husband sink down on his knees, his hands grasping at his chest and throat.

05.38

Riccardo Bucci was being led from the house, hands cuffed behind his back.

Out in the street he saw an army of men in black with masks and machine guns, the waiting *carabinieri* car, the neighbours who had come out of their houses to see what was going on. As someone put a hand on his head and forced him down, pushing him into the back of the car, he tried to count how many armed men there were.

Next thing, he was in the car, a masked man sitting on either side of him.

'Are you Martians?' Riccardo asked. 'Oi, is this a film?'

05.48

The cars and vans were travelling in convoy towards the maximum-security prison. There were no sirens or flashing lights, but the vehicles were moving fast, overtaking the sparse local traffic on the road at that time of the morning.

Overhead, a helicopter flew low, following their progress.

The other three helicopters were still hovering over the town. Then an order must have come through, because they suddenly sheered away, heading south, back to where they had come from, disappearing as three black dots behind the distant hills.

Four suspects had been arrested without a shot being fired. One hundred and five men had taken part in the assault. None of the armed forces had been injured.

Operation 'Lone Wolves' had been a success.

06.30

General Corsini and Magistrate Catapanni left the *carabinieri* station.

Outside, members of the local press were waiting in the street, firing off questions as the two men climbed into the chauffeur-driven car that would take them to the prison where the suspects were being held for interrogation. The general made a brief statement, knowing that the national press and television crews would already be on the road, heading north.

'There will be a press conference later this morning in Perugia . . .'

'What's it all about, General?'

'What's going on?'

General Corsini held up his hand for silence. 'A victory for law and order,' he said. 'Full details and press sheets will be released at midday. You are all invited to attend.'

FORTY

19 September – 10.30

Raniero was driving.

Zì Luigi filled the passenger seat, his face set hard like a widow at her husband's funeral. He hadn't said a word so far, slumped in the corner, staring morosely out of the window, as if he blamed Raniero for what had needed to be done.

There was no going back on it, that was for sure.

Zì Luigi had said it himself – Corrado was a timebomb ready to go off. If he had spoken with a magistrate, they'd all have been blown away.

Raniero pushed the button, lowered the car window, lit a cigarette then threw the car into the next bend. Driving up was Zì Luigi's idea. A fucking wake was what he wanted.

'We'll get his stuff, Raniè. His sister, Lisa, should have his stuff.'

'If that's what you want, Zì Luì,' Raniero had said.

They were heading up the mountain to the farmhouse, as if they had nothing better to do. If Corrado's sister had any sense at all she'd be glad to be shut of him.

As they pulled into the farmyard, the hens scattered before the wheels. No matter how hard you tried, you couldn't kill those fucking birds. Raniero wondered what the Zì would want to do with them. The thought of a crate of hens travelling south with Corrado's coffin made him want to laugh out loud. Instead, he pulled on the handbrake, then turned a serious face to Zì Luigi. 'This is it,' he said solemnly.

Zì Luigi ignored him, pushed the door open, got out of the car and climbed the short stone stairway up to the front door of the farm like a man who was going to the gallows.

Raniero trailed behind, then stood to face him by the front door.

Zì Luigi's mouth went tight. He laid his hand on Raniero's arm. 'Thanks, Raniè,' he said, real quiet.

Thanks, Raniè? He had never heard that word on Zì Luigi's lips.

'Let me show you the way,' Raniero said, pushing the door open. 'He never bothered to lock the place. Corrado wasn't afraid of no one.'

They stepped into the gloomy interior. One of the windows was open, thank Christ, so the place didn't smell too bad. The remains of Corrado's last meal lay decomposing on the table – half a loaf had turned black, while a lump of cheese was green and black, crawling with maggots.

'They didn't give him the time to wash the plates before they took him off.'

Raniero pointed to an empty coffee cup, a curling rind of orange peel, the stub of a cigar. 'At least he finished his dinner in peace,' he said with a shrug.

Zì Luigi stood in the doorway like an unwelcome guest.

Raniero turned to face him. 'He'd be glad to know you've come to pay your last respects,' he said. 'He really would.'

Zì Luigi took a couple of steps forward.

'It reminds me of the place where he was born,' he said in a hushed voice. 'Identical, more or less. Thirteen of them – mother, father, grandma, ten kids. Corrado was the fifth of the litter. All of them dead now, except for Lisa. Just one big room . . . They ate there, slept there, sat around the fire together at night. A door like that one, too,' he pointed to the far end of the room, 'leading to the outhouse where they kept the cows and pigs.'

Raniero pulled a chair away from the table and offered it to Zì Luigi.

The Zì sat down and shook his head.

'You didn't know Corrado like me,' he said.

Raniero pulled out another chair, dusted it off. He didn't want to ruin his suit. Still, there were more important things to clean up here than a pair of costly trousers. He sat down, wondering where to start.

'You raised him out of the dirt, Zì. You made Corrado what he was.'

He'd said the right thing evidently, because Zì Luigi let go of the breath he'd been holding down inside himself with a loud sigh.

Raniero piled it on. 'Corrado Formisano. Dead-Eye Dick . . .'

Zì Luigi nodded. 'A loaded Magnum, that's what he was. You just had to point him in the right direction. No need to tell him twice what needed doing. Not then, anyway.' He raised his hand, waved it in front of his face. 'And talk about creative . . .'

Raniero nodded.

'He rubbed them out with passion, skill . . .'

'Still,' cut in Raniero, 'hacking off a wolf's head, putting it on public show, dropping us in the shit like that . . . God knows where that idea came from.'

Zì Luigi passed his hand over the chequered plastic tablecloth as if he was wiping it clean. 'Prison burns some people up inside.'

Raniero looked around the room. It looked like a prison cell before you stuck your pin-ups on the wall. A single unmade bed in the corner, a portable TV on top of the fridge, an ancient wood-burning stove in the corner.

Raniero recalled the first time he had met Corrado. Out at Zì Luigi's country villa twenty years before. Corrado Formisano with a long-nosed pistol, showing off to Raniero and the other kids. He'd clipped a bunch of grapes off a vine twenty feet away with a single shot, then held the fruit up like a trophy. He'd been a good-looking man back then, robust and heavy, with a head of curly black hair. The day they'd brought Landini's body up, he recalled the surprise he had felt. Corrado seemed to have shrunk, his curls tinged with grey like a fresh coating of frost. Maximum-security prison had crushed the life out of him, and getting out hadn't made things any easier. Far from home, and only one bungled job to show for it, Corrado must have known that he was on the downward slope.

Raniero raised his palms in the air.

'You did the right thing, Zì. Corrado had to go.'

'He lost his head . . .' Luigi murmured. 'Lost it totally.'

Raniero lit a cigarette, didn't say a word.

'I did right by him,' Zì Luigi was saying. 'It's the first rule, Raniero: never forget the soldiers. Not when they go to jail, not even when they end up in the cemetery. They've got wives, kids, responsibilities . . .'

Raniero blew out smoke, his patience stretched, sitting there listening to the old wanker when there were more important things to do. There was nothing more to be said, in any case.

'Don't let it get to you, Zì,' he said, putting an end to the weepy pantomime. 'It's water down the toilet.'

Zì Luigi stood up and stared at him. 'Once the mud settles,' he said, 'we'll put the pieces back together.'

Raniero bit his tongue to stop himself from saying something nasty. Some people didn't know when to keep their gobs shut. He'd have given the Rolex he was wearing to hear the old man say, just once: I blew it, Raniè, I really fucked it up. Maybe I should go and have a nice lie-down and let you young lads do the business. If he'd said that, Raniero would have respected him. Instead, he blamed it all on Corrado. Raniero shook his head. Zì Luigi had been in charge. The operation was *his*. If it got fucked up – if someone fucked it up – it was *his* fault.

Zì Luigi was moving round the room, picking things up, putting them down again. Then he reached the fridge and stopped dead in his tracks. He opened the door, took a look inside, turned to Raniero and said: 'If we eat now, we won't have to stop till we're south of Naples. There's eggs, tomatoes, onions . . . I don't know about you, Raniè, but I'm starving.'

Raniero couldn't believe what he was hearing.

'It's a custom in the village me and Corrado come from,' Zì Luì was saying, 'to have a bite to eat in the house of the late departed. There's three chairs as well – two for us and one for Corrado.'

A picnic with a ghost, Raniero thought.

'Let me do it, Zì,' he said. 'Don't want you messing up your best suit, do we?'

Zì Luigi sat down like a sack of potatoes, drumming his fingers on the tabletop.

'I was hoping you'd offer,' he said. 'I ain't never cooked a thing in my life. I always had women do that stuff for me. Where did you learn, anyway?'

'In jail,' Raniero said. 'What about an omelette? In honour of Corrado.'

'Sounds good,' Zì Luigi said, smiling almost. 'With what?'

'Onions?' Raniero suggested.

Zì Luigi clicked his tongue against his teeth. 'Perfect.'

Raniero spotted a bottle of red wine that was already open, the cork pushed back to stop it turning to vinegar.

'Just think, Zì,' he said as he laid two glasses out on the table, 'he'd be chuffed to know you're drinking his wine, and in his house, too.'

'Did he suffer, do you think?' Zì Luigi said, a grimace on his face.

He was acting brave now. He hadn't wanted to know when Raniero phoned to tell him that the thing was done and the danger was past. There'd be nothing in the papers in the days to come. The authorities held back on details about prison deaths.

'It was over before he knew it,' Raniero said. 'I swear on the Holy Virgin.'

He was beginning to enjoy himself, working up an appetite now. He poured some olive oil into a frying pan and lit the gas with his lighter. He set an onion on the chopping block, took a knife from the draining board and tried the cutting edge with his thumb.

'This should be sharp enough,' he said. He chopped the onions and threw them into the pan. Then he cracked an egg against the edge of the sink, dropped it into a bowl and threw the shell in the sink.

'If you're hungry, Zì, let's make it four,' he said, cracking three more, whisking the eggs then adding salt and paper. 'The milk's off, but who cares?'

Soon, the onions began to splutter and spit.

'Don't burn them,' Luigi warned him, moving towards the cooker.

'Would I do that, Zì?'

Raniero turned to meet him, knife in hand.

Luigi looked up and Raniero pushed the knife hard into his throat, ducking to avoid the spray of blood then giving the blade a couple of twists to drive it home, the way you did when you were tightening a screw.

When he felt the muscles clench around the blade, he pulled it out.

Zì Luigi was bug-eyed, staring at him, the hole in his throat making a noise like the onions sizzling in the frying pan.

He fell down on his knees, and Raniero watched him.

A strange smell was coming from the cooker. Raniero turned towards it, meaning to shut off the gas. He saw the red stuff mixed in with the onions. *Tomatoes?* he thought. He hadn't bothered with tomatoes.

Zì Luigi's blood was frying in the oil, the red spots turning black, swelling up in bubbles until they popped. As Raniero shut off the gas, he heard the body hit the tiles behind him.

'You ruined my fucking omelette,' he said.

He glanced at Zì Luigi as he dropped the knife into the sink, ran the tap and washed the blood from his right hand beneath the ice-cold water. Then he bent down and slipped the pistol from the holster under Zì Luigi's left armpit. The grip was warm, tacky with blood.

It was the silver-grey Bersa 380 that he had always fancied. He held it under the tap by the trigger guard, saw the blood turn pink, then pale, then vanish down the drain. He stuck the gun in the back of his belt, felt a trickle of cold water running down between his buttocks and hoped it wouldn't stain his trousers.

Then he spotted the blood on the shoulder of his jacket. Fuck! Another good suit gone.

His phone was sitting on the table by the wine glass. He picked it up, made a call and heard a voice he recognized.

'You got it sorted, Raniè?'

'All sorted, Don Michè.'

FORTY-ONE

Sebastiano Cangio was halfway up the mountain road.

He and Marzio had been taking turns to feed the animals since the arrest of Corrado Formisano the week before. It was the state of the cow that worried them the most. Unless she was milked every day she might develop mastitis, and that would do her permanent damage.

He turned on the radio for the mid-morning news. The speaker was reading an item about the US president, who was due to land in Rome that afternoon for a three-day visit, including an audience with the Pope. Next came news of an explosion in Turin; a family of six had died when their apartment had blown up after a gas leak. It was the usual smattering of bland official press releases mixed in with bleak, private tragedies. He didn't bother to switch the radio off, but he wasn't paying it much attention.

Then the speaker said something which caught his attention.

'. . . *Umbria. Four men were arrested in the early hours of the morning. General Arturo Corsini, head of the national Carabinieri Special Forces squad in Rome, revealed that armed officers had taken into custody four suspects who are believed to belong to a major terrorist organization after a surprise swoop at dawn . . .*'

Cangio stood on the brake and the car skidded to the side of the road.

The Legend?

He slammed his hand on the dashboard and shouted at the radio. 'Terrorists?'

Had some stupid journalist got the news twisted? The Legend was watching the 'Ndrangheta in Umbria, keeping tabs on criminal infiltration into the area.

'. . . *The suspects are being held in the local maximum-security prison. Further details are expected later this morning in the course of a press conference in Perugia—*'

'What the fuck are you saying?' Cangio shouted at the radio.

The radio seemed to answer him back. *'That is the end of the news.'*

He rolled down the window.

His head was spinning.

He gasped for air like a fish out of water.

FORTY-TWO

19 September – midday

The conference room was packed.

Frescoed nymphs danced on the ceiling high above the assembly. Journalists from most of the national newspapers filled the seats, smartphones, iPads and mini-recorders in their hands, eager to be in on the scoop. A dozen television stations had sent along their camera crews and top reporters. Mingling with the press were members of the regional government, the local police, armed forces, members of President Pignatti's personal staff plus a lot more people who shouldn't have been there at all – people who had seen the fuss in the entrance hall and wanted to know what it was all about.

Still, a crowd was a crowd.

At twelve o'clock the spotlights came on in a blaze and the cameras were rolling. General Corsini leaned close to the microphone, tapped it in the time-honoured manner and began the proceedings.

'As most of you know, a major *carabiniere* operation took place at dawn this morning under my command. Four suspects have been arrested, and they are undergoing interrogation at this moment regarding terrorist attacks which have taken place in the region in recent months. A list of their names will be handed out at the end of this session.

'"Lone Wolves", the codename for this particular operation, was chosen to indicate the singular nature of a terrorist cell that I have been tracking for quite some time. To avoid surveillance they took to the woods and mountains to plan their criminal activities, sweeping into town to launch their attacks. As you all know, important reconstruction work has begun in the province. While much has been done to alleviate the suffering of those who lost the most in the major earthquake of 2009, rebuilding has not gone forward as swiftly as was hoped on account of opposition from certain quarters, notably those who condemn modernization and redevelopment out of hand. In most cases, the opposition has been vocal – genuine "environmentalists", let's call them, but there has also been a disturbing undercurrent of vandalism, malicious damage against property, and intimidation aimed at persons in positions of authority, notably the delivery of explosive devices by way of the public post.' He waved his hand in the direction of Donatella Pignatti, though he didn't mention the president by name. 'While purporting to be nature lovers, guardians of local history and so on, these individuals have crossed the criminal line, using threats to further their idealistic ends. Acts of violence and subversion cannot, and will not, be condoned by the State. Criminal behaviour will always be subject to the direst repression within the limits of the law.'

Pens flew furiously over lined yellow notebooks.

'In such cases, the problem is knowing when to intervene. Strike too soon and the criminals may get off lightly. But strike too late . . .' he paused for extra emphasis, '. . . and lives may be lost. After consultation with Magistrate Calisto Catapanni, who has worked closely on the case and authorized the arrests, and President Donatella Pignatti, who was the subject of the latest anonymous threat, the decision to act was taken yesterday in view of strong indications of an inevitable progression towards armed insurrection. At five o'clock this morning I gave the order for assault teams to apprehend the suspects, who were taken into custody without a single shot being fired thanks to the skill and the experience of the officers involved. I take this opportunity to congratulate my men. I am fully confident that further investigative and forensic analysis of the evidence will lead to the conviction of the people who were arrested this morning.'

General Corsini paused and looked around the room, noting with satisfaction the shocked faces of people in the audience, the racing pens of the journalists, the red lights blinking on the television cameras.

'I will now take questions regarding the logistics of the operation. Of course, I can say nothing regarding the terrorists . . . the *suspects*, that is,' he corrected himself with a smile. 'The law guarantees them the right to remain silent, and the onus will be on us to demonstrate their guilt. I have no doubts on that account.'

Hands were waving in the air, calling for his attention.

General Corsini pointed his finger at a young woman from Rome who he knew would ask the right questions. How many men were involved? How many helicopters had been used? How long had the operation taken?

Next, the television reporters staked their claim to questions. Did the fact that so many policemen had been used indicate how very dangerous the suspects were? Should the public feel reassured to know that the immediate danger was over? How long had General Corsini and his men been keeping tabs on these local activists? When the general spoke of a terrorist cell, was he suggesting that they were part of a national, or even an international, terrorist organization?

General Corsini replied with measured calm, underlining the fact that the operation had been carried out with the full cooperation of all the authorities involved. He was about to close the meeting when a man that he didn't recognize stood up, announcing that he was a reporter with a local online news site.

'General Corsini,' the man began, 'by explosive devices, I suppose you're talking about bullets, right?'

'Correct,' General Corsini snapped.

'And, er, this decapitated head of a wolf, General . . . Have you ever come across a threat like this from a terrorist group before? It's the sort of thing that you hear about down in Sicily or Calabria, where the Mafia . . .'

'There are no indications that the Mafia was involved,' Corsini said quickly.

'You are renowned for spectacular operations of this kind,' the reporter went on, refusing to sit down, 'which attract a great deal of attention in the media. Is that why everyone calls you the Legend?'

General Corsini pushed his glasses up on to his forehead and leant closer to the microphone.

'Let me ask you a question,' he said. 'If you think that I am an attention-seeker, don't you think I'd have gained far more attention by arresting important members of a Mafia clan in some other part of the country, instead off a splinter terrorist cell in Umbria that nobody has ever noticed before?'

General Corsini glanced in the direction of President Pignatti in time to see her furrowed brow relax and a broad smile appear on her lips. He waved his hand towards the microphone, inviting her to speak, moving aside as she took her place.

'I wish to express my sincere thanks to General Corsini,' she began, 'and to all the officers who played a part in the arrests which were made this morning . . .'

Corsini stood beside Calisto Catapanni.

'You handled that well,' the magistrate murmured behind his hand.

Corsini nodded. 'Any news?' he asked.

Catapanni pinched his nose and sniffed. 'I received a phone call from Milan this morning. It seems that there's a vacancy up there in the procurator's office.'

Corsini pursed his lips. 'Congratulations,' he said.

While they had been talking, the press conference had ended. President Pignatti was at the centre of a large crowd now. Journalists were swarming around her, political allies surging forward to offer their congratulations and best wishes for the future.

The same question was on everyone's lips: would she be standing in the coming parliamentary elections?

FORTY-THREE

19 September – 12.06

Cangio parked the Land Rover before he reached the farm. He could have driven all the way up to the door, but the noise of the diesel engine would have frightened the animals. He cut across the open meadow, the grass knee-high. The breeze blew fresh in his face, but the smell of manure grew stronger as he skipped over the dry-stone wall and walked along in the shadow of the barn, approaching the house and the farmyard. He still could not make any sense of what he'd heard on the news.

As he came around the corner of the barn he stopped dead in his tracks.

A silver-grey Mercedes was parked in the courtyard, where hens were pecking for worms. Had some gentleman farmer driven all the way up the mountain in such a fine car to take care of the animals?

'Hello!' he called. 'Is anyone there?'

No one answered, but the barn door was open.

Was the visitor in there milking the cow and feeding the pigs?

He made for the door, called out again, but no one answered. As he stepped into the building he was blinded for some moments by the lack of light. The pigs began to squeal and leap up on their hindlegs, trotters resting on top of the concrete wall of the sty, staring at him with unblinking eyes, their red mouths open, shrieking. It was clear that they hadn't been recently fed.

'Hello?' he called again.

At the sound of his voice, the cow let out a mournful lowing.

He turned towards the cow and saw a body lying on the ground beside the concrete trough at the far end of the barn. His first thought was that someone had come up alone to feed the beasts and been taken ill.

Cangio dashed towards him. That was when he saw the gash in the throat. Blood had stained the man's white shirt and light grey suit.

Whatever had happened, it wasn't an accident. He fumbled in his pocket, pulled out his mobile phone. He found the number and pressed the call button. It rang several times. Then he heard a voice.

'Yes?'

'General Corsini! It's me, Cangio. Sebastiano Cangio. I'm at the farm I told you about. Come up here fast. There's something you should see . . .'

A heavy blow struck him from behind.

Cangio hit the floor before his phone did.

FORTY-FOUR

19 September – 13.01

General Corsini snapped his telephone shut.

The ranger's voice had sounded like static from a distant planet.

Still, Corsini knew where he was calling from. That farm up in the mountains. The one that had belonged to Corrado Formisano. The ranger was drawn to the place like a fly to jam. The general took a deep breath, then he opened his phone again, intending to call Cangio back.

President Pignatti stepped into his line of sight as she freed herself from a platoon of journalists and came marching towards him. She was smiling broadly, as if the TV cameras were still pointed in her face.

'Are you avoiding me, General?' she hissed through the smile.

Corsini slipped his phone into his pocket. 'On the contrary,' he said. 'I didn't want to rob you of your share of the glory. You deserve it after the risk you've run—'

'Cut the bullshit!' she murmured. 'I'm no safer than I was before. Thanks to you, General Corsini. Or should I say, thanks to *them*?'

'Them?' he said, turning his ear towards her, as if he hadn't understood. 'Do you mean the terrorists we arrested this morning?'

'I'm talking about whoever sent me those bullets!' Her voice was low but it was loaded with venom. 'The people who killed my cat. That's who *I* mean, not the band of juvenile delinquents you and your army locked up in jail this morning. Now I really *am* scared shitless, while you've got what you wanted out of this charade.'

'They won't bother you,' he assured her. 'You've got the message; I'm sure you'll act upon it. And I am quieter than a grave when it comes to keeping secrets. They know that I know, and that I will not hesitate to act on what I know, if necessary.'

'Are you quite certain, General?' she said. 'You won't catch them as easily as the kids that you call terrorists. I've been reading the book you told me about. Sun Tzu? I understand what you were saying about an enemy you can beat.'

'You've beaten them, too,' he reminded her. 'Today you are reaping the rewards. The press, the compliments, the television! You'll be the talk of the town for quite some time to come. There's nothing so winning as a woman in jeopardy who sticks to her guns and weathers rough seas. The voters love that sort of thing. I wouldn't be surprised to learn that your party has already put your name on the list for the general election. And that, if I may say, you owe to me, *signora*.'

She shook her head and stared at him. 'Unexploded bullets, dead wolves . . . What happens next, General Corsini?'

The Legend shrugged his shoulders. His gold epaulettes emphasized the gesture. 'Nothing will happen. They know when they're outclassed. They realize now that you are an intelligent, perceptive woman who knows how to handle herself. They won't mess with you . . . Unless you mess with them, of course. And you're far too sensible for that. They want the same things you do, and they're ready to share the cake. Money, power . . .'

'What do *you* want, General Corsini?' ·

'Smile,' he warned her as a tall blonde reporter came rushing over towards them, microphone in hand, a camera crew trailing in her wake. 'Money and power don't interest me at all. I am not so vulgar.' He laughed out loud as the red light of the camera flashed on, and Donatella Pignatti slipped her arm into his. 'I am not a politician,' he murmured into her ear.

It reminded him of that cartoon film that his youngest niece watched over and over again. He and the president must have looked a bit like Cinderella and Prince Charming as the band struck up and the ball began.

'A big smile for the camera,' the reporter said. 'Then a word from both of you for our viewers.'

'You cannot know how grateful I am to General Corsini,' gushed Donatella Pignatti, slipping effortlessly into the role as she turned and planted a kiss on the general's cheek with her bright scarlet lips.

Lights flashed, cameras clicked and whirred.

The picture would be on the front page of the all newspapers the next day.

FORTY-FIVE

19 September – 13.06

'**W**ho the fuck are *you*?'

The question rattled around inside Cangio's brain. His head was heavier than lead. His nose felt as if it was broken. Blood clogged his mouth and throat. His stomach heaved, and he vomited on the shoes of the man who was pointing a pistol in his face.

'I'll kill you slow for that,' the gunman cursed.

Cangio opened his eyes and looked up at him.

The man was older than himself – not much, but older. A thin face, long nose, a slit of a mouth, eyes too close together. Even so, he was smartly dressed. Apart from the blood stains on his jacket.

'Who the fuck are you?' the man asked. 'What are you doing here?'

The pistol tapped Cangio's nose and a wave of nausea shot through his nervous system.

'I work in the park,' he managed to say. 'I came to feed the animals.'

The pistol caught him under the chin and lifted his head.

'And you were ordering sweet-and-sour for the three little pigs from the Chinese takeaway, I suppose?'

Cangio coughed and spat out a mouthful of blood, turning his head to avoid hitting the man, his shoes, his clothes. One thought kept going through his head: General Corsini had answered. Corsini knew where he was. The general hadn't called him back. He must have realized what was going on.

'Who were you phoning?'

It was easier to answer the first question.

'My name's Cangio. I'm a park ranger—'

The pistol jabbed at his chin, held him fixed as securely as a nail.

'Been up here before, have you, Cangio?'

'I knew the man who was living here.'

The man let out a thin whistle. 'You knew Corrado?'

'Just a bit . . .'

The man's thin face displayed a twisted smile. 'Fuck me! You're the ranger that arrested him. You were playing with fire, my friend.'

The butt of the pistol hit Cangio hard in the teeth.

'Don't fuck around with me,' the man said. 'Who were you calling?'

Cangio spat out a tooth. 'Who was he?' he said, glancing towards the body stretched out on the ground.

The man looked at him. 'Does it matter?' he smirked. 'Tell me who you were talking to or I'll throw you in the acid with him. You'll be alive, though.'

Cangio opened his mouth then closed it again. If he mentioned General Corsini, the man would shoot him. If he said nothing, the man would shoot him anyway.

'The cat got your tongue?' the man said. He took two steps to the side, never taking his eyes off his prisoner, except for one moment as he bent down and picked up Cangio's phone. 'These things never lie,' he said. He pushed a button and the number came up. He pushed another and a name appeared on the display.

This man murdered people. He wouldn't hesitate to kill again. The germ of an idea sprouted in Cangio's mind.

'You know who I was talking to,' he said.

'You didn't tell him nothing.'

'I told him enough.'

Some spark of sarcasm, a sneer or a smile, must have appeared on Cangio's face, because the man reached out with the pistol and banged it hard into his cheekbone.

'Don't you fuck with me,' he said. 'What was the message, then?'

Speak and be killed, or die for saying nothing. The odds were zero either way. The only possibility was to play for time. General Corsini must have heard enough to put two and two together.

'He knows where I am,' Cangio said. 'I didn't need to tell him anything. He's on his way, and he won't be alone. He'll bring an army of men. There's only one road leading up here. One way in, one way out. You're trapped.'

'All the way from Rome?' the man sneered. 'It's a two-hour drive.'

'He's in Umbria,' Cangio said. 'He arrested a bunch of kids . . . terrorists, in town this morning. He knows about the 'Ndrangheta, too. I told him everything. He'll drop on you like a ton of bricks. Ten minutes by car, three by helicopter. You've got blood all over you—'

A kick caught Cangio full in the face.

Before he blacked out, he remembered asking himself whether it was better to be kicked to death or take a bullet in the brain. Either alternative was better than being thrown half-dead into a bath of acid.

He felt a slap on his cheek and opened his eyes.

The man was sitting on his heels, watching him through narrowed slits, hefting the gun in his hand now, as if he had something on his mind.

'This general of yours,' he said. 'If he knew about Corrado, the wolf and us . . . why would he bother with a bunch of kids?'

Cangio spat more blood, more fragments of teeth. 'They menaced a politician, sent her bullets through the post—'

The man's sharp laughter stopped him in mid-sentence. 'Fucking hell!' He looked up at the ceiling. 'That wolf? That was Corrado, that was. Did your mighty general know, I wonder? I'm almost tempted to wait and ask him. Still, if he's going to bring the cavalry,' he said, standing up, pointing the gun at Cangio, 'we'd better get this done and get out of here.'

'I can help you,' Cangio said.

The man slid the ammunition chamber out of the pistol, then slapped it back with the palm of his hand.

'You stink of dead meat.'

'I can make him come up on his own,' Cangio said.

'Explain.'

Cangio took a deep breath and climbed to his knees. 'All I have to do is call him back—'

The kick hit him square in the balls, but it wasn't as hard as it might have been.

'If you're shitting me, you're dead,' the man said.

'He told me how he works,' Cangio lied, staring him in the eye. 'He goes scouting alone before he calls his men. I can make sure he comes up here on his own.'

When one of the pigs let out a squeal, Cangio's heart stopped dead for an instant.

'You'll breathe until the general arrives,' the man said slowly. 'If I see more than one car coming up the valley, you're dead and I take to the woods. Here, catch!'

He threw the phone to Cangio. 'Call him,' he said. 'One wrong word and it'll be your last.'

FORTY-SIX

19 September – 13.29

The general's phone trilled a military march.

President Pignatti moved away, leaving him alone to answer it.

Cangio sounded frightened. He didn't say much more than he'd said the first time. He was up at Corrado Formisano's farm. There was something Cangio wanted him to see. It was the bit at the end of the conversation that was puzzling. Cangio had reminded him of their meeting in Rome the week before, and then he had said something very odd.

Come the way you always do.

That day in Rome they had spoken of many things. The fact that he had many men under his command, men who would follow him blindly into any situation, risking their lives to obey his orders. Was that what Cangio meant?

Bring your men?

Had he found some evidence linking Corrado Formisano to the 'Ndrangheta? Something he wanted General Corsini to see before he made it public?

That conversation told him something else, too.

Cangio was all alone up there.

FORTY-SEVEN

19 September – 13.31

Raniero was seething.

The ranger hadn't been lying. He had spoken with General Corsini. Raniero was caught in a trap, and he knew it. The corpse of Zì Luigi wouldn't go away. If he killed the ranger, too, and the *carabinieri* arrested him, he'd be going down for life. But he couldn't let the ranger live.

Beads of sweat erupted on his forehead, a river of the stuff flowing down his side beneath his armpits making a wet rag of his best linen shirt.

Why the fuck had it happened? You chose the time, you chose the place, then you discovered that both the time and the place were wrong. He'd sewn himself up by killing Zì Luigi at the farm. Could he ever have imagined that some idiot of a park ranger would choose that day to feed the pigs?

Even worse was the thought of Don Michele. What would the don say when he heard that Raniero had fucked up the operation, just like Zì Luigi and Corrado? He corrected himself. He'd fucked it up worse than the two of them put together! What had Don Michele said? *We need to get this ship on course, Raniero. You answer to me, and no one else.* If he went to prison, he'd end up eating fish bones, just like Corrado. Or worse.

There was only one thing that was to his advantage: the farm was on top of the mountain. You could see the road right down into the valley. If a posse came charging up the road, he could take to the woods. By the time the cops reached the farmhouse he'd be long gone. And what would they find when they got there? Two dead bodies. One with a gun in his hand, the other holding a knife. It would take two minutes to rig the scene. Where was the proof that he had ever been up there? The cops wouldn't think of looking for a third man. Why should they? It would look like an open-and-shut case. A park ranger had tried it on with the 'Ndrangheta and lost. General Corsini would make sense of it. He'd write Cangio off as a silly fucker who had tried to grab the glory before the sheriff arrived.

A silly fucker who'd got what was coming to him!

But if the general came on his own, it would be a different story.

He could rub the bastard out, and Don Michè would see things in a different light. A dangerous enemy taken out of play. OK, there'd be a heavy military presence in the area for a while, more cops and *carabinieri*, but the dust would soon clear. How long would the coppers be able to occupy the territory? If the clan laid low, took care of business with the bankers and politicians, they'd be ready to move into top gear once the pressure eased off. And what use would an army be without the Legend to guide it?

Cangio groaned and pulled him back to reality.

The kid was more useful alive than dead. Raniero grabbed him by the hair and pulled his head up. The ranger's eyes snapped open with fright. He didn't say a word, but Raniero knew what he was thinking.

What happens now?

'I'm gonna be generous,' Raniero said. 'Give you a choice. Left or right – which is it to be?'

Cangio looked puzzled.

Raniero kicked him in the ribs. 'Left or right?' he said again with a burst of impatience. 'I haven't got all fucking day!'

Sebastiano Cangio opened his mouth to speak, closed it quickly as blood ran out of his nose, coughed, spat, then stared up at him.

'What choice?' he managed to say.

'We need to be ready to greet the general. Left or right?'

'Left or right . . . what?'

Raniero sniffed. 'Tomorrow's coming. You just missed the ferry.'

He pushed his pistol into Cangio's right thigh and fired.

The ranger went out like a lightbulb popping.

FORTY-EIGHT

19 September – 14.19

General Corsini drove carefully up the single-track road. He couldn't risk running into the drainage ditch that ran beside it; he had no way of explaining what he was doing up there on his own.

The road seemed to go on forever, twisting and turning, hardly seeming to gain in altitude, until he suddenly found himself on the ridge and an open gate in a dry-stone wall appeared ahead of him.

He braked hard, managed not to stall the engine.

There was a rundown farmhouse, a barn, a flagged courtyard between them. Sitting in the middle of the courtyard, on a white plastic chair, was Sebastiano Cangio. His face was barely recognizable. Blood was streaming from a wound in his thigh. The ranger moved his head – maybe he had heard the car – and General Corsini knew that he was still alive.

He froze behind the steering wheel.

Somebody had got to Cangio first.

His eyes darted from the house to the barn, then back again.

A man stepped out from behind a tree, a gun in his hand, and the windscreen exploded, covering him with shards of glass.

Corsini threw himself flat across the passenger seat.

There was another sharp crack and a bullet whistled above his head.

'Get out of the car!' a voice shouted. 'Show me your hands.'

Corsini opened the glovebox. His copy of Sun Tzu was there, together with the unmarked pistol he had 'requisitioned' from a seized arms haul. He unclipped the safety catch with his thumb and slipped the gun into the back of his Sam Browne belt.

'I'm coming,' he called. Then, head down, he edged out of the car, using the door as a shield.

'Stand up,' the man shouted, 'or I'll pepper the door.'

Corsini peeped over the windowsill.

A tall, slim figure in a stylish suit was standing in front of Cangio now, a black pistol held in both hands, his feet apart, sighting along the barrel.

'Show me your gun and raise your hands.'

'Don't shoot,' Corsini said, unclasping the holster flap, his fingers closing around the butt of his service pistol, holding it up in the air.

'Throw it here. Nice and slow.'

As the pistol slid across the yard and came to a halt, the man looked down for an instant. In the same instant, Cangio's heavy work boot came up sharply between the man's legs.

A shot exploded from the killer's gun, throwing up dirt ten feet to the general's left. He grabbed the pistol from behind his back and took aim. The killer's gun was pointing at the sky, his left hand holding the crotch of his trousers, his face contorted with pain. Corsini fired before the man had a chance to recover. Blood exploded from the target's head in a bright red mist, then he rolled forward and fell on his face. Cangio didn't see it happen. His eyes were closed, head lolling on his chest as he lost consciousness after the effort required to kick the man.

'Thank you, Cangio,' Corsini murmured.

He walked towards the man who was lying face down on the ground, fired another shot into the back of his head, gave the body a kick, retrieved his service pistol, and put it back in its holster.

Then he turned to Sebastiano Cangio.

FORTY-NINE

19 September – 14.40

The world seemed to shift in slow jerks.

It was like a rolling back-cloth in a run-down theatre with ancient stage machinery being turned by hand. The general's car was moving slowly out of sight, the corner of the farmhouse, too, while the woods and the mountaintop slowly began to appear.

It took an eternity before Cangio realized what was happening.

He was being shifted.

Someone had tilted the chair on to its back legs, dragging it and him across the farmyard. His saw a blue sky spotted with clusters of cotton-wool cloud, then his eyes jammed shut with pain. His heels were dragging on the ground. At every bump on the worn flagstones, a shock went through his right leg. It was like being shot all over again, not just once but dozens of times.

When he opened his eyes again there was no sky and he could smell the pigs, the sharp smell of acid. The cropped head and blue-tinted glasses of General Corsini bobbed in and out of sight. The general was taking him into the barn, out of the sun. General Corsini would lay him down to rest on the hay. Then he would call for help.

The mafioso hadn't managed to kill either of them.

He remembered kicking the bastard in the balls. It had been a miracle. Corsini must have seized the opportunity to shoot him.

'General, call your men,' he murmured. 'I'm losing blood.'

General Corsini spoke behind his shoulder, his voice soft and gentle, reassuring. Just like the voice of the maths teacher at school – the one they called *Mister Nobody*.

'Leave everything to me,' General Corsini murmured.

Cangio heard the grunting pigs, the bleating sheep. Then the chair stopped moving, dropping forward on to four legs again. His hands were untied, then two hands slid beneath his armpits and he felt himself being lifted, then dragged again. He cried out in pain, but Corsini didn't stop. Suddenly, the general let him go and he hit the ground. Pain swelled up again in a red wave.

'General . . .'

He might have been talking a language that Corsini didn't understand.

'Please . . . I'm . . .'

'Yes, I can see. You're dying, Cangio,' General Corsini said, his breath coming in gasps from the effort of shifting him. 'I'm very sorry,' he said, clapping the palms of his black leather gloves together, 'but what can I do about it? It will all be over in a matter of minutes. An 'Ndrangheta safe house, bodies all over the place – goodness knows what the local police will make of it. Well, there is one thing they'll soon find out. All three of you are . . . no, *were*, I should say, from Calabria. That fact alone explains a lot.'

General Corsini turned away and strode out of the barn.

FIFTY

19 September – 14.41

Alfredo Dandini pulled off the headset and grabbed the telephone.

A voice answered at the second ring and gave a name and rank.

'Awaiting orders, sir.'

'Call out the fifth company. An emergency. How many men can you give me?'

'Thirty-eight on duty, Supervisor. We could probably—'

'Send a helicopter assault team . . . No, make that *two* aircraft, to this location. And a medical team. There's a person bleeding to death.' He read out the OS map coordinates of the farmhouse. 'Call out the local *carabinieri*, tell them to close all roads leading up to the top of the mountain.'

'I'll need authorization . . .'

'Cable the order to me. I'll sign it.'

'Sir?'

Dandini's temper snapped. 'Are you deaf, Lieutenant? I want two helicopters on site inside ten minutes!'

'The Legend . . . General Corsini, sir. He's in Perugia, following the arrest of the terrorists in Spoleto. Shouldn't he be told that a major operation is about to begin?'

Dandini shook his head and blew out air.

Another fan of the Legend, as he had been himself until the day they had summoned him to the Ministry of Justice and given him a job to do.

'We are confident that you'll lay out the lines of battle carefully, Dandini, certain that the general will respond as he has always done.'

He had been charting General Corsini's movements for months.

Electronic bugs in his office, home and cars, a live tap on his telephones, listening in on his listeners, recording everything he said. He had set Corsini up that night in St Peter's Square, warning him that an investigation was starting, inviting him to step into a trap, knowing how he would react. Arturo Corsini wasn't interested in money or power. He wasn't greedy or corrupt. The only thing that drove him was ambition, the desire to perpetuate the Legend that he had created of himself.

'General Corsini will know soon enough,' Dandini said. 'If you find him up there, arrest him. If he's left already, put out an all points alert.'

Dandini heard the sharp intake of breath at the other end of the line.

'The Legend, sir?'

'The Legend, Lieutenant. General Corsini. I have a warrant for his arrest.'

Two minutes later, the lieutenant called back. His voice was cold, professional now, the voice of a man who knew that the pecking order was changing.

'They're on their way, sir. Do you have any other orders?'

Dandini hesitated, but only for an instant. 'Prepare a press release giving details of the operation that's under way – the time and place, the number of men, the number of vehicles and helicopters taking part. Objective? Let's keep it vague for now. Search and recover, a large-scale operation of primary importance. Oh, yes . . .' He paused briefly. 'You can name me as commander and coordinator of the forces involved.'

'And if they ask for the codename, sir?'

Dandini thought for a moment. 'Call it *Operation Sun Tzu*,' he said.

FIFTY-ONE

E veryone has wondered what it must be like to die.

Cangio found the reality strange, perplexing. There was no sudden drop into a deep, dark void. No upward surge towards a light that was welcoming and bright. He seemed to be slowly suffocating in a calm grey sea, where things lost shape and colours ceased to exist.

The pain was gone. His arms and legs were somewhere else, his broken nose an irrelevance. If he had a body, he felt the pull of it no longer.

The only sensations he would carry away with him was the stench of the pigsty and the sound of the pigs.

Far away, a faint noise began to pulse and throb.

Was it the beating of his heart, an engine running on one cylinder now, struggling to compensate for the lack of blood that was left in his veins?

Yet the noise didn't fade. It seemed to swell and grow. A regular, rhythmic beating coming closer and closer. Like the wings of some dark angel closing in on him, a word written on the flank of the creature in big white letters.

Carabinieri . . .

FIFTY-TWO

Three weeks later

Loredana had bought him a get-well present on eBay.

She was living in the house with him now, playing the nurse. She had settled him in his chair beneath the beach umbrella in the garden before going off to work.

'Got everything you need?' she asked.

He had his pills, his crutches, a phone, cigarettes and lighter, a book to read, a bottle of water, his Zeiss binoculars.

'If there's anything else, I'll . . .'

'Make a list,' she said, and laughed.

The list of names had appeared in all the newspapers. The list of names that Mayor Truini's wife had left behind the day that Loredana caught her shoplifting. Loredana had pulled the list from her bag one day while Cangio was in the hospital, told him the story of how she came to have it, and Cangio had passed it on to newly promoted Colonel Dandini when the officer came to visit him that afternoon. The *carabinieri* were amazed at how rich a lot of orphans, nuns and bedridden pensioners in town appeared to be. The bank manager, Ruggiero Franzetti, had been arrested . . .

A light flashed on the other side of the valley.

Cangio reached for Loredana's get-well present, the powerful Zeiss binoculars, and a sharp pain ripped through his right thigh. He would walk again, the doctors said, but not for a month or two.

He focused the glasses and caught another flash of light. Two of them, like the eyes of a wolf in the darkness of the woods that cloaked the mountainside.

Somebody was spying on him.

It was the third time in three days, and always in the same spot.

It might be a warning. They could be showing themselves on purpose, sending him a message: *We know where you are,* cumparu. *Why stay here? Why look for trouble?*

They had driven him out of Calabria; they weren't going to drive him out of Umbria.

He stared at the trees on the far side of the valley, close to where the wolves were living, daring whoever it was to come across and get him.

The service pistol was tucked inside his shirt, the hammer cocked.

He was ready for them . . .